NEAT

Previously by Ron Gomez

My name is Ron and I'm a recovering legislator (2000)
Zemog Publishing, P. O. Box 81397, Lafayette, LA 70508

Pelican Games (2003)
Noble House/American Literary Press, Baltimore, MD

NEAT

Ron Gomez

iUniverse, Inc.
New York Lincoln Shanghai

Neat

Copyright © 2005 by Ron Gomez

iUniverse books may be ordered through booksellers or by contacting:

iUniverse
2021 Pine Lake Road, Suite 100
Lincoln, NE 68512
www.iuniverse.com
1-800-Authors (1-800-288-4677)

This is a work of fiction. The events described here are imaginary. Although some settings are based on real locations and references made to real people, they are used fictitiously without intent to describe their actual conduct.

ISBN-13: 978-0-595-37051-1 (pbk)
ISBN-13: 978-0-595-81452-7 (ebk)
ISBN-10: 0-595-37051-9 (pbk)
ISBN-10: 0-595-81452-2 (ebk)

Printed in the United States of America

Dedication:

to my grandfather, Antoine "Neat" Gomez, a quiet, unassuming survivor, not a hero, but an uncommon man

I
February 29, 1876

The soft night breeze carried lilting string quartet music through the trees. The young man guided his horse along the long, grassy, oak-lined entrance to the stately mansion. The air was cool and damp with the last throes of a mild winter gripping the south Louisiana swampland.

Sensing other equine presence, the little mare neighed softly as she made her way toward a gathering of more than thirty horses. Most were attached to carriages and tethered to the hitching posts. Several nodded their heads, blew a fog of air through their nostrils and grunted greetings.

Neat hitched his horse and patted her affectionately on the jowl, "You'll be all right, Dancer, I won't be long." Standing in the shadows, away from the glow of the coal oil lamps on the gallery, he pulled a large mask down over his swarthy face. It was the beak-nosed, Venetian-style mask styled after the fabled Scaramouche. A friend had bought it for him as a gift on a recent trip to New Orleans. It was beautifully sculpted of papier maché brought to a hard finish with several coats of high-gloss black and vermilion red lacquer. He had carefully stored it in anticipation of this evening, Mardi Gras.

He pulled from a side pocket the cleverly duplicated invitation to the ball that a calligraphy-schooled friend had made for him. It included the warning that, though most men carried side arms as a matter of habit, firearms would not be allowed in the home for this event. He unbuckled his belt and holster holding the Colt .44 revolver and placed it in the saddlebag then reached back and made certain the Double Derringer in the small of his back was secure.

Neat looked at the imposing structure. It had been built thirty-five years earlier as the residence for a wealthy plantation owner and his family. It was the centerpiece of their seven hundred plus acre sugar cane farm. Even after being occupied and abused as a barracks for Union troops for two years during the war, it still was considered one of the most beautiful homes along the Mississippi River. Two stories of whitewashed brick were surrounded on three sides by great plastered brick columns, eight on each side. Twenty-foot wide galleries wrapped around both floors of the house. It had been commandeered by Union troops in 1863 and was now the residence of the chief administrator for the area Freedmen's Bureau. The former owner of the plantation was allowed to house his family in the small quarters in the rear once used by the slaves who worked the fields. He and his two sons still farmed the land along with several Negro men, but the bureau confiscated most of the crops and meager profits. His wife and daughter, along with two newly freed Negro women, cleaned the house, cooked most of the meals and did the laundry for the administrator's family as well as their own. The former slaves, men and women, had voluntarily stayed on through loyalty to the plantation owner and his family. It was the only life they had ever known.

The official name of the Freedmen's Bureau was Bureau of Refugees, Freedmen and Abandoned lands. It was established in the War Department in 1865 to supervise all relief and educational activities relating to refugees and freedmen (former slaves). It also assumed custody of confiscated land or property in the Confederate states. The supervisors and administrators were extremely powerful men with almost unbridled authority.

Voices and laughter mixed with the music as Neat climbed the gallery steps and crossed to the French doors opening on the great central hallway. He carried his slight frame confidently, held the invitation out for a cursory inspection and easily whisked past the bored servant posted at the entrance. Once in the hallway he was facing a graceful staircase that spiraled up through the fourteen-foot ceiling. The music was coming from the great room on his right.

He noticed thankfully that he had chosen the proper clothing. Like him, practically all of the men wore dark three-piece, four-button suits with a white shirt and dark cravat. Some of the shirts, like Neat's, were ruffled. All the men were masked though Neat's was unique and more striking than most.

Almost all of the women had their hair piled high with ringlets dangling on either side of their faces. They wore long gowns and elbow length gloves. They too were masked. Some held feather-decorated eyepieces on short wands. Others had full facial masks in varied complexions and colors.

Three huge crystal chandeliers, each with thirty-six lit candles, helped illuminate the room. Lamps in sconces on the walls around the room enhanced the glow of the chandeliers. The light of a huge, well-stoked fireplace added to the golden flush engulfing the crowd of revelers.

On close examination, the suits and gowns, though elegant, revealed the fraying and fading of age. They had seen better days. Much better. The South would never see those days again. The masks were a requirement noted on the invitation. After all, this was the main event of Mardi Gras in Iberville Parish, Louisiana. Tomorrow was Ash Wednesday, the beginning of the Lenten season for the Catholic community and generally observed by everyone in the state.

Of the nearly two hundred or so people in the gathering, about a dozen were Negro. They too were reasonably well dressed and wore the mandatory masks. Most of the other celebrants were olive-complexioned of Mediterranean descent: Spanish, French and the almost indefinable mixture called Creole. The rest were newly transplanted of mixed European descent and originally from the North, the Union states. Some were veterans of the winning army. Many of these bore the scars and missing limbs now so prevalent throughout the nation.

Mingling with the crowd, Neat tried to remain casual and inconspicuous in spite of his attention-getting mask. He was five-foot-seven, slim-as-a-reed with black hair and, under the mask, a swarthy Hispanic complexion. He was nearing his eighteenth birthday. Many young ladies cast their eye toward him not only in appreciation of his distinctive mask but also noting his easy, confident carriage. He, in turn, nodded or bowed slightly to each one and strolled casually around the room appearing to be watching the dancers and heading for the table holding the punch bowl. He was looking for Amanda.

Antoine Joseph Galvez had been called "Neat" as long as he could remember. Though not knowing the exact genesis of the sobriquet, he dimly realized that it was his four older sisters who had brought it about. They had lavished attention on him as a child, dressed him up like a little doll and marched him around to their friends to show him off. He had to admit he still enjoyed dressing up as he was tonight though such opportunities came very seldom the last several years. But, even in casual or work clothing, he was always, well—neat.

The quartet ended the tune they were playing and the chatter and laughter grew louder for a moment. Then a tall man in a feathered mask was standing on the riser next to the musicians calling for order, "Ladies and gentlemen, ladies and gentlemen, your attention please." The crowd slowly quieted and started moving toward the speaker. Neat spotted Amanda at the back of the crowd near the center of the room. His knees felt weak. *Even masked, she is so beautiful!* Dressed in a maroon, off the shoulder gown that accented her creamy skin and enchanting cleavage, her blond hair pulled up into a bun with ringlets escaping at her temples, she looked much more mature and sophisticated than her seventeen years.

She was the pride of her parents, Cora and Lawtell Pitre. Amanda's beauty was complemented by a sweet, loving personality and uncommon intelligence. Lawtell had managed to save his sugar cane farm by cooperating fully with the reconstructionists. This, in turn had cost him some friendships and respect in the area. But, he reasoned, his relationship with men like Herman Boyer allowed him to care properly for his family. It provided for his wife and beautiful daughter and ensured their recognition with the coveted invitation to tonight's festivities.

"Ladies and gentlemen, I know we're all enjoying this wonderful evening and we want to properly thank the person who is responsible for it." The man's accent was familiar but still foreign to the ears of Neat and the other Louisiana natives. "As you all know, we are the recipients of the generosity of this man who has been the leader of the United States government's reconstruction efforts in this area for the past eight years." In spite of themselves, many in the crowd let out a soft moan. "I'm sure you've heard the news that he has recently been notified of a transfer for him and his family to our unified country's Capital, Washington D. C."

The speaker turned with a slight bow to the man standing to his right with his arm draped over the shoulders of a short, stout woman wearing a white satin eye mask. "We thank you for your service here in our midst, sir, and we wish you God speed in your new assignment. I know you will all join me in warm applause for Mr. Herman Boyer, administrator of the Freedmen's Bureau for Iberville, Assumption and Ascension Parishes. Mr. Boyer."

Boyer stepped up on the riser and greeted the throng with outstretched arms. The applause was polite and under whelming. He was dressed much like the other men but his suit, shirt and tie were much newer, immaculately clean and well fitted on his portly frame. A gold watch chain looped across his ample vest. His sandy hair, beard and mustache were neatly trimmed and his eye mask was made of bright, golden satin. Even at age thirty-eight, he most assuredly had an air of authority; one might even say haughtiness.

As Boyer started talking, Neat moved cautiously through the back of the crowd until he was just behind Amanda. He leaned over her left shoulder and, in French, whispered softly, "Bon soir, mon chere, please don't look around and please don't be angry with me, I had to come." He sensed her stiffen but couldn't read her expression under the maroon mask. He slipped his right arm softly around her waist and she didn't move away. In fact, she inconspicuously leaned slightly into him. Continuing in French, he breathed quietly in her ear, "When this pompous carpetbagger is finished praising himself, the Union and the Republicans, meet me on the south gallery." She nodded her head slightly in the direction of her parents who were avidly watching Herman Boyer. Then she lifted her shoulders slightly in a questioning gesture indicating she wasn't sure she could break away from them. Neat took a deep breath, savoring the faint magnolia scent of her hair, then slipped away.

Boyer was still talking, "So, I wanted to show my appreciation for the many friends I have made here by inviting you to my home tonight for this festive occasion. As you know, this may be the last Mardi Gras my family and I get to spend with you as it appears I am being reassigned." His Pennsylvania accent and nasal twang reverberated off the walls of the huge ballroom. "My wife Hilda and my children, little Jessica and young Samuel, will all be leaving here soon and we'll always have fond memories of those of you who have welcomed us into your lives. Of course, Hilda and I and the children had never heard of Mardi Gras, Fat Tuesday, before we came down here," he chuckled. "But now, we will never forget it." Some in the crowd laughed gratuitously.

Boyer became more serious, "As you well know, things have not always been easy during this reconstruction. There are some in this area who have not yet accepted the fact that the South did not win the war and cannot continue with its old ways." There was a nervous shuffling of feet among the crowd. "Most of the Southern states have put the war behind them and moved on. I hope those of you gathered here, who have helped us in our efforts, will prevail in convincing those few stubborn, misled souls still denying reality. They must realize that their continued resistance will condemn them to being permanent outcasts of the new South just as they are tonight. You've noticed, I'm sure, that they and their kind were purposely excluded from this joyous occasion. You know who they are, they know who they are and," he smiled slightly, "I can assure you we know who they are.

"Now, let's enjoy one more dance and then we will unmask and properly greet our old friends as well as our new ones who have joined in our efforts to rebuild the new South." He signaled to the musicians who immediately began a lively reel as couples began pairing off.

Neat had ambled over to a side door and was emerging onto the gallery that encircled the house when one of Boyer's aides came around the corner of the house and shouted to him, "You, sir, I don't believe I know you. Would you please remove your mask and show your invitation?"

Neat started laughing heartily, "Of course you don't know me, my good man. I'm with the Freedmen's Bureau in Baton Rouge and, if you were listening to Mr. Boyer, you'd know it is not time to unmask yet. I was personally invited by Mr. Boyer and only just arrived after an all-day ride." He was trying hard to soften the accents that were part of his French and Spanish heritage as he waved the forged invitation in the air. "Please excuse me as I have an urgent need to find the outhouse." Neat turned and headed for the steps leading down to the yard and the herd of horses and carriages nearby.

"If you're looking for the outhouse, you're heading in the wrong direction. I don't believe anybody places their sanitary facilities in the front of their house. You just stop right there, sir."

Neat heard Boyer's voice, "What's going on here, Nathaniel? Who is that?" He was standing in the doorway.

"I don't know sir. He says he's from Baton Rouge and that you invited him. I didn't know we had invited anyone from the Baton Rouge office." He turned to see Neat quickly moving into the shadows near the hitching post. "Hold it there. Hold it, I said." Nathaniel pulled a revolver from under his coat.

Neat heard the gun being cocked but kept walking toward the horses trying to appear as nonchalant as possible. He waved a hand over his shoulder, "I'll be right with you. Don't you know what it feels like when you have got to relieve yourself? I'll just have to step behind this oak tree. I'm about to burst!" Suddenly another of Boyer's men ran up from the other side of the house. Several of the horses were startled and started pulling uneasily against their reins as the third man removed his mask and leveled his revolver on Neat.

Nathaniel and Boyer jumped down from the gallery and ran up to the two men. "Unmask him," Boyer said, "I think I know who this young rebel is. I've seen that cocky walk before." All three men were now holding revolvers in their hands.

"Now just hold on here, men." Neat turned and faced Boyer and Nathaniel. The other man was standing just off his left elbow a couple of feet away. Neat left his mask in place. He lowered his voice conspiratorially, "Herman, I was working in the governor's office with Governor Pinchback back in '72 when you needed all the help you could get down here with these damn rebels and I got help for you. Now, damn it man, get those pistols off me."

Confused, Boyer lowered his gun and the other two men slowly followed his lead. Boyer said, "I don't believe I know what you are talking about, sir. I don't recall asking the governor for help back then. Now, please identify your…" Neat suddenly ripped off the Scaramouche mask with his left hand, slashed it across the face of the closest aide, simultaneously pulled the Derringer from the small of his back and fired both barrels within two seconds. The first ball caught Nathaniel in the right shoulder and spun him around and back three yards. The second hit Boyer in the left upper chest. He went backwards as if kicked by a mule. The hard, lacquered Scaramouche mask had cut a gash across the other man's forehead. He dropped his pistol and was holding both hands to his bleeding head and moaning loudly.

Spinning into the horses tied to the rail, Neat quickly found his mare, swung up into the saddle and was flying down the pathway between the oaks when the first revelers responded to the gunshots. They very cautiously moved through the doors of the mansion. Men started running to aid Boyer and the two others on the ground. Women, seeing the blood oozing from one man's head and spreading over the front of Herman Boyer's ruffled white shirt, started screaming. Two fainted.

Neat heard the pandemonium behind him as he leaned into Dancer's neck. They reached the road and sprayed dirt as they turned north and headed for the little town of White Castle. *Goddamn it, look what they made me do. All I wanted to do was see Amanda and have a little fun,* he thought. He had to get far away quickly and he immediately knew where he had to go: into the swamp.

II
February 29–March 1, 1876

Neat galloped Dancer through the chilly night straight up the main street of the sleeping village of White Castle. He was living in the back room of a small frame house on the outskirts of town. The parents of his friend, Sherman Mayers, owned the house. The Mayers family, Sherman, his mother, father, a younger brother and two younger sisters lived in the four rooms at the front of the house. His room was a shed attached to the rear of the kitchen that was also used to store wood for the stove and fireplace. It was nearly midnight when he slowed his mount to approach the house.

The house was dark. The family was obviously in bed for the night. He eased Dancer into the backyard. Some of the chickens roosting in a lean-to next to the house started clucking nervously and the big hog being fattened in the nearby sty grunted a couple of times. He led the horse to a water trough and waited as he drank deeply. Leaving Dancer saddled and tethered behind the house, he entered as quietly as possible, felt his way around his tiny room, found and lit a lamp.

Working quickly, he threw clothing and boots into a small valise. He opened the small food cabinet where he kept a few essentials. He stuffed some of the food in the valise: a bag of rice, some coffee, a round of bread and some beef jerky. He grabbed the old Springfield rifle leaning against the wall and packed two additional saddlebags with ammunition for the rifle and both pistols.

Minutes later he led the laden horse quietly toward the road that led out of town to the west. When he was well away from the Mayers' house, he mounted the mare and eased into a slow gallop. She was blowing a cloud of condensation through her nostrils as Neat guided her into the shadows at the side of the dirt road. The new moon was just beginning to give way to a thin crescent. He would have to navigate mainly by starlight and his and Dancer's instincts. He needed to go about nine miles to get to his destination. Resting the horse and stopping for water along the way, he figured they should be near Bayou Maringouin in a couple of hours, well before sunup.

The air had turned much colder and more humid. Neat suspected the last cold snap of winter would soon hit the swampland. As they moved along, he shook his head in disbelief of what had happened and shivered with the thought of what might lay ahead for him. Just yesterday he and his best friend, Sherman Mayers, were talking about how things were beginning to get better in their lives.

Neat was born in the tiny Louisiana fishing village of Barataria on the north shore of the bay of the same name. It was once the legendary headquarters of the infamous Jean Lafitte, the pirate, or *privateer,* as he preferred to be called. Neat's mother and father spoke Spanish as a first language, French as a necessity and struggled with English when all else failed. The children became fluent in all three languages.

Neat was certain his grandfather was part of Lafitte's band of privateers though his father would never admit such and would not allow questions concerning the man's life and fate. Neat could only ascertain that the last time anyone had ever seen his grandfather was around 1817, the same year Lafitte's pirate fleet left Barataria Bay under pressure from the United States government and moved their operations to the Galveston, Texas area. Neat's grandfather, Jorge, was a first generation immigrant from the Canary Islands. Many of the islanders, called Los Isleños, had worked their way through the Caribbean Islands and settled along the Mississippi River and its tributaries and nearby swamps. Jorge would have been thirty-seven at the time of his disappearance and Lafitte's evacuation.

Neat's father, Lorenzo, was just an infant at the time. He grew up never knowing his father. As the only male in a household of six sisters and his mother, his responsibilities to his family prevented him from doing much courting at an earlier age. He did not marry until he was past thirty years old. Little Antoine was born after his four sisters when Lorenzo was over forty.

Just before the War Between the States broke out, Neat's father moved the family to a small farm on Bayou Lafourche. One of Neat's earliest memories was of his mother preparing chickens from their farm for a group of Confederate soldiers who had shown up at their doorstep near starvation. The young men, all under eighteen years old, were emaciated with threadbare remnants of uniforms hanging from their bony frames. Neat's father had greeted them with a leveled Springfield rifle as they approached the family home just after dusk. None of them was armed. In these unsettled times, one never knew what was coming down the road.

The soldiers turned their blank stares on Lorenzo and the family standing on the front gallery of the house. They held their arms away from their bodies to show they were harmless as they related that their unit had been ambushed and annihilated in a firefight near Donaldsonville several weeks earlier. They alone had escaped with their lives and little else and had been hiding during the days and traveling at night trying to find a viable Confederate Army presence somewhere along Bayou LaFourche. The young men eagerly devoured the chicken and boiled rice Neat's mother hastily prepared for them. They slept fitfully in the hayloft of the rickety barn for several hours then slipped away into the night. Neat would never forget the haunted look on the faces of the young rebels.

The Galvez family had suffered the ravages of the war as it devastated Louisiana along with the rest of the South. The systematic destruction left a once proud, thriving culture destitute. In 1860, Louisiana was the leading Southern state in per capita wealth. Its geographic location astride the Mississippi and its rich agricultural environment was a magic combination attracting commerce and industry from the heart of the young nation as well as its trading partners in Europe and Central America. The war had reversed all of that.

Louisiana now found itself in economic devastation. Great plantations with their stately mansions were in ruins. Industries in and around the once bustling port of New Orleans were wrecked. Roving bands of Union soldiers had burned many of the farmhouses, most of the fields and taken or killed almost all the livestock. Just meeting the necessities of life was an all-consuming, crushing task. There wasn't much time for schooling the children. Besides, there were practically no schools left intact or operating after the war. Neat remembered spending only about three months in a tiny classroom and a couple of years off and on with a tutor, a neighbor who had once taught school.

In addition to the destruction wreaked by enemy soldiers, roaming bands of outlaws, usually deserters from the Confederate army, were constantly marauding and plundering the countryside. They called themselves by the romantic name of "Night Riders." His father called them "Jay-Hawkers" and spoke of them with as much hatred as he usually reserved for the "scalawags," native southerners who cooperated with the Union soldiers and occupiers.

In order to build up the numbers in the depleted livestock, the families restrained from eating much meat of any kind, beef, pork or chicken. The farmers pooled their stock for breeding purposes.

After the war, Lorenzo's tiny farm barely eked out enough food for the family of seven. When Neat was twelve, he and his father had to work away from the farm as well. His mother and the four girls tended the vegetable garden and the meager livestock. Lorenzo operated a barge and young Antoine drove the mules along the banks that pulled the flatboats and barges through the shallow parts of the bayou.

Lorenzo died of malaria when Neat was fourteen. The family was devastated but his mother held it together. To help the finances of the family, the teenager struck out on his own working at the bustling Port of Donaldsonville as a dockhand loading and unloading the boats and bringing most of his earnings home to his mother and sisters. Because of the terrible human carnage of the war, there weren't many able-bodied men available for such jobs. Besides, Neat was multi-lingual and quite gregarious, a natural salesman. His young career was delayed when he contracted small pox and then barely survived yellow fever. When he recovered, He and his older sister, Corina, set out together looking for jobs. Corina found work in Donaldsonville as a seamstress. Neat found work at a nearby sugar mill. Both contributed most of their earnings to the family back on the farm.

Unfortunately the mill shut down at the end of grinding season but one of the their suppliers had taken notice of the industrious young man and was impressed by his outgoing personality and the fact that he spoke fluent Spanish and French in addition to passable English. He was given a job selling lye and other supplies to the numerous sugar mills throughout south Louisiana and he was good at it. Lye was a necessity in the sugar making process as it was used to clean the sticky residue from the cooking vats in the refineries.

Young Neat also represented a company that specialized in tools and tack for the sugar cane farmers. He was finally making enough money as a salesman to make a more substantial contribution to his mother and sisters back in Brusly McCall and still have enough to support himself and his chief hobby, playing poker.

Neat and his generation matured quickly. He was carrying a sidearm and smoking cigars by age fifteen. He learned to play poker the hard way but he learned well and, after a half-year or so of regularly losing his meager discretionary earnings, became a consistent winner.

The previous November, Neat attended a potluck supper at the Catholic Church in White Castle with some friends. While sampling the dishes, he caught sight of a young beauty serving slices of sweet potato pie. He instantly fell madly in love with Amanda Pitre. A blue-eyed, honey-haired sprite, Amanda was barely seventeen and the only daughter of the once-wealthy Pitre family who, in spite of their wartime losses, were aristocracy compared to the Galvez family. Her father, Lawtell, in his comfortable relationship with the reconstruction administrators, made regular off-the-record payments to them for the privilege of continuing the operation of his sugar cane farm and refinery. He was also one of young Neat's clients. Neat had a reputation as a high-spirited, arrogant, non-compliant young rebel and was always on the verge of crossing the line in dealing with the ruling bodies. He and Sherman and some of his other friends were frequently warned about their rowdy conduct and obvious disdain for the administrators of the Freedmen's Bureau and other authorities.

Amanda was a great attraction to many of the young men of the area but especially the Northerners who had come down to seek their golden futures in the name of "Southern Reconstruction." Her blond hair and fair complexion, inherited from her mother's Scottish side, was in stark contrast to most of the French and Spanish descendants along the west bank of the Mississippi. With born female intuition, she flirted expertly with her many admirers. She had her pick of young suitors but, as is often the case, was drawn to the rebellious, non-conforming Galvez. Neat, small, dark, slim and intense intrigued her the most.

Her parents were astounded at her attraction and did whatever they could to discourage Neat's courtship of their lovely daughter. That made it all the more magnetic for the young lovers. They devised ingenious ways to meet in secret places.

As he galloped through the shadows of the night he thought, *I may never see Amanda again. And what will happen to my mother and sisters? All they have is that tiny farm. Damn, damn, damn. Mon Dieu. This is not good at all.*

One thing he knew for sure: he could not turn himself in to the authorities and hope to convince them of his innocence. He knew he would not stand a chance in a trial conducted by the reconstructionist administration, especially considering who he had shot. Most of the judges were former Union soldiers or former slaves who had been elevated far beyond their education or training. Both groups still bore enmity for the Southerners who came into their courts.

Most of the law enforcement had also been turned over to former slaves who wielded justice according to the wishes of their carpetbagger sponsors.

Recently word had come up river from New Orleans that the carpetbaggers' days were numbered. The utter destruction during the war that had turned this once thriving land into one of abject poverty had soured a lot of them on the experience. Most of these opportunists were having difficulty maintaining a comfortable existence. In addition, the core of the South's wealth lay in the sugar cane and cotton fields of the land. Without the expertise of the previous owners and, even more importantly, without the slaves to plant and harvest and do the rest of the backbreaking labor that was required, there was no way the carpetbaggers could duplicate the profits of the past.

Louisiana was neither averse nor unfamiliar with Northern business and commerce. New Orleans, the Queen City of the Mississippi, had been a great attraction for investors and entrepreneurs. Prior to the start of the war in 1860, it had reached a pinnacle as the wealthiest city in the South. But, after the war, a different breed of Yankees had taken up residence. Many native Louisianians in and around New Orleans had fought secession and remained loyal to the Union. As the war ended, they welcomed the newcomers. They would rather cooperate than see their beloved culture totally destroyed. The returning Confederate soldiers, broken physically, mentally and economically referred to these Union supporters as "scalawags." Seeking to make their fortunes, the carpetbaggers had come in waves. More than in any other Southern state, these blatant opportunists dominated Louisiana during reconstruction.

By 1866, under carpetbagger leadership, a third of the state's House of Representatives and twenty percent of the Senate were black men. Some had been slaves. With the disenfranchisement of ex-Confederate sympathizers, blacks formed the majority of the electorate in the state. The twenty-six year old governor, Henry Clay Warmoth, was a former lieutenant colonel in the Union army. He brought the corruption in state politics to new heights.

Millions of dollars being poured into the South in the name of reconstruction were being squandered and stolen. In 1873, a federal investigating committee reported that Governor Warmoth "has been governor four years, at an annual salary of eight thousand dollars and he testified that he made far more than one hundred thousand the first year and he is now estimated to be worth from a half million to a million dollars." Taxes in the state had risen by over five hundred percent and the bonded indebtedness rose to over fifty million dollars.

Another civil war was brewing within the state. Confederate soldiers, leaders of the Democratic Party, native white supremacists and a group calling itself the Knights of the White Camellia joined forces determined to oust the invaders. Like many defeated armies before and since, they had laid aside their uniforms but not their guns and they never really surrendered. They were the new vigilantes. The decade after the war was almost as bloody as the war years in Louisiana. in 1868 alone, almost eight hundred lives were lost in Louisiana as a result of terrorist activities. Governor Warmoth was impeached by his own Republican Party and replaced by P. B. S. Pinchback, a light-complexioned black man who was the only one of his race to ever occupy the governor's office. He served thirty-five days.

Sporadic violence ensued from one end of the state to the other but especially in New Orleans. In 1874 almost four thousand heavily armed members of a paramilitary group called the White League engaged in all-out war against the state's militia and the Metropolitan New Orleans police from the foot of Canal Street to St. Charles Avenue. It was called the *Battle of Liberty Place.*

Neat, undereducated and living in the backwaters of rural Louisiana, paid little attention to the politics raging up and down the Mississippi and through the bayous but his recent travels to sugar mills as far away as Baton Rouge, Opelousas and Thibodaux made him aware that change was afoot. Many believed that the Union soldiers would be leaving soon and, without their protection and encouragement, the carpetbaggers and "the leeches serving them" would soon lose their authority.

The war and its ensuing unrest had left the state inhospitable for business by natives and invaders alike. Overall, Louisiana emerged from the war with less than half its former wealth. In 1860, she ranked second in the nation and first in the South for per capita wealth. By 1880, she ranked 17th in the nation and last in the South. Louisiana entered the war wealthy. At its close it was ruined, devastated and poverty-stricken.

Neat knew he couldn't turn himself in although he knew the sheriff well and shared a mutual respect with him. *Maybe I'll get lucky and those bastards I shot will live.* Hell, Sheriff Henry Gilmore had worked with him on the mule teams along the bayou. They had sneaked sips from bottles of whiskey behind the saloon Henry's father cleaned up at night. The sheriff was only about six years older than Neat and was a freeman-of-color. The carpetbaggers had made him sheriff along with several other Negroes who were elevated to positions of pseudo-authority in the Parish.

Just gotta get out there to our shed in the swamp and get some time to think. Hope Sherman left the pirogue well hidden on this side of the bayou. I think we left a lamp and a good supply of coal oil out there too. Probably nobody's been back since we shot that deer in December. Damn, I forgot, Henry's been to our little camp, too. He'll figure out that I'll be there. If he tells that Boyer bunch, I'm a dead man. Glad I took a lot of ammunition. There's no way I'm going to be taken in alive. Mon Dieu, what a mess.

A fine mist was in the air and a light fog clung to the banks of the bayou as Neat dismounted. He still had a couple of hours before dawn. He looped the reins over a low hanging branch and went off on foot through a thick growth of palmettos. The hand-made pirogue was lying upside down under the palmettos partially hidden with clumps of moss. Neat turned it over and the hand-hewn paddle rattled along the bottom. He dragged it into the water and pulled it along the bank until he was back to the spot where he had left Dancer.

Working quickly, Neat unbridled his horse, removed the saddle and bags and placed everything in the boat. He took the mare's head in his hands and gently kissed her snout. She whispered a low whinny. "Take care, ole girl. You'll find your way home and somebody'll take care of you." She jumped with surprise and trotted out to the road when Neat swatted her on the rump.

He got in the boat with his tack and supplies and started paddling down the bayou.

While fishing with his pal Sherman the previous summer, they had come across a small, abandoned hut probably built by a trapper several years before. It was almost totally hidden by thick underbrush and the trunk and low-hanging branches of a huge old oak. It was situated a couple of hundred feet from the edge of the bayou on a ridge nearly a half-mile long and a quarter of a mile wide. In all but the driest months, the ridge was an island in the middle of the swamp with Bayou Maringouin running along one side. Bayou Sorrel emptied into Bayou Maringouin about a mile north. The branches of century-old oak trees intertwined creating a jungle-like umbrella over the ridge while two to three-foot tall palmettos covered the floor of the small forest.

The trapper had done a good job. The hut was constructed with the bousillage method, small logs held together with a mixture of dried mud and moss. The roof was of the same construction but was also covered with several layers of dried palmetto leaves forming a nearly waterproof thatched roof. There were several long, slim horizontal openings near the roof for ventilation and a loosely fitted door.

Neat and Sherman had cleared the dirt floor and laid down a mat of dried palmetto leaves and moss over most of it. One corner was left bare where they had brought in a small pot-bellied stove for heat and rudimentary cooking. A couple of moss-stuffed, thin mattresses were rolled up and hung from the ceiling, as was a coal-oil lamp. Several three-foot long logs served as seats or tables. On their last visit Sherman and Neat had brought in a five-gallon can of coal oil. They also had some basic pots and pans and eating utensils.

The boys had spent a lot of time at their hideaway fishing, hunting, drinking and lazing around. It would now be the center of Neat's survival. Neat got the lamp going and swatted a couple of spiders and their webs from the corners of the room. He then made a quick inspection of the floor for other unwanted guests.

He suddenly realized how bone-tired he was. He grabbed a mattress down from the ceiling, unrolled it on the floor of the hut, closed the lamp and, with the crickets, cicadas, bullfrogs and alligators joining in swamp song, was deeply asleep within minutes.

III
November 3, 1958

The leathery-faced old man sat almost dead still in the rocking chair. The only indication of life was an occasional flicker of an eyelid or a slight push on the floor to set the rocker in ever-so-slow motion for a few seconds. He held the remains of an unlit cigar in his mouth and rolled it from one side to another every two or three minutes. An ancient pipe, also unlit, sat on the small table next to the rocker.

He squinted with one eye through the screen of the porch at the sound of tires on gravel. *I guess it must be most time for lunch,* he thought, *that man in the green automobile just pulled up on the side of the house. Every time he does that the little plump woman comes and calls me to eat. She says, "Your son's home…time for lunch." Guess it must be one of my sons, but he sure looks old for that. Can't hardly tell 'em apart anymore, they're all gettin' so old. Can't even remember their names most of the time. If he is my son, that little pudgy woman must be his wife. Damn, he coulda done better'n that.*

Antoine Joseph Galvez was approaching his 100th birthday. He had lived on his small sugar cane farm "back o' White Castle" up until four years ago. Then, finally acknowledging his advanced years, he grudgingly accepted the hospitality of his children. His remaining family, five daughters and four sons, moved him from house to house among themselves every couple of months. Well, some did. One daughter, Gretel, was twice divorced and presently unmarried though living with a man in New Orleans. Because of such unacceptable behavior, she had been estranged from most of the family for several decades. Another daughter, Francis, lived out of state and chose not to associate with most of the Louisiana family since she believed she had married above them.

Unlike the others, the second-to-youngest son, Edgar, had remained on the family farm. Over the past years most of the others had moved into nearby cities like Baton Rouge and New Orleans. A couple of the daughters lived out of state with their own families. Edgar, tending the farm for many years, had negotiated a buy out of the family property. After the sale, Neat remained on the farm in his original frame house even after his wife, Marie, died. Some in the family felt Edgar had manipulated the terms of the sale to cheat the other siblings of their inheritance. But they all had to admit they wanted no part of running a small sugar cane farm in Iberville Parish. The dependence on weather conditions in south Louisiana always made the value of each year's crop questionable at best.

The old man everybody called uncle or grandpa Neat (the nickname still with him since he was just a kid being spoiled by four older sisters), was easy enough to care for. He still walked reasonably well. His eyesight and hearing were remarkably good. You could still tell that his hair had once been jet black. His appetite was adequate though special care had to be given to the consistency of the food since only eleven teeth remained in his mouth. But they were fairly well aligned to allow for some careful chewing. His wife had passed away almost twenty years ago. He didn't require much company and seemed content sitting alone, chewing on an old cigar or smoking his pipe, living quietly with his memories. Those memories were not too vivid for the near past but were clear and lucid when involving his early and middle life.

His current temporary residence was one of his favorite spots in his ever-changing living status. He was in Baton Rouge and his son Louis's home had a nice screened porch on the west side where he could sit and rock and even smoke without anybody complaining. The weather had been especially mild for the past couple of weeks and he had spent most of each day in the rocker.

That boy shoulda seen the girl I had in Napoleonville back in about '82 or '83. Had my pick of 'em then. And if it hadn't been for that trouble with the damn carpetbaggers, hadn't wasted over a year of my life, hadn't lost Amanda, no tellin' what I coulda had, big business, big farm, women to mess with and poker games with the other big shots.

His daughter-in-law Tess came to the door of the porch, "Come on, Paw Paw, time for lunch. I made some spaghetti with that ground meat sauce you like so much."

Well, at least she's a good cook. Better than that crazy old coot my oldest son married. Cooks her damn crawfish etouffe with ketchup, for God's sake. Wonder when they gonna make me go back there. Christ, living with that woman will make a man get old.

Neat grunted his way off the rocker and followed Tess into the kitchen where his son Louis was already seated at the small dining table. "Hey Paw, how's it going today? Nice and cool, huh? That October was hot, wasn't it?"

He acknowledged Louis's greeting with a brief wave of his hand and sat down in his usual seat. Tess started serving him the spaghetti and ground meat sauce. The pasta had already been cut up into pieces an inch or so long. Tess had convinced him long ago to use a spoon rather than a fork for most of his food. Louis said, "Poppa, you're gonna have a visitor tomorrow." The old man looked up with wary eyes. "It's a young man that works for the newspaper in Plaquemine. He heard you were going to turn one-hundred-years old this week and wants to write a story about your life."

Neat stopped with a spoonful of spaghetti halfway up to his mouth, "Why'd he wanta do that? I ain't never done nothin', never been nowhere 'ceptin' back o' White Castle, Bayou Lafourche and up here. Hell, never done nothin', never seen nothin', what's he gonna write about?"

"Well, just talk to him. After all, not many people reach one-hundred-years old. He'll ask questions and you just answer them. Just tell him what you remember. You've got a memory like an elephant for things that happened seventy, eighty years ago even if you don't remember what you ate yesterday."

Tess added, "I'll get you all dressed up in case he wants to take a picture. After all, he'll wanta see why they call you Neat. 'Course you know we're going down to White Castle Saturday for your big birthday party. Going to be a lot of people there. We've got the American Legion Hall rented and some of Edgar's girls are going to decorate it and all." She paused, took a sip of iced tea and said, "And try not to cuss so much when you're talking to the reporter, OK?" She looked over her glasses and smiled sweetly, "We don't want all that kinda stuff in the newspaper now do we?"

Neat gave her a withering look and got busy on the spaghetti. *I know what I ate yesterday. That goddamn cabbage and ham dish I hate. Oh yeah, gonna have a great big party. Ain't gonna hardly be anybody I know at that damn party. Everybody I knew or even liked is dead and gone.*

That nosy reporter probably wants to ask me about those slimy carpetbaggers I shot. That's all anybody wanted to talk about for years. That and the year I spent hiding out in the swamp. Hell, there's a lot worse things than being alone. Kinda liked it out there in the swamp, really. 'Specially when Amanda came visitin'.

IV
November 4, 1958

Tess was ready for the interview. She had always been uncomfortable with her father-in-law's crudeness and what she considered his wild and embarrassing past. She closely monitored Neat's conversations with strangers and even family members. She did not want him talking about his poker-playing, saloon-carousing, sidearm-toting, woman-chasing past and she especially did not want him resorting to using his salty barroom language. Her own family was French with a touch of German influence originally from the oft-contested Alsace-Lorraine area on the German-French border. They were generally soft-spoken, self-effacing, courteous and devoutly Catholic. They were also known to sometimes be determinedly stubborn.

Louis's family, though also Catholic, was, in Tess's view, decidedly loud, braggadocios and confrontational. While growing up, Louis and the Galvez brothers liked nothing better than a good, bare-knuckled brawl. It was better if it involved outsiders but they would just as well fight each other if the pickings were slim. Tess had decided this newspaper interview was going to be well within her control. Neat was not going to embarrass her or the family.

She greeted the young reporter, Bob Hudson, at the door and showed him to the screened porch where Neat was waiting in the rocking chair. Tess had him dressed in his only suit, a dark gray wool that hung loosely over his thin, drooping shoulders. He wore one of Louis's regimental striped ties and a white dress shirt whose collar looked two sizes too large for his wrinkled neck. A thin wisp of smoke curled from the barely lit pipe sitting in the ashtray on the side table. He was wearing his glasses and seemed fairly anxious to meet the young man.

Tess pulled a straight-back chair up next to Neat's rocker for Bob then plopped down in another chair several feet away on the porch. She was ready for her role as censor. Hudson pulled out a pencil and a small reporter's notebook.

Over the course of an hour the young reporter took a couple of snapshots with his twin reflex, Rolleiflex camera and scribbled notes as Neat answered his questions. At first the responses were one or two words only. Though only twenty-five years old, Hudson was a thorough interviewer. He had a homey, north Louisiana accent and a low-key personality that usually evoked trust from his subject. As the time wore on, Neat grew more comfortable with the questions and started to drift off into his memories and tended to ramble into a sort of stream-of-consciousness reminiscence. Bob let him wander. "There was one time when I didn't think I'd make it. I had smallpox *and* yellow fever. Both at the same damn time. Couldn't do a thing. Burned up with fever. Just wanted to sleep all the time. Didn't have no doctors either with all that medicine they give you nowadays. Hell no! Just mustard packs and some of mama's potions. 'Tween her and the pox and the fever, damn near killed me." Tess cleared her throat loudly. Neat looked at her, "Well, it did. Did damn near kill me! But that was the only time I been sick all my life. After Doctor Ourso treated me for that snakebite in '77, hadn't even seen another doctor 'til a couple of years ago. One of my daughters took me. I was having trouble pissing…getting up all night." Tess went into a fit of coughing. Neat gave her a wicked grin, "I think they just wanted the doctor to tell 'em how much longer they was gonna have to put up with me."

He recounted moving with his mother and four sisters to Brusly McCall after his father died. "Betcha don't even know where that is now." Hudson shook his head and waited for an explanation. "It's down toward Donaldsonville. 'Bout seven miles below White Castle. You go on that road that leads west back of Donaldsonville 'bout three miles. Don't know what's left but there used to be a couple dozen houses, a saloon and general merchandise store and all. Hell, it may be all gone now. I don't know, hadn't been there since before 1900."

Bob asked him about his immediate family. "Well, I got a late start so we only had nine children. Nine that lived. All still living, right?" Neat looked to Tess for affirmation. She nodded and started to say something but he picked up where he had left off. "Lost a couple of little girl babies. But, hell, I didn't get married 'til I was thirty-six. Too damn much to do to worry 'bout getting married." Tess started coughing again on the "hell" and kept it up through the "damn". Neat squinted at her. "You catchin' a cold, woman? Maybe you better get yourself inside off this porch. Go see a doctor or something." Bob suppressed a smile and went on with the interview.

"Having a birthday party?" he asked.

"That's what they tell me. Going back down to the Legion hall in White Castle. That's where my farm was, you know, 'bout ninety arpents of sugarcane. Me and some old mules, my sons, when they was home, and a couple of hired hands during cutting time. That's all they was. That was some hard work, boy. Sunup to sundown. And the boys was in and out through the years, what with going off to wars and then getting married and moving away to the big cities. Thank the Lord for the good niggras we had. The girls all took off soon as they got growed up. Grabbed a man and off they went. All but one of 'em. Hell, that one grabbed every man she saw."

Tess interrupted, "All of his nine children and their families will be at the party at the Legion home and, look at this." Hoping to distract Bob from the personal questions, she handed him a stack of envelopes. "He got birthday cards and messages from Congressman Jimmy Morrison and President Eisenhower and he was made a colonel on Governor Earl Long's staff. How about that?"

"Notice they didn't send any money or presents, typical politicians." Neat grumbled. He squinted through the porch screen. "I wonder if that Boyer kid is gonna make it to the party. He's been following me around off and on for damn near eighty years. Probably not even still alive. He'd be getting pretty old by now, somewhere in his '90's. Wonder if he ever got his face fixed. Damn shame what happened to his daddy. But, hell, I couldn't help it."

Before he could say another word, Tess was on her feet, "Well, that's about it, Bob. He's getting tired, talking nonsense. I'm sure you have enough for a real good story. Thank you so much for coming." She had him by the arm and was leading him back into the house and toward the front door.

"Thank you for your time, Mr. Galvez," Bob said over his shoulder as he was being hustled out, "and happy birthday and, well, many more, I guess. I'll see you at the party Saturday." He turned to Tess when he got to the front door. "Who's this 'Boyer kid' he said has been following him around for eighty years. That sounds interesting."

"Did he say Boyer? I thought he said Sawyer. Don't matter, it's nobody, just something he dreams up ever now and then. After all, he *is* a hundred years old." She opened the door and guided him through it. "I'll be looking forward to reading the story you write. Bye now." She closed the door, leaned against it and let out a slow moan. *That old man will be the death of me yet.*

V
March 2, 1876

The Boyer family and friends were gathered at the house that served as an undertaking establishment on White Castle's main street. The family living in the large home rented out the parlor and dining area for wakes and funerals. They even hosted an occasional wedding. Horses and carriages were tethered at every available space along the dirt road. Inside, seated in the front row of the parlor, closest to the pinewood casket, were Herman's thirty-five year old widow, Hilda, her twelve-year old son, Samuel and her ten-year old daughter Jessica.

The Episcopal minister, brought in from Baton Rouge, had just finished a brief service and people were offering condolences as they filed by the family.

"He was a wonderful man."

"If we can do anything, anything at all, please let us know."

"We'll be by your home later to bring some food."

Hilda was still in shock and the children in a state of total confusion. Hilda's mother, a widow for seven years, had moved down from Pottstown, Pennsylvania to join the Boyer family when she lost her husband and was now holding the children close and whispering to them.

Outside, a large group of men, black and white, gathered on the side of the road speaking in hushed tones. Occasionally, a voice was raised in anger. In the center of the group was Henry Gilmore, the tall, extremely slim, twenty-five-year old black sheriff of Iberville Parish. Most of the men around him were associated with reconstruction and the Freedmen's Bureau. The others were white natives of the area who had cast their lot with the Union forces. Some of the blacks were former slaves others freemen-of-color. The mood was ugly. Andrew Becker, brother of Boyer's aide Nathaniel, whispered, "My brother may be dying at this moment. If he lives, he won't have use of his right arm. I want to get that rebel rat and string him up right now. We need to hang him right here in the middle of town to let these low-life rebels know who's boss. We won the goddamn war and it's time they understand that."

William Simpson, wearing a huge, bloodstained bandage around his head agreed, "He didn't give us a chance. Sliced me with that damn mask of his and shot poor Herman and Nathaniel in cold blood, they never had a prayer."

Others were urging a more cautious approach. Eyeing the crowd of native whites who had gathered on the other side of the street, Sheriff Gilmore sensed big trouble brewing. He held his big hands up for quiet and spoke slowly and softly. "I understand how ya'll feel but we gotta go about this thing right. Remember that situation in Colfax a coupla three years ago. And ya'll know what's been going on in New Orleans and them other places. Them Knights of the White Camellia is headquartered right over there in Opelousas, just 'bout fifty miles from here and we don't have many troops or arms left around here to put down any kinda uprising."

The sheriff was referring to the massacre at the Grant Parish Courthouse in Colfax in north Louisiana three years prior. The state was split into two hostile, warring governments with the gubernatorial election of 1872. Both the reconstructionist Radical Republicans and the white supremacist Democrats claimed victory. The Democrats swore in John McEnery as governor and the Republicans, ignoring the obviously fraudulent ruling of the election board, declared William Pitt Kellogg the winner. For two years both men served as governor of the state simultaneously, neither ruled. Violence did. On Easter Sunday, 1873, dozens of black Democrats were killed in Colfax. Many were gunned down coming out of the courthouse with their hands in the air after they surrendered and a cease-fire had been declared. By the time the federal government finally intervened and declared Kellogg the governor, anarchy, led by the White League of Opelousas, was rampant.

Meanwhile, a seriously wounded and divided nation was also in the throes of an election for president scheduled for later in the year. Some reconstructionists in the South were now of the opinion that almost any concessions were worth it for peace and a chance at prosperity in controlling the spoils of war.

Many of the friends and allies of Herman Boyer were of the mind to form a posse immediately and go after Antoine Galvez with a hanging party. They just didn't know where to find him. Sheriff Gilmore and some of the cooler heads finally convinced them to wait for a more formal justice to prevail. "I know this man called Neat, Antoine, he has been a friend of mine," Gilmore told the group. "I may even know where he is. Let me try to find him and talk to him. I may be able to bring him in peacefully and we can set up a proper trial." The grumbling rose and ebbed and William Simpson said, "All right, you do that Henry, but I want somebody to pay for what they did to me, Herman and Nathaniel. And soon! We'll just see about that trial."

Across the street, Sherman Mayers and a dozen of Neat's friends watched the heated discussion. "We've gotta get word to Opelousas or New Orleans about what's going on here. Pokey, you got nothing going on. Why don't you take my pa's good horse and get on over to Opelousas. You should be able to make it in a day and a half. Get a hold of some of them knights. Let'em know what's going on here."

Arthur "Pokey" Lafleur, so named for his lack of speed of foot and mind, looked at Sherman with wide eyes and mouth agape. "Well damn, Sherm, why me? I never been out West afore in my life."

"Cause you can ride better'n any man here. Hell, we got any volunteers to go with him?" Three hands shot up. "See there, Pokey? You're the leader. Which one you want, Pierre, Gustav or David?"

Pokey grabbed Pierre Bourgeois by the shoulder and they split from the group and started making plans for their trip. Pokey looked back at Sherman, "Pierre says they's a great big ole river 'tween here and Opelousas. How you 'spect we gonna get across that, Sherm?"

"Ever heard of a ferry, Pokey? Here, we'll take up a collection so you and Pierre'll have some money for the ferry and some food." He held out his hat and the group started digging for coins. One of the group threw a handful in and laughed, "Don't go spendin' it all on liquor now, boys."

Sheriff Gilmore had been watching the action and slipped out of the center of his group to speak quietly to one of his most trusted black deputies. The man turned and headed down an alley.

VI
March 2, 1876

Neat awakened with a start. It was midmorning in the swamp. Disoriented, he was aware only of the sounds of the creatures he now lived among. Not only was he cramped from the hard mattress, cold air and the previous nights exertions, he found he was exceedingly hungry.

For now, the beef jerky he had stuffed into his saddlebag and some water from his canteen would have to do. Later, he would scout out the ridge for some fruit, maybe some root vegetables and, if he was lucky, a sleepy rabbit or squirrel.

Though he had slept soundly for over six hours, he still remembered fragments of a vivid dream. He was riding in a carriage with Amanda along the river road that ran north from White Castle to the beautiful mansion at Nottoway Plantation. Neat had felt a connection to the plantation home since he learned it was built the year he was born, 1858. It was one of the few truly grand plantation homes he had seen. With sixty-four rooms and fifty thousand square feet, it was the largest surviving the war mostly intact. It was not the magnanimity of the Union gunboats, artillery or infantry that saved Nottoway. It was the sheer audacity and courage of the mistress of the plantation, Emily Jane Randolph. When her husband took himself and his slaves to Texas to escape the war and protect his wealth, the forty-five-year old Mrs. Randolph remained at the house with her personal slaves and small children. With a dagger stuffed in her waistband, she faced down both the Yankees who would attack her and the Confederate soldiers who volunteered to defend her. She told them she could manage her family and home without either one. She gained their respect. The magnificent home was barely damaged.

In his dream, Neat and Amanda were entering the grounds of the Greek-revival mansion on the banks of the Mississippi. But when he glanced over at his beautiful friend, she was wearing his lacquered Scaramouche mask and blood was running out of the eyeholes. Neat tried to scream but nothing came out. Suddenly, Herman Boyer was running alongside the carriage. His face was gray as in death and his chest covered with blood. He was grinning crazily. Amanda suddenly whispered, "I know you did it for me. I will never forget you. I love you. I always will."

He shook off the chill brought on by the memory of his dream, strapped on his Colt .44, grabbed the Springfield rifle his daddy had left him and an ammunition bag and went off on his hunt.

For the next couple of days he tramped over almost every square foot of the ridge. He thought of his new surroundings as the Garden of Eden. There was foliage and wildlife of every description. Several persimmon trees were beginning to bud and would bear fruit soon. There was a stand of fig trees that he would have to fight the birds for the fruit in the summer. Squirrels scampered through the treetops as he rustled through the palmetto leaves. There were numerous droppings indicating a large rabbit population. Along the way, he found some edible greens and berries.

On the way back to his new home, he spotted a couple of squirrels playing in an oak several hundred feet ahead. He readied his rifle and moved stealthily forward, stopping, statue-still for minutes on end until he got within range. He dropped one young squirrel with a single shot. When he got back to his camp he skinned, gutted and roasted his prize over an open fire at the campsite. He felt as though he was attending a feast.

With a charred piece of wood he sketched a crude calendar on a flattened section of log in the wall. Neat was beginning to realize that his exile could be an extended one. He wanted to be aware of the passage of time. The shooting had occurred on Tuesday, Mardi Gras night. It was now Friday. He was sitting on a log in front of his new home, puffing on a corncob pipe, wondering where this would all lead. He had no plan of action. Giving up was not an option in his mind. He felt that would be committing suicide. Leaving the area, maybe even the state, was his most logical option but the logistics were daunting; little money, no transportation, no destination.

The soft whinny of a horse drifted across the waters of Bayou Maringouin and brought Neat to attention, his heart pounding. He quickly snuffed out the pipe in a nearby pile of dirt, unsnapped his holster, cradled the rifle in his arms and moved into the shadows of the old oak. He glanced back at the cabin for reassurance that he had not left a fire burning with its tell tale smoke. He could now see some movement through the drooping moss far off on the other side of the bayou. Again, the horse neighed and blew through its lips as if recognizing his presence nearby. Neat quietly cocked and checked the load on both of his firearms. He heard the unmistakable creak of a person dismounting from a saddle followed by the brush of footsteps through the dry leaves.

"Neat, oh Neat," a voice called out, "Hello, Neat. Come on, Neat. I know you're around here. I found your little horse just up the road."

It was his erstwhile friend Sheriff Henry Gilmore. Neat stayed in the shadows, unmoving, silent.

"Neat, they's some of 'em wants to come after you with a noose, you know? I told 'em, 'no, they's a better way. They's a right way.' I don't s'pose you've heard; that big shot Boyer done died and the other one you shot probably won't use that arm anymore." Neat's heart sank. "You know I respect you, Neat. But, I also respect the law and I know you respect the law too. We friends, Neat. Hell, we even got drunk together once, remember?" Silence. Even the birds, crickets, bugs and animals were waiting for an answer. "Now, Neat, they wants me to take you in. I told 'em I'd do that only if I got the promise that you'd get a fair trial, with a fair jury. So I'm here all alone. Just you and me, Neat. I swear ain't nobody knows where I am. I'm here to promise you a fair trial and to bring you in, Neat. I'm gonna be right there standing with you. Nobody's gonna do you no harm. So come on, come on out and let's get this over with."

Another ten seconds of silence. "You wanna bring me in, Henry? Come and get me." It was almost a whisper but in the hush of the moment easily carried across the water.

Henry heard it clearly. He made his own voice and manner a little lighter. "Now, how I'm gonna do that, Neat? How'm I gonna come and get you? You know I cain't swim and neither can this ole horse of mine and I know you done took the pirogue over with you so how you think I'm gonna come and get you, huh?"

The quiet was all consuming. Neat let it fester. "Well, if you ain't coming to get me, I guess you might as soon go on back and tell 'em you can't find me. 'Cause, if you go back and says you found me and couldn't bring me back they gonna be awful mad. Probably take that star off your chest and start treating you like a darkie again. Remember how that was? So, I guess you better go on back and say, 'he ain't where I thought he was, les go look somewheres else.' Ain't that right, Henry?"

Henry paced up and down the bank for almost a minute. "Aw, come on, Neat. Stop messin' with me. I done told you I promised you a fair trial, a fair jury and, *and* a good lawyer."

"Ain't no such thing as a good lawyer, Henry. Go on, get outta here. Go back to town and tell 'em I musta gone to Donaldsonville and jumped on a packet heading for New Orleans. Ain't that what you woulda done?"

"Neat, I can't go back there and tell 'em that, I…"

A pistol shot shattered the air and whistled through the branches of the trees. Henry dropped to the ground. Leaves and wisps of moss floated down into the bayou. "I ain't messin with you, Henry. I am Goddamn serious! I ain't going back to swing from some chinaball tree for shooting a couple of scavenging, wormy carpetbaggers. Besides, they was going to shoot me if I hadn't shot them first. And that's the truth…and that's the end of this conversation." As punctuation he fired another shot from the .44 through the canopy of trees. A great blue heron broke out of its hiding place on the side of the stream screeching and flapping and heading away from this invasion of its serenity.

Henry backed off toward his skittery horse. "All right, all right, Neat. I'm gonna try to reason some sense with 'em. If you right and Boyer and Becker were about to shoot you, than you got a self-defense argument and ought not to be convicted. So, I'll see you soon, Neat. Don't you do nothin' stupid now. You need anything? You got yoself enough to eat?"

"Don't you worry 'bout me, Sheriff. Just don't let on that you know where I'm at."

"You ain't got no problem with me, Neat. I'm just trying to do my job and it ain't getting any easier." Henry turned, wheeled onto his horse and spurred her into a fast trot.

Neat walked slowly back to his shack, reloading his pistol. He looked up into the umbrella of oak limbs and leaves fighting back tears. *Right. Self-defense. No witnesses other than that slimeball Simpson. Ain't no self-defense when they drop that trap door out from under your feet.*

VII
March 5, 1876

Shortly after midday, Neat finished testing his new rabbit and squirrel trap. He had fashioned a little box out of small tree limbs tied together with marsh grass. He turned it upside down, tied a piece of twine to a chunk of potato and ran the twine through the back of the box. The string then went over the top and was tied to a small stick propping the other end of the box off the ground. The trap was set. When the animal pulled on the bait, the string tightened and pulled the propping stick loose and the box dropped over the unfortunate rodent who immediately qualified as Neat's next couple of meals. He proudly set up his contraption on the far side of the big oak tree about fifty feet away from his cabin.

Just as he was carefully adjusting the propping stick the swamp suddenly became very quiet and he heard the sound of hooves and the crush of carriage wheels on the road across the bayou.

Several times in the last couple of days he had been brought to attention with the passing of travelers along the road. He suspected that some of them might have been soldiers or deputies looking for him. Other than Sheriff Gilmore, none had stopped.

He moved carefully back to the hut and grabbed the rifle leaning against the front wall. His pistol was already strapped on. The carriage came to a stop and he heard two voices murmuring in the distance. He could not make out the words or even the gender of the voices. Didn't matter, he wasn't taking any chances. He settled behind the trunk of the oak and waited. Two forms took shape on the far bank. *Oh hell, this don't look good,* he thought. They were still partially obscured by the hanging limbs and moss. Then, he heard Sherman's voice call out in a loud whisper, "Neat, it's me, Sherman. I have Amanda with me; just the two of us. Come on across. I don't have a boat and I know you must have the pirogue over there."

Neat was still suspicious. *Is this a trap? Did Henry tell Sherman where I was? Naw, Sherman and Amanda would never do that.* He eased closer to his side of the bayou staying in the shadows. He could now plainly see Sherman and Amanda. The sight of her made his knees weak. She was dressed in what was obviously her Sunday best, a dark blue silk dress with a scoop neck. Over her shoulders was a powder blue shawl. "Sherman, you sure you weren't followed?" Neat asked in a low whisper.

Sherman and Amanda heard him and immediately looked directly at the spot from which the sound came. "Oh yeah, I'm sure, Neat. We stopped about a half-mile back and then doubled back for another half-mile before coming on over here. Come on, hurry. Amanda can't be gone all day and it took us almost two hours to get here."

"Ok, ok, I'm coming." Neat moved out of the shadows, uncovered the pirogue hidden under moss on the bank, turned it over and launched it into the bayou as he jumped in. He still carried his rifle with him. It took him less than two minutes to cross to where Sherman and Amanda were waiting.

Sherman grabbed the front of the boat as it touched ground and pulled it partially up on the bank. "Neat, you're looking good. Got a little beard going but it looks good."

Amanda blinked tears from her eyes, "Hello, Neat. You look wonderful."

Neat could not resist. He pulled her toward him and wrapped his arms around her. She eagerly responded. "Oh, Amanda, I've missed you. I'm so sorry I've created such a problem. I don't know where this is going to end up but, I want you to know how much I care for you and…and I'll do whatever it takes to make this work out.

They moved further away from the road and sat on a felled tree. Sherman quickly brought him up to date on the situation in town. Amanda held Neat's hand tightly and never took her eyes off of him. "I sent Pokey and Pierre to Opelousas to let the White League people know that we got problems here. Don't know if they'll help but we sure need something. That bunch wants you at the end of a rope real soon. I think Henry's trying to help you. He let on to me that he knows about this place but he done told Boyer's people he thinks you hopped a packet in Donaldsonville and ran off to New Orleans. I know they sent a message to the law down there to be on the look out for you. Says you're wanted for murder and attempted murder, Neat. That's bad."

"I know, I know, Sherman. Henry's playing this real smart but I don't know how long he can hold them off. I may have to find a way to get over to Texas. I don't think I can win a trial here even if I could prove that they was going to kill me that night."

Amanda spoke very softly and slowly, "Neat, if you go to trial, I'll testify that I saw them shoot at you before you pulled your gun. I'll tell 'em I was on the gallery and saw the whole thing. Nobody else was out there. I'm the only witness."

Sherman and Neat looked at her in amazement, "Damn," Sherman said, "that would do it, Neat! She can be your proof it was self-defense."

"I don't know." Neat was still staring in wonder at Amanda. "I didn't see you come out on the gallery. Are you sure you saw them shoot at me?" Amanda nodded a slow but decided yes. "We don't know what they'd throw at us in a trial. I gotta think about it. Amanda, how'd you get away to come out here? What'd you tell your folks?"

"Elizabeth and I told our families we were going to Donaldsonville for a picnic with some friends and Sherman was taking us. That gives me until around sunset to get back. I guess we should be leaving soon."

"Look, you two take a little walk in the woods while I go take care of the horse," Sherman said with a wink to Neat as he started walking back toward the carriage.

Neat and Amanda, hand in hand, followed Sherman's suggestion. Once deeper into the brush they stopped and embraced. In the months since they had met and fallen in love they had cautiously explored the wonders of each other's bodies. They had never consummated their intimacy but the temptation was getting stronger. They held each other tightly and kissed passionately. Neat let his hands slip down her back and cup her buttocks. He pulled her even tighter to him. She could feel his arousal and pushed even harder into him. After several minutes, at Amanda's urging, they started back for Sherman's carriage. "I've really got to get back. We left right after Mass this morning and my folks will be concerned." When they got back to the road, Sherman was waiting with the carriage. Neat cautiously looked up and down the dirt road. Amanda reached into the back of the carriage, "Oh, I almost forgot, here are some things you might be able to use." She handed him a gunney sack that seemed to weigh about ten pounds. "Some fruit, vegetables, extra clothes and some soap." She wrinkled her nose cutely.

Neat asked, "Thank you, you're wonderful. How soon can you come back? I don't know how long I'll be out here."

"I'm trying for two weeks from yesterday. Elizabeth and I have planned a visit to one of her aunts' homes in Plaquemine. She'll cover for me and Sherman can bring me back. That's a Saturday so we can get an early start and I'll be able to stay longer, maybe even cross the bayou and see your cabin." She smiled sweetly.

Neat grinned, "I'll have to do some spring cleaning. Might even have some curtains hung."

"Yea, if you're gonna do that you might better make some windows for the curtains while you're at it," Sherman laughed.

Amanda and Neat kissed once more, Neat shook hands with Sherman, then grabbed him and gave him a hug and pat on the back. "Thanks, mon ami. Be careful on the way back."

Neat watched them move off through the rutted road. He had to wait several minutes to let the ache in his groin subside before he could board the pirogue and return to his lonely existence.

VIII
March 10, 1876

The sheriff's office in White Castle was jammed with men. Voices were raised in argument and vehemence. "Damn it sheriff it's been almost two weeks and you ain't got a clue yet where that little rebel bastard has disappeared to!" It was William Simpson shouting at Henry Gilmore. His head was still heavily bandaged from the gash inflicted by Neat's Scaramouche mask on the night of the shootings. Others joined in a chorus of vilification against the young, black sheriff. "We put you in this office and by God we can take you out, maybe even feet first!"

"Just hold on now men," Henry said rising from his desk. At six-feet-three, he towered over the men in the room. His right hand was on the butt of his holstered pistol and his left held a serious looking billy club. "I might just let you have this thankless job if any of you thinks you can do it better. Now I done searched everywheres I could think of and we wired down river to New Orleans. So far we done got sightings of fourteen men all fitting the description of Antoine Galvez. You know it's not like we be looking for a Chinaman or something. This *is* Louisiana and there are a few black-haired, five-foot-seven, one-hundred-thirty-five pound Spaniards and Creoles in and around these parts."

"Well, let me tell you something else, Gilmore," It was Nathaniel Becker's brother, Andrew. "My brother is looking at the rest of his life without the use of his right arm and you been sitting around here with your black thumb up your black ass sending telegrams and acting like you conducting an investigation." Henry gave him a withering look but Andrew continued, "And what you doing about those six strangers that rode into town last night? You checked 'em out? You know who they are? They been hanging around with Galvez's friends. They gotta be some of them White Camellia or White League or whatever they call those bastards. You gonna just let 'em set up shop here. It's bad enough they 'bout to take over New Orleans and Baton Rouge. Now we got'em out here too."

It had been like this all week. The frustration of the Boyer administrators, friends and their sympathizers had reached a fever pitch. The killing had only exacerbated the growing awareness that their days as rulers of a defeated but unrepentant South were numbered. Sheriff Gilmore still staunchly claimed he knew nothing of Neat's whereabouts and that he was doing everything within his power to find the man. The insults and threats coming from his supposed friends and benefactors were only deepening his resentment of them and his resolve to protect his friend.

Down river at the Boyer residence, preparations were being made for the family to make the long journey back to Pennsylvania after burying their husband and father, Herman. As a handful of black servants loaded furnishings and crates onto two large wagons parked in front of the home, Hilda sat on the gallery with little Jessica and Samuel. She patiently explained to them the calamity that had suddenly and forever changed their lives. Samuel wanted to know why "that bad man" killed his daddy and if someone was going to kill "the bad man" in return.

Hilda tried the Christian approach. She stroked Samuel's blond hair and said, "we don't know why God lets people like that man do such terrible things but we must trust in God's judgment. That man will have to answer to Him." She pointed to the heavens, "You know your daddy would want you to go on with your life and live it in such a way to make him proud. We must forgive and forget."

Samuel's eyes filled with tears. Little did Hilda realize that they were not tears of sadness but tears of rage. The boy was thinking very adult thoughts. *I'm going to kill that man! I will never forget! I will never forgive!*

IX
March 18, 1876

Neat hardly slept Friday night. Amanda was coming today. He was up with the singing mockingbirds at dawn. He straightened up his meager belongings within the cabin; then went downstream several hundred yards to a secluded pool of water out of the main channel. Shivering in the cool morning breeze, he bathed, using the soap Amanda had brought.

He had washed and hung to dry a change of clothes a couple of days before. He put on the clean clothes and ran his fingers through his lengthening hair. Now it was time to wait. He lit the corncob pipe and sat on the log at the front door.

Time had passed slowly and uneventfully since Amanda and Sherman's last visit. His hand-made trap had caught two rabbits that were summarily roasted and eaten. He decided to set the trap only once a week to avoid depleting the population of his special treats. Several times during the week he scrambled for his rifle when he heard horses or carriages passing on the distant road. None stopped at the bayou. And he continued his treks around the ridge that was now his world.

Finally, about mid-morning, he heard a single horse and carriage coming down the road. Moving stealthily toward the bayou's edge, he remained hidden by the thick palmetto growth and underbrush. The carriage halted. In a couple of minutes Sherman called out from the far side. Neat checked the scene to be sure it was only the two of them then launched himself in the pirogue to cross the bayou.

Amanda was wearing a bright yellow dress with a white sweater and carry-ing a covered straw basket. She put the basket down when Neat approached and they embraced. Sherman offered his hand and quickly said, "Look, I'm gonna go on back down the road a piece and have myself a little nap. That way I'll know if anyone's coming this way. Ya'll go on across and I'll whistle when I come back in about an hour and a half, okay?"

Naturally they agreed. Neat helped Amanda and her basket of goodies into the narrow boat and paddled back across the small stream. He pulled the pirogue up on the grass and under some protective covering then led Amanda by the hand to his "castle."

She walked into the hut as if she were entering a grand ballroom. Once inside she whirled around, spread her arms and said, "It is absolutely beautiful, my dear man. A home fit for a king. I think I'll stay."

Neat took her in his arms and they kissed long and hard. He softly caressed her downy cheeks and slowly removed her sweater. She untied the cord at the bodice of her dress and slipped it down to her waist. She stood looking into his eyes with no embarrassment as he bared her small, firm breasts and placed his thumbs over her rosy-pink, now-erect nipples. They were young, they were inexperienced but they were not hesitant. They knew what they wanted.

Neat was passionate but gentle and after a few moments of discomfort, Amanda joined him in his passion.

A half-hour later, Neat rose from the moss-filled mattress and poured a mug of water from his canteen for Amanda. He told her that he regularly boiled water from the bayou so that he would always have a good supply for drinking and cooking.

They sat, partially clothed and completely unselfconscious, and talked for another half-hour. She told him of how she was spending her days in the one-room White Castle schoolhouse. Her eyes were wide and bright as she told him her decision to become a teacher. He described how he spent his days of solitude.

She looked sad and said, "Oh Neat, we've got to find a way for you to come back and be free again. Maybe my father would agree to hire a lawyer for you."

"Somehow I doubt that he would do that. Have you seen or talked with Henry Gilmore at all? How long do you think they'll keep on looking?"

"I don't know but I've heard the Boyer bunch is still very angry and even have talked about firing Sheriff Gilmore and bringing in federal agents or soldiers to try to find you."

"Damn, it isn't fair. It *was* self-defense, wasn't it?" He looked into her eyes.

"Yes, Neat. It was self-defense. I'll swear to that."

They heard Sherman's bird-like whistle from across the bayou.

Neat brought Amanda over. He and Sherman exchanged a brotherly embrace. Again, Amanda's eyes filled with tears. "Maybe I'll be able to get back again in a couple of weeks. I'll see what Elizabeth and I can cook up." Neat grabbed her and held on as if he were drowning. She whispered in his ear, "I love you. I always will."

X
April, 1876

With springtime, the daylight hours grew longer and the days seemed endless
for Neat. Sherman visited a couple of times in the last two weeks of March, but
Amanda had not been able to concoct a logical excuse for her family that
would work for the four hours it took to make the round trip plus some reasonable time to visit. Neat wondered if she was having regrets about their last
meeting; if maybe he had moved too quickly in his desire for her.

Sherman always brought new supplies to him: vegetables, fruit, even coffee
and a briefing of the news of the day. Today he also brought a small bottle of
bourbon. They were sitting under the big oak in front of the hut. Sherman
took a swig from the bottle and handed it to Neat. "I don't know what's going
on but Boyer's people, all the carpetbaggers and their buddies, seem mighty
distracted. They's stopped talking about you so much, far as I can tell." He said,
"They kinda worried 'bout what's been happening in New Orleans, Baton
Rouge and a lot of other places in the state. Sounds to me like they losing control.

"Our friends from Opelousas let it be known that they didn't like the talk of
hanging a young southern boy just because he defended hisself against three
armed men. You gotta meet these folks, Neat. They is some tough. Don't take
no shit from nobody. You'd like'em. And, then too, Mrs. Boyer and the kids are
gone. They left on a steamer a couple of weeks ago so they're not around to
remind people. You just hang on. It ain't gonna be much longer. We can get
you in, get some judge to do some justice and you'll be free again."

Neat passed the bottle back to him. Sherman sipped and went on, "The
Becker boys also moved on. I heard they went to New Orleans but were heading back to their home in New York and Willie Simpson told somebody he's

going back to Illinois soon's he can. That's a bad-looking scar you gave him, Neat. Run's across his forehead from temple to temple."

"Hope he tells people where he got it. I just want to be left alone."

Sherman also brought news of Neat's family. Neat had asked him to check on them and let them know that he was all right. Sherman rode down to Brusly McCall one Sunday afternoon to visit them. Neat had warned him to just let them know he was doing fine but not to disclose his hiding place. "You know how people slip up when they're talking to friends," he said. Sherman said the women seemed to doing as well as could be expected but seemed to be just eking out an existence on their tiny spread. He said one of their mules died in early March and Neat's mother had a bad case of the flu but seemed to have recovered except for a persistent cough.

Neat brought Sherman back across the bayou about an hour before sundown. He swayed a little as he mounted the carriage, gave Neat a salute and was on his way.

Neat woke the next morning with a headache that lasted well into the afternoon.

On some days, to relieve the boredom, Neat paddled his pirogue across the bayou and took a walk along the dirt road leading back to White Castle. It was just an exercise in hopefulness, imagining that he was free to go home again. Once, a team of mules pulling a large wagon loaded with fence posts and barbed wire surprised him as it rounded a turn in the road without his noticing the approaching sound. He had been "gathering wool," off in a daydream of his last day with Amanda, reliving the warmth and passion of this wondrous young woman who, for reasons beyond his imagination, obviously loved him and had given herself lovingly to him.

Neat dived into the brush on the side of the road just in time to avoid being seen by the muleskinner and the young black man riding on the rear of the wagon. He severely bruised his right shoulder in the evasion and vowed to be more careful in the future.

Sometimes he would take the pirogue up the bayou to a spot where Bayou Sorrel emptied into the stream. Almost every time he went he was able to land a fish with his simple pole rigged with twine and a small fishhook that Sherman had brought. He would bait it with worms he had dug up in the soft dirt around the oak tree at his hut. Now that was a treat, fresh fish.

A couple of his days were filled with rebuilding his rabbit trap after an armadillo wandered into it one night and proceeded to rip it apart during its frenzied escape. The thrashing of the animal awakened Neat with a start. He couldn't get back to sleep the rest of the night.

Though still keeping his crude calendar, he sort of lost track of the seasonal events. He did not realize on April 15th that it was the day before Easter. Around noon he was in the midst of cleaning his small arsenal of guns when he became aware of the approach of a single horse at a very slow, and seemingly stealthy, gait. He quickly reloaded and moved into a hidden position. The creak of a saddle being dismounted and the sound of soft footfalls through the brush drifted across the bayou.

"Neat." It was Sheriff Gilmore.

Aw, shit, I thought he'd given up, Neat thought.

"Neat, let's talk. Come on, Neat, let me know you're there, we need to talk. I got problems."

Neat quietly changed his position so he could get a better look through the foliage to the road beyond the sheriff and his horse. He waited and listened. Finally, feeling secure, he said, "What you mean you got problems, Henry? You think I ain't got enough problems I gotta take on yours too?"

Gilmore found a convenient log on the far shore and folded his lanky frame down on it with a sigh. "I know, I know, Neat, but just hear me out. I don't know how much you know 'bout what's been going on, but I been a loyal friend to you. I ain't told 'em nothing 'bout your whereabouts, nothing 'bout your little hideout. But now, I need your help. I really do." Silence. Henry sounded as if he was about to cry. "Come on, Neat, I need your help, man. They's ain't nobody with me. Nobody followed me. Come on, talk to me."

Neat whispered across the water, "Go on, I'm listenin'."

Gilmore got up and walked to the bank of the bayou. He unhitched his pistol belt and holster and laid it on the ground. "See there, Neat. I'm not armed, just wanna talk, face to face, not across the bayou."

Neat said, "Pull your horse away from the road. Tie her up over there by those canes where she can't be seen from the road and don't pick up your gun. I'm coming over."

Henry helped pull the pirogue up on the bank when Neat glided over some five minutes later. "You looking good, boy," he said smiling, "a little shaggy for a lad that goes by the name, Neat, but not all that bad for a swamp rat."

"What's going on, Henry? Sherman tells me things may be cooling off for me and that the carpetbaggers seem to be jumping ship. They still giving you a hard time? You still got your job?"

"Yeh, yeh, I'm still the sheriff but I don't know anymore who's in charge. With the Boyer family and the Beckers gone and Simpson about ready to run too, they's nobody in control. The bureau ain't sent nobody out to replace Boyer. Ain't nobody talked to me about nothing for days. But that worries me. Last I heard those folks had reported me to the bosses in Baton Rouge or New Orleans or wherever the hell they is. I heard they told'em I couldn't even find one skinny little rebel that killed the head of the reconstruction down here."

"Hey, Henry, I appreciate what you been doing. I'm sorry I put you in this position. But, how the hell can I help you? I can't even help myself. Look at me."

"I want you to talk to Sherman. I know he's been coming out here regular. He don't know it but I've had one of my people keeping an eye on him." Neat stiffened. Henry held out his hands and quickly continued, "I just wanted to make sure nobody else followed him. I'm telling you, your secret's safe with me. I just need you to convince Sherman to tell those bad hands from Opelousas, that White League bunch, that I'm one of the good guys, even if I am a darkie, I'm your friend and I done proved it. Now they gotta help me and protect me from that Freedmen's Bureau and that reconstruction gang." Henry was pleading now. "I know that bunch was just using me and God knows what they got in mind for me now. But, damn it, Neat, I've been a good sheriff. I know who the good guys are and who the bad guys are. When all of this shakes down, I wanna still be standing...with the good guys. I want us to be friends like we was before." Gilmore's eyes were glistening with unspilled tears.

Neat put his hand on Henry's shoulder. It was a reach since he was eight inches shorter than the black man. "I understand, Henry, and you're right. You've been a true friend. If anybody could have betrayed me and given me up, it sure could've been you. I'll talk to Sherman. You know he likes you too. I'm sure he'll do everything he can for you."

"Thanks. Never thought when they made me sheriff I'd need to be protected from them." Henry looked to the west through the brush and trees at the sinking sun. "You gonna be all right? You need anything? I gotta be getting back."

"I'm good as can be. Sherman's been real good about bringing me things I need. Don't need nothing but to get back home."

"Maybe we can work something out to do that soon. Things are changing fast. If they move out that judge and that D. A. in Napoleonville and put in some local folks, I think you'd be all right. I'll get back to you." He gave Neat a friendly punch in the shoulder, led his horse out of the trees, swung up on the saddle and headed back east.

Neither man could have imagined how long Neat's ordeal would last before it was resolved. Neither could have, in their wildest dreams, thought that the resolution would hinge on the outcome of an unprecedented, contentious, bizarre election for president of the newly reformed, but still deeply divided, United States of America.

XI
April, 1876

The sad, tedious journey of the small family finally ended in Pottstown, Pennsylvania. The young widow, Hilda Boyer, twelve-year old Samuel, ten-year old Jessica and Hilda's widowed mother, Gretel, were physically and emotionally exhausted. Two weeks of cramped quarters on steamboats and finally several long, jolting rides by horse drawn coach had brought them through the heart of the expanding nation.

This should have been an exhilarating experience for the youngsters. It would have been a magnificent experience as an exploratory vacation. They were still babies when Herman was assigned the administrative duties in Louisiana. Neither remembered the trip down river.

There were splendid vistas along the Mississippi and Ohio rivers; views of the bluffs of Natchez, the skylines of Memphis, Louisville, Cincinnati and other growing river cities; beautiful sunrises and sunsets, blue skies and thunderstorms, river mists and rain showers as they passed through the hills and mountains of the Appalachians. They saw every manifestation of river transportation, wildlife along the shores, birds and fish of every description. All that wondrous beauty, all that splendid discovery was marred by the fact that they were on this journey without their father, Herman Boyer.

Hilda and her mother did their best to keep the children occupied and upbeat about the trip. Hilda bought maps and books to accompany them and educate them on the sights. Still, the enormity of their loss cast a crushing pall over each day and night.

Pottstown, fifty or so miles northwest of Philadelphia, was where Hilda and Herman grew up. Their families lived on either side of the small, hilly village but their parents had attended the same Episcopal Church for years. Hilda's mother, sixty-year old Gretel Whitten, was the only survivor of the in-laws. She still owned the modest family home on the west side of the town. Her sole surviving sister, Polly, had been living in the house since Gretel had moved to Louisiana to join her daughter after her husband, Laurence, passed away some seven years ago.

The telegram with the news of Herman's death had arrived three weeks ago. Since then, Hilda's elderly aunt Polly had been making plans for her sister and the grieving family to move in with her. It would not be easy. She was barely able to support herself from the meager savings left after her own husband's death. At their age and with no training, she and her sister had little ability to earn more money. Herman had left Hilda with a modest amount of cash. She had raised more by selling much of their furniture and belongings before leaving Louisiana. There was still some jewelry that could be sold. All this would get her through the first year or so if she was very careful, but she had no skills or training and, of course, the youngsters were not old enough to work.

Polly did the best she could. Her gingham apron neatly tied over her housedress, she smiled and hugged Gretel, Hilda and the children when they arrived. She had a hot meal waiting and clean linens on the three small cots in the extra bedroom for Hilda and the children. Gretel would share Polly's bedroom. The four travelers slept for most of two days after their arrival and then slowly settled in to their new life.

Hilda got a job at the local inn doing menial cleaning jobs and started learning some office skills. Jessica, a mild-mannered, quiet young lady, received tutoring from one of Gretel's older friends. Samuel, temperamental and rebellious, attended a school administered by the Episcopal Church. He was in constant trouble, fighting with classmates, clashing with his teachers and the clergy and generally showing his contempt for the current circumstances of his life.

Though Pottstown had escaped the ravages of the war, and after twelve years had settled into a quiet, peaceful existence, it offered an uninspiring, dreary, mind-numbing life for Samuel. Many nights he lay in his cot listening to the soft, sleepy breathing of his mother and sister while thoughts of revenge swept through his brain. *He took my father away from me. Now I'm stuck in this nowhere place. I will never forgive. I will never forget. I know your name and I'll find you, you murderer. I know you, Antoine Galvez!*

XII
Summer 1876

The long nightmare was ending. The grand adventure was imploding. Post-war reconstruction of the South was, in most cases, and particularly in Louisiana, a disaster. Tens of thousands of opportunists had poured into the old Confederacy. Many of them were former Union Army soldiers who had been in the area during the war and returned or remained to seek their fortunes. Some of them were driven by honest ambition and well-meaning motives. Some had even fallen in love with and married Southern girls. All wanted to have a part in the reconstruction of the South and pursue the promise of property and perhaps prosperity for themselves and their families in the process.

Unfortunately, the majority of the new migrants were greedily self-serving. They had descended on the war-ravaged South fully expecting to reap the rewards of victory with their mere presence and by dealing off of the misery of the people and the innocent hopes of the newly freed slaves. Louisiana attracted a great number of the reconstructionists because of their awareness of its prewar wealth, its agricultural riches, its majestic mansions, the mighty Mississippi River and the mystical allure of the city of New Orleans.

As the Civil War approached, New Orleans had a population four times that of any other Southern city. It was easily as large as Cincinnati, St. Louis, Baltimore and Boston. It was the banking and commercial center of the South. The wealth generated by the Mississippi River and the rich agricultural areas bordering it was enormous.

By the mid 1870's, under Radical Republican Reconstruction rule, New Orleans city property had depreciated forty per cent, parish (county) property fifty per cent. One hundred and forty million dollars in federal enhancements had been squandered and pilfered with nothing to show for it. State debt increased by more than forty million dollars.

The plain, simple truth was that the engine that drove the economy of the South, slavery, no longer existed and an entire new structure and culture would have to be created before a real recovery could take place. The reckless adventurers who followed the victorious Union Army into the region found the pickings slim. Much of the arable land had been burned or otherwise damaged. In some areas of south Louisiana, Union troops had loaded drums of salt from the mines at Jefferson and Avery Islands and systematically salted the sugar cane fields rendering them unusable for years. Without slaves there were not enough laborers who could profitably reconstitute the ruined land.

In addition, corruption among the new rulers was rampant. The principled elements of the ruling group were in the minority and realized that the grand reconstruction plan was doomed.

An ominous precursor of the collapse of reconstruction in Louisiana, *The Battle of Liberty Place,* occurred September 14, 1874. President Ulysses S. Grant had assumed a policy of leniency toward the South rather than the harsh measures some in his party urged. Federal troops had been reduced to minimum numbers in most of the states but the stubborn and violent resistance still prevalent throughout the state required a continued ominous presence in Louisiana. The White League, organized with Confederate Army veterans and others, numbered more than fourteen thousand members throughout the state. Their continuing raids and sniper attacks dictated the ongoing presence of the troops.

Republican Governor William Kellog was considered one of the more corrupt of the carpetbaggers who had risen to power. Mistakenly thinking they would further encourage the hands-off policy of the federal government, nearly four thousand armed White Leaguers gathered in New Orleans to demand Kellog's resignation. The governor responded by calling out over thirty-six hundred policemen and black militia troops. Further enraging the White Leaguers was the fact that former Confederate General James Longstreet now commanded the governor's small army. The general formed his troops into a battle line stretching from Jackson Square to Canal Street. It included two Gatling guns and a battery of artillery. His priority was protecting the Customs House, that served as the state Capitol and where the governor and other Republican officials had taken refuge.

In an hour-long firefight, the White Leaguers charged the line, captured Longstreet and routed his troops. The streets of the French Quarter were awash with the blood of the battle. In all, thirty-eight men were killed and seventy-nine wounded.

Kellog was deposed, replaced by White Leaguer John McEnery. The coup lasted three days. Alarmed at the insurrection, President Grant reluctantly agreed to order more federal troops and gunboats into New Orleans. The insurgents' strategy had backfired. In the face of vastly superior firepower, the Leaguers and their governor withdrew and Kellog was reinstated as governor. The slightly wounded General Longstreet was released. One White League officer said he had great difficulty restraining his men from killing the general when they saw him "leading niggra troops against his own."

The Battle of Liberty Place was an attention-getting event. The chilling account of the carnage on the streets of the Queen City of the South crackled across the divided nation on the telegraph wires. The news signaled the beginning of the end of reconstruction.

For the next two years the Democratic Party grew whiter and stronger. Only the presence of federal troops protected whatever power the Radical Republican carpetbagger and scalawag administrators and office holders still wielded. More and more unspeakable corruption in Governor Kellog's administration was unearthed. The state government was in disarray. His own party finally impeached Kellog.

❧   ❧   ❧

In the swampland along Bayou Maringouin the hot days and humid nights dragged on for Neat. Oblivious to the historic events that would eventually restructure his life, he had fashioned lazy days of fishing, trapping, whittling and, with the help of materials brought by Amanda and Sherman, teaching himself to read beyond his woefully inadequate previous skills. On her last visit, Amanda had introduced him to a book on arithmetic and presented him with a somewhat worn but still usable abacus. He was fascinated with her instruction on its uses.

Practicing for her career as a teacher, she presented her pupil with a three-page, hand printed study plan and a two-page test to be taken when the plan was completed. Neat was as ardent a pupil as he was a lover.

Amanda's visits were limited to only once every four or five weeks due to the difficulty of finding believable excuses to be away from home for five or six hours at a time. She and Neat cherished the little time they had together and made good use of the short visits, physically and emotionally.

Sherman visited more often and kept the little camp well supplied with food and other amenities.

Once the Boyer family and some of the other principals in the night of the shooting had moved away, Neat was almost forgotten as a fugitive. He and Sherman arranged for several visits into the town during quiet evening hours. Neat would visit with old friends, have dinner at their homes and stay overnight. The ever-faithful Sherman would return him to the hideout before daybreak or after dark the next evening. Always slender, Neat was now sinewy and tanned and sported a full black beard and shoulder-length hair that he tied back under a big hat on his visits to town.

The summer brought other inconveniences. The rains increased and the hut was in need of constant repairs and patching. And then, there were the mosquitoes. They were overwhelming. It was only fitting since maringouin is the French word for mosquito. By day they were distracting, by evening they were swarming. Sherman brought several yards of netting that he and Neat carefully suspended from the ceiling of the hut to protect the sleeping mat area.

Through experimentation, Neat concocted a mixture of water and coal oil that served as a repellant. His first attempts left his skin irritated by the petroleum but he eventually found a comfortable mixture that was sufficiently diluted and yet effective. Every morning and every evening he would carefully coat every inch of exposed skin. He apologized to Amanda for his new aura of coal oil. Not only did she understand, she insisted that he give her a similar treatment when she shed her clothes during their lovemaking. One evening when returning to her home, she froze when her mother greeted her at the back door sniffing at her odd aroma. Amanda, thinking quickly, explained that she was helping a friend's family store some coal oil and had spilled a bit. She breathed a big sigh of relief when Cora apparently accepted the explanation.

As fall approached, Neat and Sherman arranged to meet secretly with a young attorney, Norman Goldsmith. Sherman's father had mentioned Goldsmith during supper one evening. He had met him during an organizational meeting of area farmers. The group wanted to form a legal coalition aimed at strengthening their position regarding the new posture of the Freedmen's Bureau. The elder Mayers was impressed with the young attorney.

Goldsmith was from Illinois. He migrated south after the war to practice in a law firm owned by his uncle, Jacob Hermann. Two years later he married the daughter of a once-prominent planter and thus solidified his acceptability among the natives. He practiced in Napoleonville where most legal matters were resolved in the tri-parish area of Iberville, Assumption and Ascension.

Goldsmith was sympathetic to Neat's situation but explained that, though the reconstructionists were obviously weakened and beginning to retreat back to the North, they still controlled the vital functions of government and were supported by the occupying Union Army. After Liberty Place, Washington, D. C. insisted on an even larger presence of federal troops in Louisiana and effectively propped up the failing carpetbagger regimes. Goldsmith felt it would still be risky for Neat to surrender himself to a trial.

Neat and Sherman advised him that there was a star witness waiting to vouch for Neat's self-defense claim. "Amanda Pitre was there. She was standing on the gallery and saw it all," Neat told him. "She saw them shoot at me first and saw me shoot back only to defend myself. She's told us she'll testify to that. She's Lawtell Pitre's daughter. He's well respected and has even worked with the carpetbaggers to keep his plantation going. And when a jury sees Amanda, all sweet and truthful and innocent, they'll love her and believe her. I know it."

Goldsmith said, "That's one witness, Neat. You have nobody else to corroborate that account and we won't know until we have pretrial hearings who or how many the prosecutors have to counter her testimony."

Neat hung his head and shook it side to side. "I'll never get out of that damn swamp."

"Well, just hold on now. Things are getting better every day and we may see something big happening in November. There's a presidential election coming up and this whole matter could get cleared up either way it goes."

"A presidential election? What's the hell's a presidential election got to do with me for God's sake?"

"Just listen, this is a really important election. The new president of the United States of America will decide the future of the South and thus, of Louisiana. The Democrats are running a man by the name of Samuel Tilden, he's the governor of New York. Now, with all those big states up there like Connecticut, New Jersey and his home state going for him plus most of the South, hell, he should win. Now you know the Democrats want to forget all about reconstruction and let us get back to running the South the way it used to be. On the other hand, the Republican candidate is Governor Rutherford Hayes of Ohio. If he should win, there's a lot of folks thinking the Republicans have had about as much of reconstructing the South and dealing with the ex-slaves as they can stand. The feeling is that Hayes would look the other way if we took back our government down here and, so long as we don't have slaves, leave us the hell alone! You see? Either way, we win!"

"Well, I'll be damned." Neat was in awe of Goldsmith's explanation. He got up and strutted around the room. "Little ole Antoine 'Neat' Galvez has got a stake in who becomes the next president of the United States of America. Doesn't that just kick over your outhouse!"

They all had a good laugh over the incongruous prospects.

Goldsmith explained the election timeline to them. The election was set for the first week in November. He urged patience for just a few more months to let matters settle. He told Neat and Sherman that if a few judges were changed after the presidential vote he'd be glad to take on the case for just two-hundred-fifty dollars. Sherman and Neat stared at him with their jaws open. "Start saving your money boys, freedom ain't cheap."

Sherman and Neat looked at each other. Two hundred-fifty dollars was more than both had earned in their entire lives. "I ain't ever even seen a hunnerd at one time, myself," Neat said.

XIII
November, 1876

The mind-numbing, soul-crushing, lonely existence dragged on. Neat concentrated on the self-teaching exercises Amanda had supplied. As the days grew shorter and the nights somewhat cooler, he occasionally squeezed in clandestine visits into town. The rare, amorous visits with Amanda and the thought that he might soon be free to emerge from the swamp barely sustained his spirits.

On one visit Amanda divulged the discouraging news that her parents were now planning for her to attend a private teachers' college in New Orleans. Neat could not imagine living without her. Their occasional lovemaking became even more passionate and meaningful.

🍁   🍁   🍁

In July, the recovering nation had celebrated its first one hundred years with celebrations and parades. Understandably, little of this revelry occurred in the South. A massive event called *The World's Fair*, the first held in the United States, opened in Philadelphia. The proudest example of American democracy, a presidential election, was culminating on Tuesday, November 7. Some saw it as a golden opportunity to further unite the still painfully divided nation. Others intended to use the election to further serve their own self-interests.

As the first election returns trickled into Washington and New York via the nation's still fledgling telegraph system, indications were that, as expected, Democrat Samuel J. Tilden would be a clear winner. The governor had swept his home state, New York and swing states Connecticut, New Jersey and Indiana and was expected to carry the *solid South* and most of the newly emerged populations in the West.

Both Tilden and his Republican opponent, Ohio Governor Rutherford B. Hayes, went to bed assuming the Democrats had captured the White House for the first time in twenty years.

The *New York Tribune* and several other major newspapers in the East put their morning editions to bed with the headlines proclaiming Tilden's victory. However, *The New York Times* edition of November 8th stated cautiously, ***"The Results Still Uncertain."***

Around midnight, former Republican Congressman Daniel Sickles, a former Union general who had lost a leg in the Battle of Gettysburg in 1863, limped over to the Republican headquarters in Manhattan to check the returns.

After careful analysis, Sickles realized that Hayes just might be able to salvage the election. If he lost no more northern states and won the states of Florida, Louisiana and South Carolina he would win the Electoral College by one vote regardless of the outcome of the popular tally.

Sickles fired off telegrams to Republican leaders in the three southern states. At three in the morning a reply was received from South Carolina's Republican Governor Daniel Chamberlain: "All right. South Carolina is for Hayes. Need more troops." That left Louisiana, Florida and one lone maverick elector out West to deal with.

By six Wednesday morning Hayes was projected to have 165 electoral votes and Tilden 184 with 185 needed to win. If the 7 votes in South Carolina were truly in Hayes' column, he had 172 with only 13 electoral votes remaining in dispute: 4 in Florida, 8 in Louisiana and the one wild card in Oregon. Hayes needed to win them all.

When the total votes were finally counted, Tilden won the popular vote with 51% to Hayes's 48%, a nationwide margin of less than a quarter of a million votes.

Pandemonium ruled in the disputed southern states. The Republicans still held the seats of power in those states and thus controlled the "returning boards," the certifying authorities for the elections.

The returning boards in all three of the disputed states threw out enough Democratic votes to give the election in their states to Hayes and the Republican gubernatorial candidates. In Florida, the state Supreme Court ruled in favor of the Democratic gubernatorial candidate, but let Hayes's margin of victory in that state stand. The new governor promptly overrode the court's ruling by appointing a Democratic returning board that announced that Tilden carried the state.

In Louisiana and South Carolina, Democrats declared their gubernatorial candidates elected and established state administrations prepared to take office simultaneously with Republican administrations.

The United States was in the midst of an unprecedented Constitutional crisis. Only once before, in 1824, the lack of an Electoral College majority among four nominees had resulted in the election being thrown to the House of Representatives. It chose John Quincy Adams over the winner of the popular vote, Andrew Jackson.

Manipulation, closed-door dealing and outright corruption ran rampant in Washington and in the states in question. The returning board in Louisiana rejected over 13,000 Democratic ballots and nearly 2,500 Republican ones. The result was the declaration of Hayes as the winner of the eight electoral votes and Republican Stephen Packard's election as governor. This was strongly disputed by the Democrats. Federal troops surrounded the St. Louis Hotel in New Orleans that was then acting as the State Capitol when Packard took the oath of office. Meanwhile, several blocks away at St. Patrick's Hall, the Democrats inaugurated a former Confederate Brigadier General, Francis T. Nicholls, as governor. The two were the twelfth and thirteenth men to serve as governor of the tumultuous state government in the past sixteen years.

Nicholls, a Rebel hero, had lost his left arm at the Battle of Winchester and his left foot one year later in the Battle of Chancellorsville. One of his first acts as governor was to name his own returning board and have it rule that Louisiana's eight electoral votes would be cast for Tilden.

Meanwhile, unknown to either governor, the head of Louisiana's Republican returning board, James Madison Wells, nefariously offered to sell the state's electoral votes for $200,000 per board member. Amazingly, he got no takers. Three of the board would later be indicted for various crimes of fraud and bribery.

The national standoff got so contentious that four artillery companies were summoned to the nation's capital to maintain order. Democratic newspapers trumpeted headlines like: "Tilden or War!" To make matters worse, Republican President U. S. Grant refused to recognize the Republican gubernatorial administrations in Louisiana and South Carolina even further emboldening the Democrats in those state.

The holdout elector in Oregon seemed to have disappeared from the face of the earth. Foul play was suspected but meanwhile both parties attempted to have him replaced with one of their own. Naturally, litigation ensued and the standoff continued.

The Democrats in Florida and Louisiana got word that Tilden, in a show of amazingly naïve political judgment, had promised the eastern powers of the party that he would not grant concessions to the former rebels. Southern Democrats were in shock. Their own party was denying them their claims to the controlling political offices of their states. They were in a deep quandary: should they give their electoral votes to the Republican candidate, Hayes, when their very existence was still being threatened by his party's representatives in their states? But, they obviously could not trust their party's nominee since he seemed to be succumbing to the South's enemies in the heavily populated northeast. The dilemma led to a month's long standoff.

The post-election war raged on through the winter. Partisan wrangling shot down one solution after another. Behind the scenes negotiations continued to unfold without success. President Grant seemed to have gone into hiding while the country waited for his successor to be chosen. A bill was introduced in congress to allow the election to be decided by the U. S. Supreme Court. Many vowed that would "never, ever happen in this democracy." The measure was resoundingly defeated in the Senate.

A Constitutional amendment was introduced by joint resolution to allow the direct popular election of the President and Vice President. The language made the effect of the bill retroactive. It would have elected Tilden. It too failed. Debate raged in the newspapers, street corners, back rooms, plowed fields and legislative halls of the nation.

Finally on January 25, 1877, almost three months after the election, agreement was reached to form a commission made up of ten highly respected members of both houses of congress (five from each party) and five members of the Supreme Court chosen based on geographic diversity.

Louisiana Democratic Governor Francis T. Nicholls decided to deal from what he considered a win-win deck. In spite of his deeply held party loyalty, he was afraid to trust his future to Tilden's New York, Connecticut and New Jersey advisers. So he ordered his Democratic representatives involved in the negotiations to offer the Hayes camp Louisiana's electoral votes without dispute. He and many in his camp correctly surmised that Northern Republican commitment to reconstruction and black civil rights had seriously waned. During the campaign, candidate Hayes had talked vaguely of a fair and just policy for the South. He had continued to espouse such a position during the electoral college controversy.

Nicholls' contingent and others suggested a solution to the stalemate. The Democrats in congress would agree to stop the House filibuster that was blocking the final count. Louisiana's votes going to Hayes would give him the presidency. In return, Hayes would agree to immediately withdraw the federal troops guarding the statehouses in the contested southern states. This would allow the Democratic governors to take office virtually uncontested. There were more considerations, such as railroad and waterway project funding and consultation on thousands of patronage jobs, but for all practical purposes, Rutherford B. Hayes was now assured the presidency.

The final details and resolution dragged on almost to inauguration day, March 5, 1877. Hayes won the Electoral College vote with 185 to Tilden's 184.

XIV
Winter 1876–1877

Sherman kept Neat posted on the political situation. According to the attorney Goldsmith, the deliberations in Washington D. C. would greatly impact his life. Neither of the young men could fully comprehend or fathom how the election of a president would allow Neat to seek his redemption and freedom but they were willing to believe.

Neat quietly celebrated his eighteenth birthday on November 5th, two days before the presidential election. He hoped his birthday present would be news that would allow him to come out of the swamp and seek an end to his exile. Sherman transported him by buggy into White Castle buried under several layers of sugar cane stalks. Neat's friends gathered in a barn on the outskirts of the town and toasted him with bad corn liquor and home made beer. Amanda even sneaked away from her family to join the party for half an hour or so.

Goldsmith sent word to Neat that, however the election was decided, he was prepared to defend him in a trial or, better yet, negotiate charges being dropped. However, he related that could not be done until the Union soldiers were withdrawn or ordered to cease their guardianship of the Republican officials especially the judgeships. Therefore, Goldman reiterated, Neat should not leave his hiding place and should not risk being sighted by unfriendly eyes.

With Sherman's help, Neat reluctantly retreated to his hideout the day after his birthday party and continued his wait. He was finding it harder to return to the wilderness each time he left.

The weeks slowly passed while the nation and its constitutional feasibility were being severely tested. Louisiana was, for all practical purposes, a state with two governors, two legislators and no governance. The institutions of government were in total chaos. Federal troops still marched the streets of New

Orleans, Baton Rouge and several other cities to support the Republican office holders while Democratic politicians continued to challenge their right to govern the state.

❋   ❋   ❋

A month before Hayes was inaugurated, word went out that federal troops would soon be withdrawn from Louisiana. It need not be said that the institutions controlled by the carpetbaggers and scalawags would no longer be protected. They and their associates fully understood the finality of the announcement. Many of their office holders and public workers started resigning or simply did not show up for their duties.

In Iberville, Assumption and Ascension Parishes the turnover in civil offices was almost total by the end of February. New governing bodies were formed, new appointments made and elections planned for the near future. The Republican appointed district judge, who sat for most cases for the three parishes in the Napoleonville courthouse, walked out of his courtroom on Friday, February 23rd, and never returned. The native Ohioan packed a few belongings, rode his horse to Donaldsonville, boarded a steamer for New Orleans and was never heard from again.

After officially taking office in January, Governor Nicholls wasted no time in assembling a new legislature. State department heads that had been named by the Republican administration were quickly replaced. Government workers were canvassed for their loyalty to the new ruling party. Their retention was dependent on their pledge of fidelity. Parish and city governments voted to immediately recognize the Democratic governor's authority. The governor appointed an entire new Supreme Court. It immediately began holding sessions. In many cases, it reversed previous decisions made during the past dozen or so years. Of great importance, tax collectors also recognized the Nicholls government and started diverting money to his treasury.

Across town, Republican Governor Packard's followers deserted in droves. Expatriate northerners fleeing the new regime overran the wharves along the Mississippi waterfront, where passenger boats docked.

Frantic messages to outgoing President U. S. Grant to permit the federal troops to interfere with the takeover were ignored or refused.

The shift was like a huge tectonic earthquake throughout the state. It rippled through the cypress swamps of the south and the piney hills of the north. Within days it jolted every city, town, village and crossroads of the state.

Reconstruction was over. The carpetbaggers were through. Louisiana could truly begin to rebuild. The stark reality was, however, there was little to build on and no slaves to do the basic, grueling labor.

❁   ❁   ❁

In Iberville Parish, the historic tremors were greeted with quiet celebrations and organizational work. Sherman Mayers father, Benjamin, had successfully maintained his farm through all the adversities of the post-war years and was considered a levelheaded, reasonable leader in the area. He was asked to serve on several of the councils and committees being formed.

He sat on one committee that was asked to submit names for judgeships and other courthouse positions in the three-parish area. One of the other committee members was attorney Jacob Hermann of Napoleonville, the uncle and partner of Neat's defense attorney, Norman Goldsmith.

The committee quickly settled on a slate of nominees and fired it off to the governor's office with the plea that appointments be made quickly so as to alleviate the large docket of cases that had piled up during the past months of confusion. Alcide Ricard, a native of Governor Nicholls' hometown, Donaldsonville, was the nominee for chief judge of the three-parish district. The fifty-year-old attorney was highly respected and was immediately accepted by the administration.

Simultaneously, thirty-one-year old Leland Bergeron, a well-connected young attorney, was named district attorney. He was to be aided by two assistants also nominated by the committee.

At supper on the evening the appointments were made official, Benjamin Mayers told his son, Sherman, about them. He smiled slyly at his son, "If you happen to know the whereabouts of your friend Antoine Galvez, you might get word to him that it's time to come in and face a trial. I can't assure him that he will be found not guilty, but I can personally guarantee that he'll be treated fairly." Sherman swallowed hard and nodded but could not keep the look of elation off his face. He could hardly wait to get the word to Neat.

❁   ❁   ❁

The month of February had been particularly hard on Neat. The tedium and cold dreariness of the winter months had taken their toll and his frustration level was reaching the breaking point. In addition, torrential rains had soaked his hideaway almost every day of the month. His hut was leaking most of the time. The water level around the ridge was unusually high. The floor was seeping mud and insects and critters were constantly trying to share his once relatively dry home.

Just before dawn on the morning of February 28th, Neat was deeply involved with a dream of floating on a grand steamboat up the Mississippi with Amanda. She was dressed in a magnificent white hoop skirt with a scoop neck modestly showing the beginning of cleavage. They were laughing and sharing a sweet, cool lemonade.

He suddenly came awake to an unidentifiable sound. The sound stopped when he jerked into consciousness. He sat up and listened carefully as he reached for and cocked his revolver. Nothing. His sleep-fogged recollection was that it was a swishing sound, as though something was being dragged over the straw and palmetto floor. The predawn light seeping under the door and through the vents gave little illumination to the room.

Neat rose slowly and quietly stepped off his sleeping mat. His bare right foot landed on what felt like a writhing rope of muscle. As he recoiled, he felt a sharp, burning stab just above his right ankle. He reacted by kicking out violently and heard the body of the snake hit the side wall then watched in horror as the shadowy black body slithered under the door and out into the swamp. Even in the low light, Neat was almost positive it was a venomous cotton-mouth moccasin.

He grabbed his canteen of water and splashed it on the burning spot on his leg. He desperately tried to calm himself.

Got to think this through. Breathe deep. This is damn serious.

He had heard that one should suck the venom out of a snake bite but, even with his lithe body, there was no way he could get the right side of his right ankle anywhere near his mouth. He had been sleeping in his trousers and an undershirt. He quickly pulled on his left boot and grabbed a long boot sock. Rolling up the right trouser leg to knee height, he tied the sock tightly around the injured leg just above the calf.

He opened the door of the hut and looked across the grass in the growing light. Not surprisingly, there was no sign of the snake.

Shit. There's no other way. I gotta get some help.

With his revolver stuck in his waistband, he used his rifle as a crutch and hopped down to the pirogue, launched it into the bayou and paddled across. His leg felt as though it was buried in white-hot coals. It was beginning to throb as he hobbled through the underbrush to the dirt road. He stopped, undecided. There was a small group of houses about three miles to the north-west. It wasn't a town, there were no doctors and he knew no one there. People simply called the spot in the road, Bayou Sorrel. And, of course, to the east, some nine miles or more, was home. He chose to start hopping to the east through the muddy ruts of the road to White Castle. Surely some Good Samaritan would come along.

Almost an hour later, only two miles into his journey, Neat felt a wave of nausea wash over him. The pain in his leg was almost unbearable. He had to sit and rest. It was almost eight in the morning and not one person had passed along the road. He found a fallen tree on the side of the path and lowered himself into a sitting position with the throbbing leg extended out. He twisted it around to get a better look. It was the first time he had seen the wound in full light. He gasped audibly as he saw the two bloody fang marks. The ankle was a dark purple and very swollen.

Oh, mon Dieu, after all this. One little damn snake's gonna do me in. I ain't gonna make it.

It suddenly occurred to him that it was exactly one year since the shooting. He dimly wondered about Divine intervention. He sensed the light diminishing and wondered briefly if dark clouds had suddenly obscured the sun. He lost consciousness and crumpled to the side of the road.

Some twenty minutes later Odon Garcia, a fur trapper, came splashing through the mud with his mule pulling a flatbed dray heading east. He saw the body on the side of the road and pulled the mule to a stop.

What we got here? Somebody drinking too much 'pone? Accident?

He got off his cart and slowly approached and circled the body. He took in the fact that the man had a rifle and revolver.

A hunter?

Then he saw the bloated leg with the makeshift tourniquet.

Oh, oh he done met "Johnny No Ears." Monsieur snake. Bad news.

The muscular Garcia had no problem lifting Neat's limp, 130 pound body into the back of his two wheel dray where he was carrying piles of beaver and mink hides. He jumped back on the cart and snapped the reins over the back of his mule.

"Come on, Bébé, we got to hurry."

Back in White Castle, Sherman was hurrying through his morning chores. He intended to round up Pokey and some other friends to ride with him out to the swamp to inform Neat of his change of fortune. He wanted it to be a "coming out" party. In spite of his father's warning that the matter was not settled by a long shot, Sherman felt good about the future.

XV
February 28, 1877

Odon Garcia guided his mule through a light, chilling rain onto the main street of the tiny town of White Castle about 11 o'clock in the morning. Still unconscious but moaning softly every few minutes, Neat was mostly covered by the hides in the back of the cart and virtually unnoticeable. The trapper could not remember if there was a doctor in the town or where he might be located but he knew where the sheriff's office and jail was. He pulled up in front of the office, tied his mule to the hitching post and went inside.

Sheriff Henry Gilmore's main office was in the parish seat, Plaquemine, but he had smaller offices and holding cells in a couple of other little towns in Iberville Parish. He was born and raised on a farm near White Castle and spent most of his time at his small office there. He came to town that morning to release a prisoner from the two-cell jail. The man had spent a couple of nights for disturbing the peace by urinating in the middle of main street at five o'clock one afternoon. The sheriff was sifting through a new batch of "Wanted" posters that had arrived that morning. He looked up at the trapper, "Yassuh, what can I do for you?"

Garcia saw the star on Henry's shirt, "I found a little man, bad hurt on the road out by Bayou Maringouin, sheriff. Believe he got himself bit by a poisonous snake. He's still alive but his leg's all swoll up and purple."

Gilmore uncoiled his long frame from behind the desk, strapped on his pistol belt and followed Garcia out to the cart. They pulled hides off the crumpled body and Gilmore rolled it over. He gasped, "I don' believe it. It's Neat. Oh, my God."

Odon looked at him curiously, "you know this man? What you mean 'it's neat?'"

"No, I mean yes, I know him. That's his name, Neat. Come on, unhitch your mule and follow me. Doc Ourso's right around the corner down there. Let's get him there quick."

At the doctor's house, Henry carried Neat from the cart. Garcia pushed the door open and called for the doctor who yelled back from somewhere in the back of the shotgun house. Henry laid the limp body on a small cot at the side of the front office and heard a low moan.

Doc Ourso emerged from the back of the house looking a little rumpled and out of sorts. The sleeves on his white shirt were rolled up to the elbows, his string tie loosened at the neck. A stethoscope dangled from his neck and hung over his white apron that had small dark stains in several spots. "Dang kids," he spit out, "always breaking something. If they'd stay out of the dang china ball trees they might stay in one piece. I told his momma…" He caught sight of Neat lying on the cot and saw the discolored and swollen leg. He immediately put his stethoscope into his ears. He put the listening cup to the chest, to the sides of the neck and back to the chest. Squinting at the swollen leg with its bloody fang marks, he asked, "How long ago this happen?"

Henry looked at Garcia. "I don't know. I found him on the side of the road out by Bayou Maringouin a couple hours ago," the trapper said. "You think he's gonna live, doc?"

The doctor was already stripping off Neat's clothes. He told the sheriff to fill a pot with hot water from the kettle sizzling on the stove in the back. "Don't know. Reckon it had to be a cottonmouth. By the width of the fang marks it doesn't seem to be from a very large one and that can make a difference; also how long it held on after digging in. Big ones carry more venom and can hold on longer." Neat's eyes began to flutter. His tongue flicked out and moistened his dry lips. He moaned loudly. "Watch him…er, what's your name?"

"Odon Garcia."

"Watch him for me, Monsieur Garcia. See if you can get him to drink some cool water. Don't let him sit up. Keep that leg elevated. I've got to finish with that kid in the back room and get some things from my instrument cabinet."

Garcia sat on the side of the cot and placed his large hand on Neat's shoulder. Neat opened his eyes, then blinked several times trying to focus on the round, dark, bearded face of the trapper. He let out a yelp and tried to get up. Garcia held him firmly to the cot. "Wh…who are you?" His eyes darted around the room wildly, "where am I?" His right hand went to the spot where his pistol should have been. "What the hell's going on? Let me up, you bastard." He struggled weakly and Garcia easily subdued him.

Henry walked into the room with a steaming pot of water. He quickly put it on the doctor's examination table and moved to the bed. "It's all right, Neat. It's me, Henry. You gonna be all right. We at Doctor Ourso's place. You got yoself bit by a snake, boy. Mr. Garcia here brought you in from Bayou Marinquoin. You just lay there and let the doc take care of you."

The memory of that morning came flooding back to Neat. He felt feverish yet chilled. He started shaking all over. "What's happening? He whispered, "am I dying? Who's this man?"

"Done told you. This here's Odon Garcia. He done probably saved your life, Neat. Found you out cold on the side of the road. Did you see the snake? How big was it?"

"Hell, I don't know, Henry. I just kicked him off me as fast as possible and he didn't stick around to get measured."

Ourso returned with a handful of instruments. "Just hush all that talking, boy. You're gonna be all right. Old Doc Ourso got a hold of you now. First thing we've got to do is get this wound cleaned out. One of you guys get at his head and the other at his feet. Isn't this Antoine Galvez, the young man you've been looking for in that Herman Boyer murder last Mardi Gras?"

Garcia's eyes widened as Sheriff Gilmore acknowledged that it was indeed the wanted man. Neat, drifting in and out of consciousness, stuttered, "It, it, w-w-wasn't murder. They shot first."

"Sure, they all say that. Now you just close your eyes and keep real quiet. We don't want a lot of movement shaking that poison up inside you." It took the doctor twenty minutes to minister to Neat. He thoroughly cleansed the wound, poured alcohol on it, then used a suction device to attempt to remove some of the venom. He withdrew a couple of ounces of watery red liquid then bandaged the area. He had Neat drink a small container of a clear liquid that he identified as laudanum. "This'll kill some of that pain and let you sleep comfortably," he told him. "You need to stay off that leg, keep it elevated and sleep for the rest of the day and maybe longer."

Doc Ourso placed a couple of pillows under the wounded leg. He nodded for the men to follow him onto the front porch. "Henry, do you need to bring him to jail? That case is still pending, isn't it?"

"Yassuh, it's still out there even though they's hardly anybody still here that cares much about it. But I guess I gotta put him under arrest 'til we find out what the new district attorney wants to do. But can I leave him here 'til tonight? I got no way to take care of him at the jail. He is gonna be all right, ain't he?"

"Well, I think so. These bites usually aren't fatal. He may lose some tissue around the wound. I might have to cut some dead flesh out later and stitch him up but, he should come out of it. And yes, I would like to keep him here until tonight to keep an eye on him. You have a deputy to come watch him?"

"Aw doc, Neat ain't going nowheres. He was about to turn himself in anyways…. I mean, that's what some of his friends had told me. Tell you what. I'll go find Sherman Mayers, that's his best friend, I know he'll come and sit with him."

"Okay, but I'm not gonna be responsible if that boy decides to run for the swamps again," the doctor said, "I got my reputation to uphold, you understand?"

Gilmore nodded, "I gotcha. Never you worry. He gonna be all right. I'll be back in about an hour."

He was out in the road heading back toward his office when Garcia pulled his cart up alongside him, "Say sheriff, I heard what you and the doc was saying about that guy, Neat. Is there some kinda reward for bringing him in? After all, I done wasted half of my day doing my duty here and I still got to get to Donaldsonville and back home again."

"No suh," Gilmore said smiling, "I can give you our thanks for what you did but ain't no reward. Sorry about that. But I tell you what, if you coming back this way this evening and it's getting too late to head for home, you just stop by the jail and I'll let you stay in the other empty cell, give you supper and feed you in the morning. I'll even take care of your old mule."

Garcia looked blankly at him, shook his head, let out an oath under his breath and slapped the reins over the back of his mule. They took off down the road. He looked back once more about twenty yards out and shook his head again. Henry thought he might have even heard him utter an oath.

Henry found Sherman in a field behind his family home trying to free a cow from a mud hole. When he told him about Neat's situation, Sherman dropped the rope, left the cow to its problems and took off running to the barn.

Taking one of his father's horses, he galloped to where Pokey Lafleur and Pierre Bourgeois were cleaning stalls at Pierre's father's blacksmith shop. "We ain't making that trip to the swamp, boys. Neat done already come in." Pokey and Pierre stood with mouths agape as Sherman breathlessly related the story Henry had told him. On Sherman's orders, Pokey took off for the Pitre farm to tell Amanda. "But quietly, Pokey, quietly. Tell only Amanda, okay?" Pierre was dispatched to Napoleonville to notify the lawyer Goldsmith. Sherman then sped back to Doctor Ourso's house.

As he raced through the screen door at the front of the house, Ourso rose from his desk with both hands out and shushed him. "Hold it, young man, your friend is sleeping and needs to stay like that." The doctor indicated that Neat was in a room just down the hall from the front office. Sherman tiptoed back and looked in. He went pale when he saw Neat's slight form covered to the bearded chin with a white sheet. He looked as though he was in a mortuary. The swollen, discolored ankle, wrapped in gauze was protruding from the bottom of the cot.

"Mon Dieu, doc, is he gonna make it?"

"I'm pretty sure he will, Sherman. Now why don't you just pull up this chair and sit with him. If he wakes up, which I doubt he will for a couple or more hours, just keep him calm and off his feet. Give him lots of water to drink. Oh yea, the bedpan's right under here. Meanwhile, I've got a few house calls to make. There's a list on my desk of where I'm going if you absolutely have to come find me." Doctor Ourso walked to the rear of the house and out the back door. Sherman heard him mount and walk his horse slowly past the side of the house and down the street.

XVI
March, 1877

With the approaching inauguration of Rutherford B. Hayes as president of the United States, Union soldiers and Northern opportunists had been preparing for weeks to depart Louisiana. There was no doubt that the "reconstruction" effort was over. Governor Nicholls' administration had already appointed hundreds of Democrats to state, parish and city positions. The business of government was in high gear. New fortune hunters were on the prowl. They had the same goals, same principles, same methods, just different accents. Louisiana was quickly reverting to a pre-war way of life. The Democratic, white-dominated political system was back. Now the only things missing were the wealth and the slaves. Both were gone from the state forever. Without the latter, there would never again be the former.

When Norman Goldsmith got the news that his client, Antoine Galvez, was in custody in the White Castle jail, he immediately asked for a meeting with newly appointed District Attorney Leland Bergeron. The meeting was set for Bergeron's office in the courthouse in Napoleonville for the morning of Tuesday, March 6th, the day after the inauguration in Washington, D. C.

Goldsmith arrived at the courthouse twenty minutes early and started nosing around, looking for the D. A.'s office. The three-story brick building was filled with people carrying loads of papers, chairs, desks, lamps, everything imaginable that would fit in an office. The attorney stopped several times to ask someone scurrying by for the location of the district attorney's office with no success. He finally started a floor-by-floor canvass of the building, looking in and calling the name of his expected conferee in each office. Finally, midway along the third floor, Goldsmith opened the door to a cluttered office. A florid-faced young man popped up from behind a box-laden desk saying, "I'm District Attorney Bergeron. Are you Goldsmith?"

They shook hands. Bergeron cleared off part of his desk and moved boxes off a chair so Norman could sit.

"Trying to get settled in, huh?" he said. "Sorry to bother you with this so soon, before you're all moved in and all, but it's an old case and I think we can handle it to everybody's satisfaction pretty quickly and move on." Goldsmith smiled hopefully. "By the way, I know your father and have great respect for him. I'm happy to see he's handling things in the district for our new governor."

Bergeron was only thirty-one and had practiced law for seven years. Most who knew him surmised that his appointment was very much family related. He was short and soft and round and had avoided military service because of respiratory problems suffered from birth. His father was an old boyhood friend of the governor and one of the leaders of the Nicholls' supporters in Assumption Parish.

After a frantic search, Leland pulled a file from the middle of a stack and said, "Ah yes, the Galvez murder and attempted murder case, right?" Goldsmith nodded. Bergeron had a worried look on his face that Goldsmith didn't like. "I've done some inquiring around since you sent word last Friday. I'm not sure how fast we can move this to trial, Mr. Goldsmith. I haven't been able to find many of the original witnesses and participants. As you know, most of them were involved in the Freedmen's Bureau and the reconstruction administration and they've moved on since the incident." He flipped through several more pages and then sighed, "I'm afraid I'll need more time to familiarize myself with the whole situation."

Goldsmith reluctantly nodded understanding, "I'm sure you'll find some folks who can bring you up to date on the case, Mr. Bergeron. You should know that my client has a witness who saw the shooting, maybe the only person still around who did. She will describe the alleged victims drawing weapons and firing on Mr. Galvez before he returned fire in self-defense."

Bergeron was totally focused on Goldsmith's testimony. He seemed empathetic but suspicious. "But didn't he then run away and stay hidden for a year? That sounds a lot like a guilty man to me, sir."

"On the contrary. With all due respect, Mr. District Attorney, my client rightfully feared for his life. You well know the caliber of people who were in office at the time and the vengefulness of that group would have, undoubtedly, denied Mr. Galvez any semblance of a fair trial. He had no choice but to disappear until things changed."

"Still," Bergeron mused, "it took a cottonmouth moccasin to bring him in. He didn't exactly volunteer to give himself up, did he?"

Goldsmith blanched slightly, "I can assure you he was about to come in when the unfortunate snake bite occurred," he said. "But now that he's in, I appeal to you to get this behind us so this young man, a victim of the national horror we have all lived through, can move on with his life." He reached into the leather satchel he had carried into the office and withdrew a sheaf of papers. "I have prepared a brief for you and a motion to dismiss all charges based on, not only the facts of the case and our witness's testimony, but on the fact that there are no witnesses that I know of for the prosecution. My witness's sworn deposition is included here." He continued pulling papers from the satchel. "While you are considering that, I have a motion here that Mr. Galvez be released on his own recognizance pending further action."

Bergeron was obviously overwhelmed by Goldsmith's barrage of papers. He held up both hands, "Hold on now. Just slow down there, Mr. Goldsmith. As you can see, I'm just setting up this office and I have stacks and stacks of cases to get familiar with. I'll need to bring this up with Judge Ricard before we move any further. Until then, tell your client to rest and recuperate from that snakebite while he's being well taken care of in jail. I'll get back to you as soon as I get with the judge." He stood and extended his pudgy hand. "Thank you for coming to this mess of an office. I hope to be sending word to you soon."

Goldsmith shook hands, thanked him profusely for his time and consideration and tried not to show his disappointment as he left the cluttered office. *I guess I need to get word to Benjamin Mayers up in White Castle to remind young Mr. Bergeron how he got to be Mr. District Attorney.*

As Goldsmith was retrieving his horse from the hitching post on the side of the building, he heard his name being called from above. Looking up he saw Leland Bergeron leaning out his third-story window. "Mr. Goldsmith, thought you'd like to know. We just got word that President Hayes has ordered all Union soldiers out of Louisiana by April 24th. Ain't that good news?"

"Sure is! Absolutely! Sure is," Goldsmith shouted back and waved. *April 24th,* he thought, *almost exactly fifteen years to the day that the feds had taken the City of New Orleans; fifteen long, bloody, miserable years. At least this president, even though he's a Republican, has been true to his word.*

Neat was sitting on the cot in his cell finishing a meal of red beans and rice when Sherman and Sheriff Gilmore came into the tiny jail house. He was finishing his sixth day of incarceration. It was already growing dark outside and the deputy had lit a couple of lamps inside. Sherman walked up to the bars with a sad look on his face. "Bad news, huh?" Neat said.

"Yea, the D. A. don't want to take any chances. Goldsmith said he's probably scared to get off on the wrong foot so he's gonna take his advice from the old judge." Sherman kicked a booted toe at a roach scooting by in front of the cell. "But, it shouldn't be long, maybe a week or so, Neat."

Neat sat on the cot looking down at the cell floor for a long time. He finally mumbled, "Well, what the hell. I guess this is better than freezing in the swamp with the snakes." His leg was still heavily bandaged and painful. Doctor Ourso said it could be a couple of weeks before the swelling went all the way down and the pain ebbed. Then, the doctor said, he might have to do a little "scouring out of the wound." Neat wasn't looking forward to that.

Gilmore put a key in the cell door and opened it, "Come on out, Neat. Ain't no sense in your sitting around in there. Did Amanda come by today?"

"Naw, she said when she was here Sunday she wouldn't be back 'til the end of the week but to let her know what Goldsmith said."

"I'll go by to see her when I leave here," Sherman said. "I talked to my daddy, Neat. He'll lend us the money for the lawyer and we can work it off on the farm when you get free. He said he'd even give me one of the spring calves to sell off and use some of that money. He'll pay us enough to have a little spending money on top of the pay-off and we should be able to finish it up in about six months. That ain't bad, huh?"

Neat got up from the cot and hobbled out of the cell into the tiny office. He glanced at the rack of guns behind the desk and caught Henry giving him a warning look as he did. "Don't worry Henry, I ain't even thinkin' what you think I'm thinkin'. But I hope you're taking good care of my guns for when I get outta here. And Sherman, what you mean your daddy will lend 'us' the money? I'm the one who owes the lawyer, not you. I'm the one gonna borrow the money. You tell your daddy I appreciate what he's doing but that I'm the one that's gonna pay it off, not you, even if it takes a year or more."

"Aw, Neat, it don't make no never mind. I don't need much money and I just want you to be free, free out of here and free from owing money."

❧   ❧   ❧

The following Monday, District Attorney Bergeron sent word to the sheriff that he needed the prisoner, Antoine Galvez, at the Napoleonville courthouse at ten in the morning of March 16th for a pretrial hearing before Judge Alcide Ricard. Obviously Goldsmith had twisted a few arms to get the DA moving.

Sherman, Pokey and Pierre were waiting on the steps of the courthouse when Sheriff Gilmore and a deputy pulled the closed carriage up to the steps, hitched the two-horse team and unloaded the shackled prisoner. Neat looked small, scared and nervous as he waddled up the steps and down the hall into the holding room next to the judge's chambers. Sherman had offered to bring Amanda to the session but her father would not hear of it. Lawtell had not been told yet that his daughter intended to testify for Neat. He had reluctantly agreed to let her be questioned, "deposed" as they called it, by that smart-alecky little lawyer. Amanda decided she would wait until the last minute to confront him with the decision to appear at the trial. She hoped the charges might be dropped making her testimony unnecessary and thus avoiding what surely would be a nasty scene with her parents.

Chief Judge Alcide Ricard, at age fifty, was a commanding figure in the courtroom. Six-feet tall and sturdily built, he had been prematurely gray since he was forty. He wore his wavy, silver shock of hair long, below his collar and tolerated no nonsense in his bailiwick. He convened the hearing by first having the charges read by the clerk. He asked Goldsmith to step forward with the accused. "Antoine Joseph Galvez, you are charged with the murder of Herman Boyer and the attempted murder of Nathaniel Becker. How do you plead?"

Goldsmith nudged Neat lightly with his right elbow. Neat, looking directly at the judge, said, "Not guilty, sir. It was self-defense."

"Yes, we'll see," said Judge Ricard.

He then asked Bergeron about his witness list and how long his prosecution phase of the trial would take. "I don't intend to take more than a couple of hours, your honor. Frankly, there are not many witnesses for the prosecution who were at the scene of the shooting. Most of them have left the area, if not the state. I will have one of Herman Boyer's former assistants who knew both him and the other man who was shot, Nathaniel Becker. He will testify concerning the temperament of the two men and their possible proclivity to using firearms. I'll also have the doctor who was acting coroner at the time and who also treated the other victim who was wounded and we'll call Sheriff Gilmore to the fact that Mr. Galvez was a fugitive and recount his efforts in searching for the accused for the past year. That will complete our case except for possible cross-examination or any unknown circumstances that might arise."

"Very good, Mr. Bergeron." The judge turned to the defense table. Norman Goldsmith was nattily attired in a cream-colored linen suit with a red cravat,

Neat sat next to him in a khaki shirt and trousers. He was clean-shaven and his hair had been trimmed to a reasonable length. He looked small and drawn and very vulnerable. "Mr. Goldsmith?"

"Yes, your honor. Our presentation will be very brief. I intend to call one eyewitness, the only one, I might add. Then we'll call Mr. Galvez to testify in his behalf. That will be all, and frankly, I think it will be plenty enough for acquittal."

Judge Ricard banged his gavel and looked at Goldsmith in astonishment, "Sir, you know better than to make such a statement before this bench. If there were jurors in the room I would hold you in contempt.

Judge Ricard fussed with the papers on his bench, glared at Goldsmith once more and said, "We will schedule the trial for two days. We'll begin at ten next Thursday morning, March 22nd. First day we'll do jury selection; I'll round up a pool of thirty men. You should be able to get nine acceptable ones out of that. Friday we'll give the prosecution two hours in the morning and the same for the defense after lunch. With closing arguments limited to fifteen minutes apiece, the jury should get the case by mid-afternoon and, with any luck we'll have us a verdict by nightfall." He banged the gavel again, then scowled down at Norman Goldsmith. He quietly, almost without moving his lips, said, "I hope you appreciate the fact that I am expediting this trial because of some interested parties who are mutual friends. Don't make me regret it. Watch yourself, son." He rose and walked out of the courtroom.

The defense attorney turned to Neat just as Sheriff Gilmore took him by one arm and Sherman, Pokey and Pierre came up to the rail. He whispered loudly, "You all better make damn sure Miss Pitre is ready for her role. If she doesn't testify, you're a goner."

"We're all three going over there right now," Sherman said. "She hasn't told her mother and father what she's gonna do yet and I know she's gonna need our support."

❦   ❦   ❦

"You are all out of your simple minds!" Lawtell yelled. He was standing on the front porch of his farmhouse just north of White Castle. Neat's three friends were standing just off the steps to the porch in the front yard. A couple of small white hens circled the boys, pecking curiously at their boots. Amanda and her mother, Cora were seated in the swing. Pitre's face was red. He was having a hard time breathing.

"Now, Lawtell, please calm down," Cora pleaded, "you're gonna pop something if you keep on like this. We can talk about what Amanda and the boys want without shouting."

"Talk about what they want?" Lawtell continued shouting, "What *they* want? They want our sweet, innocent daughter to stand up in a public courtroom at a murder trial...a MURDER TRIAL," he shouted louder, "and say she saw something she didn't see?"

"But, daddy," Amanda said in a small voice, "I did see it. I saw those men with guns shoot at Neat and he shot back. I saw it, I did." She started sobbing, her head falling into her mother's lap.

Sherman cleared his throat and tentatively raised his hand as if asking permission to speak, "Mr. Pitre, it won't take long. She'll only be on the stand a few minutes and, once she tells her story, it'll be all over. Lawyer Goldsmith said so himself. Neat will be set free and this will all be over with."

"It's over with now, young man. The answer is no. That is final. My little girl is not going to be subjected to this humiliation and potential ridicule. If that little punk is innocent he'll have to prove it himself." Amanda started sobbing louder. Cora stroked her hair and clucked soothingly.

"Well, they's gonna hang him, that's for sure." Pokey said as he kicked a rock from the yard under the porch sending the hens scuttling away. Pierre jabbed him in the ribs with an elbow. Pokey pushed back, "Well, they is. They's gonna hang him, sure as shootin'. You heard lawyer Goldsmith, without Amanda testifying he's good as hanged."

"That's for true, Mr. Pitre." Sherman said, "You gotta let Amanda do this, it's Neat's life we're talking about."

"It's my *daughter's* life *I'm* talking about. It's my *family's* life I'm talking about. It's *my* life I'm talking about. No! No! No! Do you understand one simple word? No! Now you all go on home. Get off my property." He turned and stomped into the house, slamming the screen door behind him.

Amanda pulled herself up from her mother's lap. "Oh, mama, what am I gonna do? I've got to save Neat. I've got to."

Cora stood up slowly, still holding her weeping daughter's hands, "I'll try to reason with him. Let him calm down some and we'll talk about it again tonight. You boys run on now, you're just making it worse hanging around here. He needs some time to cool off."

The three nodded agreement, waved weakly to her and Amanda and retreated to their horses tethered at the front gate.

They slowly made their way back into town. "Who's gonna tell him?" Pokey asked. The wind picked up under threatening skies and kicked dust devils across the dirt road.

"Ain't got to tell him nothing," Sherman snapped, "They's still talking it over. He ain't decided yet."

"Ain't decided?" Pokey was incredulous. "If that man ain't decided I wanna see somebody that is."

Sherman kept on shaking his head affirmatively, "It's gonna be all right. Amanda's gonna testify and…" A huge thunder clap drowned out his words and lightning flashed almost simultaneously. The horses all reared and pulled against their leads. A hard driving rain poured down on the group as they raced down the road seeking shelter.

XVII
March 22nd, 1877

Spring was in the air. The day was cool and sunny with a light southerly breeze. The pecan trees were sprouting, a sure sign that cold weather was over. It was the time of renewal and growth.

Neat was brought to the courthouse in Napoleonville early in the morning. He was held in one of two windowless cells at the back of the building on the third floor. The courtroom where his trial would be held was on the second floor. The trial was the hottest topic on the river. Word had traveled south down Bayou LaFourche and north to Baton Rouge: a teenaged rebel, a fugitive from justice for over a year who had shot and killed an important reconstruction administrator and wounded a key aide was being tried for murder and attempted murder. Two and four-wheel carriages, some drawn by horses, some by mules, were packed into the yard surrounding the courthouse and down the converging streets.

Shortly after eight o'clock Norman Goldsmith entered Neat's cell. He sat on the opposite cot and didn't speak for a full minute. Neat sensed the depressing news. "Still no word from Mr. Pitre?"

"No. He won't give in. Says his little girl is not going to be subjected to this embarrassment." Goldsmith was wringing his hands. "I've got one other shot. My Uncle Jacob is close to Clarence Bergeron, the D. A.'s father. He's heading over to Donaldsonville right now to talk to him. He's going to try to convince him to talk with Lawtell Pitre. He needs to understand that his son can't start his career this way; convicting a young man who was defending himself against people who had raped and pillaged our land for their own profit?

Old man Bergeron is also a big supporter and old friend of the governor. He'll get some kind of appointment or stipend from Nicholls for Pitre if he lets his daughter come down here. She'll be a heroine." Goldsmith looked directly into Neat's eyes. He said emphatically, "He can't turn that down." Neat found it hard to share the attorney's optimism.

❦   ❦   ❦

Jury selection went quickly. By noon four men had been selected. One was a clerk at the bank in Napoleonville, two were farmhands from around Donald-sonville and the fourth was a carpenter from Bayou Goula. Only four others had been excused for various reasons so there were still twenty-two left in the pool to fill the other five seats and an alternate position. Judge Ricard called an hour and a half recess.

❦   ❦   ❦

Just past three o'clock in the afternoon, Jacob Hermann and Clarence Berg-eron pulled up to the front of Lawtell Pitre's home in Bergeron's enclosed cab drawn by two matched chestnut horses being handled by a black driver. Cora greeted the two well-dressed men at the door with awe and curiosity.

"Good afternoon, Madame Pitre, I am Clarence Bergeron, Governor Nicholls representative in Assumption, Ascension and Iberville Parishes and this is barrister Jacob Hermann who practices the law in Napoleonville. We are sorry to intrude on you on this lovely day but we must speak to your husband. Is Mr. Pitre available?"

Cora was confused and a bit anxious. What could these men want with her husband? She opened the door wide and beckoned them to step inside. "My husband, Lawtell, is out back with some of the hands planning next week's work schedule. I'll get him. Would you all like something cool to drink."

"Water would be fine, madam," Bergeron bowed slightly as Cora scurried out of the room. The two men studied the room and its furnishings. Cora was a fastidious housekeeper. There wasn't a speck of dust visible on the old but well-kept end tables, sofa and chairs. The rug was a little threadbare but obviously clean. The room was light and airy with chintz curtains on the three windows letting in a good deal of sunlight. Cora came rushing back in with a tray loaded with a pitcher and tumblers. Moments later Lawtell Pitre came huffing in. He was dressed in dusty coveralls, a denim shirt and scuffed, dirty boots. He felt a little embarrassed of his appearance in the presence of the well-dressed visitors and apologized for it.

"Not at all, sir, it's good to see an honest working man taking care of business." Bergeron stood up and greeted him. He gripped Lawtell's hand firmly with both of his own, and reintroduced himself and Jacob though Lawtell knew both of them slightly. He was very aware of their reputations as power brokers.

"Thank you for seeing us, Mr. Pitre. I know this is a busy time for you with the preparation and planting of your fields. There is a matter of utmost urgency that we must discuss with you."

"Certainly, sir," Pitre said." He was puzzled by the surprise visit of these two important men he barely knew. Their exaggerated formality made him uneasy. "How may I be of service to you?"

"Mr. Pitre, you know, of course, of the trial of young Mr. Antoine Galvez for murder and attempted murder. It opened this morning in Napoleonville."

Pitre immediately took a step back and his entire demeanor changed. He could not believe that these two highly esteemed, dignified gentlemen were here on behalf of that rogue, Galvez. Both hands clenched into fists, his voice trembled slightly as he said, "My daughter is not going to testify in that trial, gentlemen. I emphasize. She is not." He took a step back and glanced at his wife. Her eyes were averted from all three men. "I hope that is not why you came all the way up here."

Jacob Hermann spoke for the first time, "Let's not draw any hard lines in the dirt, Mr. Pitre. Hear us out first. Please, may we all sit?"

Pitre reluctantly took a chair and said, "There is nothing to discuss." The other two sat on the edge of the sofa.

For twenty minutes they explained, cajoled, reasoned and argued the case of the need for Amanda Pitre to testify the next day in Napoleonville. Bergeron pleaded that his son would make a good and fair district attorney but he very much needed to gracefully lose this, his first major trial. He would be forever remembered as the man who sent a teenage southern native to the gallows for shooting two "no good carpetbaggers." He apologized for that characterization when he saw Pitre recoil. "That, of course, is not how I feel but it is the prevailing sense of the people in these parts." Hermann assured Lawtell that he and his nephew Norman would be forever grateful to the Pitre family and would certainly handle any of their future legal needs at no cost or, at most, for expenses.

Pitre was unrelenting. His head dropped lower and lower and he refused to utter a word. Bergeron stopped talking. There was silence for a full minute. Clarence turned to Jacob. "Sir, would you do me the great favor of stepping outside to see if my driver needs anything. I'd like a private word with Mr. Pitre."

Clarence stood up from the sofa as Jacob left the room. He walked over to Pitre's chair and placed a hand on his shoulder. "Mr. Pitre. Lawtell. I'm a father too. I have a daughter a little older than Amanda and I understand your concerns. I'm asking you as a friend, Lawtell. Let her testify. We'll see to it that she is treated with utmost courtesy and respect. You and Mrs. Pitre can accompany her to the courthouse in my cab and Jacob and I will be seated with you in the courtroom. Do this for all of us and I can assure you that Governor Nicholls will be advised of your cooperation and will show his gratitude." Bergeron put his hands on either side of Lawtell's shoulders and coaxed him into an upright stance. He cupped a hand under Pitre's chin and looked into his eyes. "Listen to me, son," he said, "There are several important appointments still pending in the district and they each carry a generous stipend. The governor can use your farming expertise." He paused to see if Pitre would respond. "On the other hand, there is a lot of competition for state funds for farming operations such as you have been receiving." He took his hand from Pitre's face but continued his stare. Finally, he extended his hand to Lawtell. "Let's make this thing right, Mr. Pitre. Let's get this distasteful business behind us so that we may enjoy the new day that is dawning."

Pitre was very still. He looked down at the floor for a long time. When he looked into Bergeron's eyes again there were tears streaming down his cheeks. His lips were quivering and he swallowed hard several times. Then Lawtell took Bergeron's hand and they sealed the deal.

As a prearranged signal, Jacob, listening at the door, cleared his throat loudly before reentering the room. Clarence turned to him and winked. "Mr. Pitre has just graciously and wisely agreed to allow Amanda to testify."

Pitre had turned his back and was rubbing his shirtsleeves over his face. When he turned back, Jacob grabbed Lawtell's hand and pumped it. "That's wonderful, Mr. Pitre, I know you won't regret it. Amanda will be spoken of with reverence for years to come for what she is about to do."

Cora, listening just beyond the door to the parlor, had tears streaming down her cheeks. Amanda had not heard the previous conversation but was now standing on the bottom step of the staircase. She paled visibly as she heard the decision. Her knees weakened and she almost fainted.

Bergeron quickly said, "My driver will pick you all up at six in the morning. It's a pretty good ride to Napoleonville. But it's a very comfortable carriage, you'll be home by nightfall and it will be all over. Thank you, sir, thank you."

He pumped Lawtell's hand again. "You are an honorable man. We look forward to seeing you tomorrow."

The two negotiators could hardly wait to get in the cab and pull away from the homestead before letting out simultaneous whoops and cracking open a bottle of Tennessee sour mash. "Damnation," said Bergeron, "the things you got to do to see to it that justice and good government prevails."

XVIII
March 23rd, 1877
morning

"And in conclusion, we will show that Mr. Galvez went to the ball in good faith and in a spirit of adventure and fun. After all, it *was* Mardi Gras. He had no intention of confronting or causing any harm to Mr. Boyer, Mr. Becker or anyone else. It was only when he was challenged by three armed men, only when he was threatened and shot at that he drew his pistol and defended himself just as any of you would have done."

Goldsmith, immaculately dressed in a light gray suit and a gold silk cravat, concluded his opening statement to the nine-man jury and took his seat next to Neat. He had a decidedly self-satisfied look on his face. The courtroom was filled to standing room only. The crush of the crowd made the atmosphere hot and humid. Many of the women were waving fans in front of their faces to keep cool air circulating. Earlier, District Attorney Leland Bergeron had used only ten minutes outlining the case for the prosecution.

The all male jury was completed with two more farmers from Iberville Parish and three young men from Napoleonville who had served in the Confederate Army. Two of them were amputees. One had lost a leg below the knee and the other his right arm at the shoulder. The alternate was an elderly man from Samstown whose main occupation was whittling in front of the livery stable there.

In the front row, just behind the defense table, sat Neat's mother and two of his sisters. Sherman had arranged for Pokey to pick them up in Brusly McCall and bring them to the courthouse. The other two sisters were married and living in Beaumont, Texas and Mobile, Alabama. Their mother had notified them but they were unable to make the tedious journeys. They both sent word that they were saying novenas for their brother. Not yet fifty-years old, his mother was thin and frail and her skin looked translucent. She had suffered severe respiratory problems over the winter including a bout with flu and pneumonia. His sisters, small and dark like Neat, were dressed in obviously handmade clothing. Neat guessed the material had come from flour sacks the women had scrounged from a mercantile store. A pang of guilt hit him in the gut. Filling out the row of seats were Sherman Mayers and his father Benjamin, Pokey Lafleur and Pierre Bourgeois.

Mr. and Mrs. Pitre and their two young sons, a Catholic priest they had invited and two of Sheriff Gilmore's black deputies occupied the second row. Clarence Bergeron and Jacob Hermann were seated directly behind Cora and Lawtell.

"Proceed with your case, Mr. Bergeron."

Bergeron, wearing his usual uniform: black suit, black string tie and scuffed, dusty black boots, stood and said, "The state calls Mr. Joseph Darnell to the stand."

Darnell was one of Herman Boyer's assistants at the time of the shootings. He had been in charge of agriculture oversight in the district. His duties included inspecting the farms to ascertain that the proper balance of crops was being planted. Certain farms were to plant sugar cane, others cotton and smaller ones were assigned vegetable and fruit cultivation. It didn't matter if the farmers had previously raised other crops and had no expertise in the ones assigned by the bureaucracy; the government knew best.

In the course of his inspections, farmers were expected to show their gratitude for his important and meticulous work by leaving sacks of produce, cured meats and small bags of currency in his carriage while he was inspecting their fields and barns. Being a graduate of a teachers' college in upstate New York had not equipped him for such a job, but he was loyal to Boyer and to the Union, in that order, and thus qualified.

The district attorney ran him through a recitation of his background and his association with the reconstruction administrator. He related that he was at the Mardi Gras ball on the evening in question.

"Mr. Darnell, the invitations to the ball specifically noted that participants should not carry any weapons or firearms of any kind onto the premises, correct?"

"That's correct, sir. I helped write the calligraphy on many of the invitations myself. It's an art I acquired while in college." He gave the courtroom a self-satisfied smile.

"Very well. Now, would that admonishment about weapons also apply to Mr. Boyer, Mr. Becker or any of his staff?"

"Of course not," Darnell sniffed, "Mr. Boyer knew he was always in danger because some people had never accepted the new regime that he represented. He knew he had to be ready to defend himself at all times. Mr. Becker and Mr. William Simpson were two of his most trusted aides and they were always armed. I too was very close to Mr. Boyer but I, well I just have never felt comfortable around guns." There were some deep-throated chuckles in the audience.

"So, Mr. Boyer and his aides were ready to use their weapons at any time if they were threatened?" Bergeron asked.

"Oh, I'm sure they were. Thank the Lord such a time had never before come up. Frankly, I'm not sure Herman ever had fired his revolver. Now, Nathaniel, I saw him taking target practice behind the Boyer barn a couple of times. He was good at it, too. You know he had been in the Union cavalry. He looked great in that uniform and, could he ever ride a horse!"

"Okay fine, Mr. Darnell," Mr. Bergeron interrupted. "Were you present, did you witness the incident? Did you see Mr. Boyer and Mr. Becker get shot.?

Darnell visibly winced, "Thank God, no! I'd have never been able to forget that if I had seen it. It was horrid enough just coming out of the house and seeing all that blood. Oh, just horrid." He cringed and covered his eyes with his hands.

Bergeron pressed on. "The guns belonging to Mr. Boyer, Mr. Becker and Mr. Simpson seem to have disappeared. Did you see them the night of the incident? Were they lying on the ground when you arrived at the scene?"

"Lord knows what happened with them." Darnell put an open hand on the side of his cheek, "There was such pandemonium out there. Women were screaming, men were yelling. When I got out front I saw Herman and Nathaniel lying there with blood everywhere. I got weak in the knees myself. William was screaming and holding this terrible gash in his forehead." He choked back a sob. "Some men brought a carriage around and loaded all three of them in it and took off for the doctor's house. Nobody paid any attention to looking for any guns on the ground or any kind of evidence. It wasn't until the next day when Sheriff Gilmore came out to the house that we started looking around. We found that ghastly beak-nosed mask with crusted blood on it but I never saw any guns. Miz Hilda, Mr. Boyer's wife? She said she knew nothing about the guns. I don't know what happened to them. Could have been some opportunists at the ball taking advantage of the chaos to pick up some new weapons." He gave a big shoulder shrug.

"But, you're sure the men did have guns on them?"

"Well, yea, I guess. They always did carry them. They must have had 'em that night."

Bergeron then led Darnell through an obviously rehearsed account of the temperament of the three men. According to the aide they were all very calm, deliberate and peace-loving individuals who would only resort to violence if there lives or their families were threatened.

Bergeron turned to the judge and said, "No further questions, your honor." Goldsmith surprised everyone by waiving cross-examination.

The district attorney quickly went back to his table, consulted a sheaf of papers and announced, "The state calls Doctor Jesse Ourso."

The doctor, wearing his customary black suit and string tie took the oath and was seated in the witness box.

He recited his credentials and the fact that he was acting coroner for the three-parish district at the time of the incident. He recalled being awakened near midnight Mardi Gras night by the sound of nearly a dozen horses and shouting men converging on his home.

"I knew two of the men they hauled in right off. It was obvious to me that Herman Boyer was dead the second I looked at him so I just left him be. Nathaniel Becker was damn near dead. That ball broke a bone in his shoulder and barely missed a major artery. He'd lost a lot of blood. The other guy just had a bad cut to the head so I started in on Becker first. Took me most of an hour to get him patched up and then I wasn't too sure he'd make it. Other gent I didn't know. Might not of recognized him anyway. His face was covered with blood; most of it caked dry. Had this nasty open gash five inches long in his forehead, just over his eyebrows. After I got him cleaned up, it took a gang of stitches to close it up. Did the best I could, but he ain't never gonna win any handsomest man contests, I can tell you." Nervous laughter rippled through the courtroom and Judge Ricard banged his gavel.

Bergeron asked the doctor if he had any knowledge of the men having fired their weapons during the confrontation.

Ourso tugged on his white beard for a couple of moments, "No sir, never looked for any signs. I was too damn busy patching and sewing and nobody mentioned anything other than them being shot down in cold blood."

Goldsmith jumped to his feet. "Objection, hearsay!"

"Sustained." Judge Ricard looked menacingly at the doctor.

Bergeron continued, "Now, doctor, I call your attention to the defense table. Are you familiar with Mr. Antoine Galvez and do you see him here."

"Why sure, that's him right there. I just treated him a couple of weeks ago for a snakebite. He's lucky to be here." He thought better of that statement. "Well, I guess he's just lucky to be alive if not exactly lucky to be…ah, hell, you know what I mean—he's lucky to be anywhere." The audience appreciated the doctor's explanation. Some started to clap their hands but were quickly stared down by a stern look from the judge.

"Would you say Mr. Galvez came to you for treatment voluntarily?"

Ourso was beginning to enjoy the attention of the courtroom crowd, "If you call getting' hisself bit by a moccasin and being carried in unconscious voluntary." There was some giggling. "Naw. Some trapper from around Bayou Sorrel hauled him into town and the sheriff carried him into my office. He was in toxic shock at the time. He never knew where he was 'til that night."

"So you don't think he gave himself up after hiding out for over a year."

"Oh yeah, he almost gave himself up to the Lord when he messed with that cottonmouth. But he never gave himself up to Sheriff Gilmore voluntarily, no." The crowd in the courtroom appreciated the doc's sense of humor once more.

Again, Goldsmith waived cross-examination.

Neat leaned over and whispered to him, "Are you going to get involved in this here trial or not? What the hell you doin' just sitting here?"

Goldsmith shushed him, "I know what I'm doing. They have no case. Now that Amanda's coming they stand no chance. Trust me."

Bergeron called Sheriff Henry Gilmore to the stand.

After several minutes of preliminaries he asked, "Sheriff, to your knowledge, what happened at the Boyer's home on the night of February 29th, last year?"

Goldsmith was on his feet, "Objection, the sheriff was not at the scene of the altercation. The prosecution obviously cannot produce an eye witness to the alleged crime. Therefore anything the sheriff might say would be hearsay or conjecture on his part."

Judge Ricard looked over his reading glasses at Bergeron, "That sounds about right to me, what do you say Mr. D. A.?"

"Well judge," Bergeron whined, "I gotta have somebody tell what happened on that night."

The judge pondered Bergeron's plight for several seconds before relenting, "You're right. You should have somebody. But, you ain't got nobody. I'm gonna make an exception though and allow this hearsay evidence just once and let the sheriff tell us what he thinks happened and how he identified a suspect." Goldsmith was up like a shot but the judge had already fixed him with a nasty look and a finger pointed at his chair. "No, Mr. Goldsmith. Sheriff? Go on."

Gilmore flashed his set of perfect teeth in a nervous smile. "Well sir, judge, the people that was at the ball all recognized the mask that the supposed shooter wore. It wasn't like nothing nobody else had. It was made of papier maché and was very hard, like plaster. It was used to hit one of Mr. Boyer's aides, matter of fact gave him a terrible cut across his head. When the shooter ran off, he left that mask on the ground next to the victims. We found blood on it. Some people were sure the mask belonged to Neat, I mean, uh, Mr. Galvez." The sheriff glanced at the defense table. Neat sat frozen with a pained look on his face. "When we went looking for him where he stayed at Mr. Mayers' house, it looked like he had taken his guns and some other stuff and high-tailed it out of town. His unsaddled horse showed up a few days later. Then we got some reports that he was seen in Donaldsonville buying passage on a packet to New Orleans. We figured he must be our man." Neat's expression eased into a very slight smile.

Bergeron retreated behind the prosecution desk referring to his notes. He looked up again at the sheriff, "Tell us how you pursued the man who shot Mr. Boyer and Mr...."

Goldsmith was up again before the question was finished, "Object. The sheriff doesn't know and nobody else knows for sure who shot those gentlemen."

Ricard said in a bored voice, "Sustained. Restate your question, Mr. Bergeron."

The D. A. tried again, "All I'm saying judge is the sheriff knew somebody got shot and he was searching for the shooter."

Bergeron was pushing Judge Ricard's patience. "I said restate your question, sir. You do know what that means don't you?"

"Yes sir, yes sir." He turned back to the witness stand. "So, sheriff, did you have a suspect in the shooting in question, sir?" He sneaked a quick peek at Goldsmith who smiled slightly but remained seated.

"Yes, I did."

"And who was that?"

"The prisoner there, Antoine Galvez."

Bergeron closed his eyes and waited for an explosion from Goldsmith. It didn't come. The defense attorney sat complacently at his desk writing notes.

A nervous smile crossed the prosecutor's face, "How did you go about pursuing Mr. Galvez?" he asked tentatively.

Gilmore recounted his procedures of searching the area, sending out deputies to question Neat's friends and associates and wiring the information to New Orleans when it was suspected he had hopped a packet out of Donaldsonville.

"What were the results of your investigation?"

"Didn't have no results. I mean we just couldn't find him. Oh, we had a bunch of reports of him being seen in a lot of different places but it never turned out to be him. You know they's a lot of men in south Louisiana that look a lot like Mr. Galvez there."

"So how did you finally capture the fugitive?" Bergeron asked with growing confidence.

Gilmore looked a little embarrassed. "He was brought in unconscious after being bit by a snake."

A ripple of laughter crossed the courtroom. The gavel slammed down.

"Do you know where he had been for the past year?"

"Yassuh, he say he was living in the swamp."

"In the swamp?"

"Yassuh, he say he had a cabin in the swamp up on Bayou Maringouin and he be up there all year."

"Well now, he had to have some help from somebody or some *bodies* to stay in the swamp for a year. You knew Mr. Galvez pretty well, didn't you, sheriff? You'd never heard of this, um, cabin in the swamp? Never considered looking for him there?"

"I did send some deputies up in that area to look for him. They said they had no sign of his being up there. But, you see that little cabin was in the woods on the other side of the bayou. The deputies didn't cross the bayou and go to the trapper's hut."

"Somebody had to be bringing him food and things, don't you think? He was out there over a year."

Gilmore bit his lower lip and shot a nervous glance at Sherman in the first row. Sherman was holding his breath. "I don't rightly know 'bout that, sir. He didn't say but I would suppose he needed some help from time to time. He sho nuff needed it when that moccasin got a hold of him." Again the crowd snickered and the judge banged his gavel.

After several more questions aimed at exposing anyone who might have aided or abetted Neat, Bergeron gave up. He had now quickly exhausted all his witnesses. He had no choice but to rest his case.

Judge Ricard pulled a silver pocket watch from under his robe, snapped the cover open and announced, "We'll take a recess now until one thirty when the defense will present its case. Everybody be on time." He rapped the gavel once more and exited the courtroom.

The crowd started buzzing and milling toward the exits. Several friends came to the rail to pat Neat on the back and wish him well. He looked over Pokey's shoulder and caught the full force of Lawtell Pitre's hatred. The man was looking at him through eyes that looked like burning coals. *Jesus God*, Neat thought, *the man hates me now, wonder what he'd be like if he knew about everything Amanda and me did?*

The bailiff took Neat by the arm and led him out of the courtroom back to the holding cell. As they went up the back stairwell he heard a familiar voice and looked down. There was the beautiful, honey-blond hair he loved so much. Amanda was being escorted by one of Judge Ricard's assistants to the judge's chambers where they would share a lunch with her parents and pastor.

XIX
March 23rd, 1877
afternoon

At exactly one thirty the bailiff called the court to order and the judge seated himself, "Mr. Goldsmith, are you prepared to offer your case?"

"I am, your honor." The attorney slowly walked to the bench, turned and took a dramatic stance with the thumb of his right hand hooked into a vest pocket. In a stentorian tone he said, "The defense calls Mr. Antoine Galvez." Bergeron looked up in surprise. A low murmur swept the room. Everyone was expecting the appearance of Amanda Pitre. Goldsmith had changed his mind during the recess. He reasoned that Amanda's testimony would be so dramatic, so conclusive anything after would be virtually ignored. He wanted Neat to be heard first.

Looking small and scared, Neat limped slowly to the witness stand, raised his right hand and swore to tell the truth.

Goldsmith led him gently through the circumstances leading up to his arrival at the site of the Mardi Gras ball.

"But you knew you weren't invited. You knew you were not wanted there. Why did you go?"

Neat shrugged his shoulders and replied weakly, "It was Mardi Gras. I had this great looking mask a friend had brought me from New Orleans and several of my friends had been invited including Miss Amanda Pitre and I just wanted to kind of surprise them and have some fun. I didn't mean no harm by it."

"Didn't you know that you were not supposed to carry a firearm into the Boyer home?"

"I don't know, I mean yes sir, I guess so." Goldsmith had warned Neat about being evasive or untruthful. He was glaring at him now. "Th-th-that's why I left my forty-four revolver in my saddle bag," Neat stammered.

"But you still carried a Double Derringer."

"Well, yea, but that was just for an emergency."

"So you felt you couldn't carry your revolver but you could carry the Derringer…for an emergency."

"That's kinda what it's for. That's why it's so little and easy to hide…"

Goldsmith interrupted him, "Okay Mr. Galvez, you felt as though you needed the little gun to protect yourself since you knew you shouldn't be there in the first place. Now, did you talk to any of your friends?"

"The only one I recognized, with the masks and all, was Miss Amanda. I recognized her in the crowd by the color of her hair. I went up behind her and whispered for her to meet me out on the gallery so I could find out where the others were, what their masks looked like."

"What happened when you went outside?"

Neat fiddled with a thread that was hanging from his cuff, he reached up and pushed his hair back from his forehead, "Well sir, one of those men, you know the ones in charge of this reconstruction stuff, came around the corner of the house out on the gallery and yelled at me to show him my invitation. I knew I could be in trouble and decided I just wanted to get out of there. I headed for where my horse was but the man kept coming at me and yelling. Then another one came from around the side of the house. I could see he had a gun drawn, cocked and pointed at me.

Then I heard Mr. Boyer coming out on the gallery asking what was going on. I knew this was his house and he was the one that had sent out the invitations. I tried to bluff 'em, told 'em I was one of them that worked in Baton Rouge but they heard the way I talked, with this accent, and Mr. Boyer, he say, 'Stop or we'll shoot.' I stopped."

"Go on, what happened then."

The courtroom was absolutely silent; so quiet that a horse neighing in the yard below could be heard clearly through the open windows. "All three had their guns cocked and pointed at me. I figured they was gonna shoot me when they found out who I was so I kept on bluffing. They told me to take off my mask. When I did, it's a big mask, I swung it off my head real fast and it spooked the guy holding the gun next to me. He jumped back and I saw fire spit out of his pistol so I hit him with the mask. When he fell back, I saw that other man, not Mr. Boyer, bring his pistol up to shoot, I fell backward as he fired. I grabbed the Derringer I had in my belt and fired both barrels. I guess I hit both of 'em. All three of 'em were down. The one I hit with the mask was screaming and holding his head; the other two were just lying on the ground. People started pouring out of the house. I got to my horse and got out of there as fast as I could."

"As you were leaving, did you see Miss Amanda Pitre on the gallery of the house?"

Neat thought for a long time. He avoided looking at Mr. Pitre's burning eyes in the second row. "No sir, I can't rightly say that I did. I wasn't looking back. I was just getting out of there as fast as I could. She may have been there though, 'cause I had asked her to come out to meet me."

"Where did you go when you left Mr. Boyer's home?"

"I was scared. I knew I was in trouble. But, I didn't know how bad those men had been hit. I went to my room at the Mayers' place in White Castle. I grabbed some supplies and headed out. I didn't know where I was going but I ended up at a little hut me and my friends used for hunting and fishing out in the swamp by Bayou Maringouin."

Goldsmith circled the defense table. He was obviously being very careful with the next question. "Did you know you had killed a man?"

"No sir. I knew they could be all bad hurt but I didn't know anybody was dead. I didn't want that to happen."

"Why didn't you turn yourself in? You know Sheriff Gilmore, don't you? Weren't ya'll friends?"

"Yessir, but Henry, I mean Sheriff Gilmore worked for those people, they the ones gave him the star. He'd have to do what they said, 'bout that time I figured I couldn't trust nobody."

"How long before you knew you were wanted for murder?"

Neat caught Henry's worried look as he thought about his answer. "Out at my little camp in the swamp there's a road that runs just on the other side of the bayou. A couple of days after I was out there I heard a couple of riders coming along the road. They stopped right across from my hideout and walked their horses up to the bayou to drink. They couldn't see me at all. They was two of those Union soldiers. I could tell they was looking for me. I heard one of 'em say that I'd be better off being shot trying to run then to come in and get hung. I knew then I had to stay away. I thought about running to Texas but I had already sent my horse off and didn't have no money or nothing so I just stayed put." Henry's eyebrows lifted slightly as if to signal "thank you."

"Now, Mr. Galvez, you told me that you were planning to come in and give yourself up in a few days when you made the mistake of stepping on that cottonmouth. Why were you ready to give up?"

"To tell you the truth, I been thinking about it a long time. I'd taken to coming into town every so often at night. With my beard and long hair nobody knew me. I stopped by the saloon a couple of times and picked up the news that the Union soldiers and carpetbaggers were packing up and going back north. I figured maybe now we would get some fair judges and juries and I could get a fair trial." The crowd reacted with nods and whispers. Neat sneaked a look at Judge Ricard. He was staring straight ahead. "So here I am."

Goldsmith spun around to District Attorney Bergeron, "No further questions. Your witness, my good man."

Bergeron stepped around the desk and up to the witness stand. "You didn't get an invitation to that Mardi Gras Ball, did you?"

"No, sir, I…"

Bergeron interrupted, "You had a fake invitation, didn't you?"

"Yes, sir, I had…"

"So you knew you weren't welcome at that house, didn't you, Mr. Galvez?"

Neat's eyes flitted from the prosecutor to Goldsmith, to the ceiling, to the floor and back to Bergeron. "Yes, sir, I guess so, but I…"

"You knew you were not supposed to be carrying a weapon at that ball didn't you?"

Neat stuttered, "Y-y-yes, sir."

Goldsmith was on his feet. "Judge, the district attorney is badgering my client. He will not let him give complete answers."

"Sit down Mr. Goldsmith. He's answering as much as he needs to. Get on with it Mr. Bergeron."

Bergeron looked smug. "So, Mr. Galvez, when you were challenged out on the gallery, you didn't really believe those men were going to shoot you, did you?"

"No, sir, I mean, yes, sir. I did believe they was gonna shoot me. I most certainly did!"

"You shot them so that they would not have you arrested and then you ran away because you knew you were guilty; guilty of murdering Herman Boyer and attempting to murder Nathaniel Becker."

"No, sir," Neat was becoming flustered and confused, "It was self-defense. They was trying to kill me. I didn't mean nobody no harm, leastwise to kill anybody." Neat's eyes were filled with tears.

Bergeron's voice went up an octave. He shouted, "You left a widow, two orphans and a crippled man and ran away to save your skin."

"I object!" Goldsmith roared. "Mr. Bergeron is using intimidation tactics to disorient Mr. Galvez."

Bergeron started to defend his actions but was cut off by the judge, "Objection sustained." Ricard looked over his glasses and cautioned, "Mr. Bergeron, let's get back to some proper decorum."

"Sorry, your honor." He turned back and shuffled some papers on the prosecution desk, "Mr. Galvez, who were your collaborators while you were in the swamp?"

Neat was trying to interpret "collaborator" in three languages when Goldsmith again objected, "Irrelevant, your honor. It might make for interesting gossip in the streets but it has nothing to do with the charges in this case."

"Sustained. Mr. Bergeron, I think you're finished with this witness, aren't you?"

Bergeron stammered, "Well, your honor, I would like to pursue…"

"No, you're finished here." The judge turned to Goldsmith, "Next witness."

Norman felt all eyes on him as Neat, breathing heavily, stepped down from the witness box and took his seat at the table. The defense attorney took his time, milking the tension in the room, before turning to the jury and saying, almost in a whisper, "The defense calls Miss Amanda Claire Pitre." The double doors in the back of the room swung open as if Goldsmith's announcement was a cue to part a giant curtain. Amanda swept through the doors accompanied by a court matron.

She was radiant. Her hair was swept up and tied with a light blue ribbon into a chignon. Her dress was a deep blue. Her shoulders were covered with a shawl that matched the ribbon in her hair. She and the female deputy walked slowly down the aisle. Women in the courtroom were whispering admiration of her clothing and carriage like participants at a wedding. Her face was flushed as she stepped into the witness stand. The crowd had inhaled as one when she walked through the doors and now seemed to exhale simultaneously as she sat. She acknowledged the oath. Her blue eyes locked onto Neat. She smiled ever so slightly.

Lawtell and Cora Pitre both breathed deeply. Cora could hear Lawtell's teeth grinding. She said a prayer quickly and crossed herself.

Goldsmith stepped forward being very careful not to block the view of a single juror. "Miss Pitre, I will make this very brief. I know it is difficult for you to recall that terrible night and we all appreciate your assisting us here today."

Amanda nodded and briefly caught sight of her mother and father seated in the second row. Her mother had a lace handkerchief in one hand held near her face. Her father was staring straight ahead as though refusing to acknowledge her presence.

The defense attorney led her through the preliminaries, why she and her family had received invitations to the ball, which of her friends were there and so on. Then he walked over to the front of the jury box and took a stance at the corner, facing Amanda, with both hands leaning back on the railing. He made sure the jury got the full force of Amanda's eyes and radiance. "Mr. Galvez has told us he found you among the crowd at the ball. He said he asked you to meet him out on the gallery of the house that evening after Mr. Boyer's speech in the ball room."

"That is correct, sir. He said he wanted to know where some of his friends were, what kind of masks they were wearing so he could recognize them and he wanted to show off his 'Scaramouche' mask to them."

"So after Mr. Boyer's talk you went out to the gallery."

"Yes, sir. I had seen the door Mr. Galvez went out of so I went to the same one."

"Tell us what happened then."

Amanda took a deep breath. Her face seemed to flush even more. She looked down at her hands then up at Neat. "As I came through the door I could see Neat's, I mean, Mr. Galvez's mask just beyond the bottom of the steps to the gallery. The light from the lamps there was very dim but I could see one man was standing to the right of Mr. Galvez. Two other men were just coming off the steps and all three of them were holding guns."

Goldsmith interrupted, "You are absolutely sure these men were holding guns?"

"Oh yes, sir. Absolutely sure. I was so frightened."

"Was Mr. Galvez armed? Did you see a gun in his hands."

"Oh, no sir. He was holding his hands out away from his sides. The men were yelling at him to take off his mask. He pulled the mask off very fast and the man at his side jumped back and his gun went off. Mr. Galvez seemed to swing the mask at him and hit him in the head. I don't know if he meant to but he did hit him. Then," Amanda stopped. She swallowed hard and seemed to be breathing more quickly, almost panting. "Then one of the other men fired his pistol at Neat, I screamed, Neat fell backwards and I saw two flashes of flame come out of his hand. He must have had a gun hidden somewhere. Everything was so fast. All of a sudden there was blood everywhere and people screaming and yelling and I saw Neat run to the horses and…" She suddenly stopped. Her face drained of color. She looked around in panic, put her hand to her mouth and vomited all over the witness stand.

The matron and bailiff quickly rushed to the stand. Amanda's mother, father and priest were right behind them. The judge banged the gavel a dozen times. He could have been tapping a pencil on the desk. Mrs. Pitre started fanning Amanda's now pale face and begging people to back off and "give her some air." They finally got her on her feet and retreated to the judge's chambers.

Judge Ricard tried again. He hammered the gavel repeatedly until some semblance of order was restored. He then announced in a loud voice, "It is now two forty-five. We will stand in recess until three fifteen. Bailiff, get these jurors out of here."

Doctor Ourso was called into the judge's chambers to minister to Amanda. He did a perfunctory physical examination then leaned over and held a whispered conversation with her for several minutes. Amanda started crying. "What in the name of God did you say to her, doctor?" Lawtell Pitre said in a loud voice.

Doc Ourso looked at him and Cora and said, "I said she needs to get home and get some rest." He smiled knowingly at Amanda's mother and winked. "She's gonna need a lot of rest for the next few months."

Cora gave the doctor a curious look that soon changed to shocked understanding. Amanda's father looked at him with disdain, "Well, it certainly didn't take a doctor to figure that out. She should have never been here in the first place." He grabbed Amanda's arm, pulling her roughly to her feet. "Let's go. We're getting out of here and going home."

The doctor leaned in close to him and said in a whisper, "Be gentle with her. She's pregnant."

❈   ❈   ❈

A long primordial howl echoed through the courthouse, "Nooooooooooooooooooooooooooo!"

The small huddle around the defense table, Neat, his friends and family froze and looked toward the door leading to the judge's chambers. They heard loud voices and then doors slamming. Pokey ran over to the courtroom window. After a few moments he yelled out, "Don't know what's going on but the

Pitre's and that priest is leaving. Somebody just pulled this big old carriage around and they poured outta the building."

Goldsmith, Sherman and Neat exchanged puzzled looks. The bailiff came huffing back into the room, "The judge says don't anybody go anywheres. I'm going to get the jury and we gonna get started again in fifteen minutes." He scooted over to Norman Goldsmith and beckoned District Attorney Bergeron to join them. "The judge said to get this over with as soon as possible. His words were, 'Tell them lawyers no messing around. Close your case and set down.'" He pulled Goldsmith along with him toward the side door and, out of range of Bergeron, whispered, "You don't want them jurors hearing 'bout what just went on in the judge's office before they make a decision, you understand?"

Goldsmith tried to ask him a question, "But, what's going..." The bailiff was out the door, down the hall heading to the jury holding room.

The entire courthouse was buzzing with rumor and speculation. By the time the jury was reseated and the judge entered the room, twice as many people were jammed in. The bailiff's warning had shaken the defense attorney and Neat could see his hand trembling as he tried to write some notes on a pad. Neat whispered, "What the hell's going on, Mr. Goldsmith? I thought we had this thing in the bag."

Goldsmith ignored Neat as Judge Ricard instructed him in a loud voice to get on with his closing statement. The judge banged the gavel loudly and shouted over the din of the crowd, "And I don't want to hear a whisper from any of you out there. Don't even let me hear a feather drop. Proceed, Mr. Goldsmith."

Goldsmith rose slowly and stepped before the jury box. He made eye contact one by one with all nine men. *I know I've got 'em after Amanda's testimony, just gotta be calm and not make it too long. Remember what the judge said,* he thought. He cleared his throat and said, "Self-defense." Again he looked into the eyes of each juror one by one. "Self-defense. It is one of a human being's most basic reactions. Self-defense. You *know* instinctively when someone is going to try to harm you and you react. Self-defense. You veterans know the feeling of being aimed at and shot at. What do you do? You defend yourself. Sure, Mr. Galvez should not have been where he was. But, did he break the law by merely showing up uninvited? Should he have been shot for that? He's a young man who wanted to have fun on one of the fun days of the year. He wanted to be with his friends and his special friend, Miss Pitre." Judge Ricard cleared his throat loudly. Goldsmith looked at him curiously but the judge was looking down and writing on his pad.

"Why was he armed? Aren't most of you armed most of the time when you leave your home, especially at night? These are still dangerous times with unstable and desperate people out and about. Fortunately he had the good sense to carry a Double Derringer when he left his revolver in his saddlebag. If he had not we would be trying someone else today for the murder of Antoine Galvez, and there could be no plea of self-defense.

"Gentlemen of the jury, this was a truly unfortunate incident. No one's life should end like that or no one crippled like that. No family should be left without a father. But we cannot go back and undo any of that. No one should point a gun at another person and expect no retaliation. No one should fire that gun without expecting…self-defense. You heard Miss Pitre describe the sequence of events. Mr. Galvez was fired upon before he retaliated. It was a basic human reaction. He was fired upon. He fired back. Mr. Galvez is sorry for the outcome of the evening's events, truly sorry. But, it *was* self-defense. Without a doubt, it was self-defense." He again engaged the eyes of each member of the jury, quietly said, "Thank you," and sat down.

As Goldsmith returned to his seat, the crowd started buzzing again. Judge Ricard again banged his gavel several times and warned, "I'm not fooling, folks. I'll clear this dadgum courtroom if I don't have absolute quiet. I might even make a few arrests for contempt. Now, just sit back and keep your traps shut." He looked out across the room menacingly as the crowd settled into silence. "Okay, Mr. Bergeron, get on with it. Make it quick."

The jury watched intently as the young D. A. rose and approached. "Gentlemen, a person must be held responsible for his mistakes. This defendant has made many mistakes and they all led to the death of one prominent man, the crippling of another, the widowing of a good young mother and denied her two innocent children the love, guidance and companionship of their father. Can we ignore all of that by saying he deserved to have his fun on Mardi Gras night? No! He was not invited to that home that night. In fact, he was trespassing. He knew that weapons were barred from the gathering. But he carried a murderous weapon in spite of that knowledge. When he was first asked to stop and unmask, he disobeyed. We don't really know if a shot had been fired when he chose to slash Mr. William Simpson with his mask. We have only one witness. And that witness is obviously very emotional about what she claims to have seen. It could be that it was Mr. Simpson who fired in self-defense."

Jacob Herman leaned over to Clarence Bergeron, covered his mouth with one hand and whispered, "He does understand he's got to lose this, doesn't he? He's doing too good a job." Leland's uncle nodded affirmation, glanced over at Jacob and motioned that it would be all right.

Bergeron's training and passion had taken over. He truly had forgotten that he was supposed to lose. He was now engrossed in his argument, "...cannot let this atrocity go unanswered. Mr. Galvez must pay for his irresponsibility, for his arrogance in believing that he could just walk into a man's home while he was entertaining his chosen friends and, when challenged, react like a thug."

Leland was now in a rhythm much like an evangelist preacher. "Gentlemen of the jury. It could have been your home. It could have been your family. It could have been you and your friends who were shot. This man is guilty. He is guilty of destroying a family. He is guilty of ruining the lives of two men forever marked by his folly. He is guilty of attempted murder. He is guilty of murder. Yes, he is guilty of murder and you," he pointed at the first juror on the right and continued through all nine, "and you, and you, and you, and you, and you, and you, and you, and you. You must bring him to justice."

Again the whispering began as Bergeron returned to his place. Ricard looked at his pocket watch. It was three forty-five.

Good, he thought, *we can probably get a decision before nightfall. If we don't that boy's ass is hung 'cause the jury will damn well find out overnight what went on back there in my chambers.*

He looked at the jury box, "Gentlemen, you've heard the case. It is in your hands. Please consider carefully all the testimony and the logic of the two attorneys. Consider how your decision will affect future actions by people placed in similar circumstances. Consider how your decision will affect your family and friends. Please give this decision your very best effort." Judge Ricard carefully went over each of the options open to the jurymen. When he finished he asked if there were any questions. "The bailiff will be with you at all times. Send him to me for any thing you may need and to let me know when you have reached a decision. With any luck we can all sleep peacefully in our own beds tonight. May God go with you."

Well, that's a hell of a thing to say, Bergeron thought. *It's like he's pushing the jury to hurry up and bring in a verdict just to get this over with. What's wrong with Judge Ricard? What happened back in those chambers?*

The jury was lead out of the courtroom and Neat was escorted back to the third floor cell. Just before he entered it, the deputy escorting him said with a chuckle, "Sounds to me like you had a damn good time in the swamp with that pretty little Pitre gal. If the jury lets you go you better hope the daddy's not waiting for you outside the door."

Neat slumped back on the hard cot. *What happened in the judge's chambers? Did Amanda suddenly tell them of their intimate times in the swamp? That's impossible.*

The secret was beginning to seep through the courthouse. Goldsmith heard about it as he was standing in the yard outside the west entrance trying to get some fresh air and prepare himself for the decision. He was feeling good about Neat's chances of acquittal until Sherman, Pokey and Pierre came bounding down the steps. "Did you hear what we heard?" Pokey whispered.

"What?" Asked Goldsmith.

Sherman cupped his hands up to the lawyer's ears and whispered feverishly. Goldsmith turned ashen. "Oh, Jesus. Oh, no. Who told you that?"

"One of them deputies. They said that's why Amanda threw up on the stand and why we heard her daddy howling like a wolf in there. He said they had to almost tie him down to keep him from going after Neat. The judge told him he'd put him in jail right there and then if he didn't take his wife and daughter and leave town right away."

Goldsmith sat heavily on the bottom step, held his head in his hands and whispered hoarsely, "If word gets through to the jury, they'll turn on him like a cat on a rat. They ain't gonna be feeling sorry for that boy spending all that time in the swamp if they figure he was having his way with that innocent little girl the whole time. Oh, damnation."

The district attorney sat in his office in the courthouse drinking black, bitter coffee. His father, Clarence, and Goldsmith's uncle, Jacob Hermann, sat across the desk. Clarence had his feet up on a spare chair. Jacob had the stub of an unlit cigar clamped in his mouth, he looked at his pocket watch, "Damn, it's after six, they been in there three hours, the sun's going down. I don't know how long Alcide's gonna be able to keep'em deliberating once it gets darker. He ain't gonna want to burn up all that oil in the jury room and courtroom too."

Clarence looked at his son. With a bit of irony he said, "You did too good a job, boy. You challenged that jury real good. I just hope they still hate carpetbaggers enough to let Galvez go. You just don't need that on your record, even though you really did a good job."

A sharp rap on the door brought the three of them immediately out of their chairs. "It's open!" The D. A. shouted.

A breathless, red-faced deputy looked in the half-opened door and said, "The jury's coming in. They just sent word to Judge Ricard."

No one had left the courthouse since the recess. The courtroom quickly filled to four-deep standing against three walls. The jury filed back into their positions. Most kept their eyes averted downward. Nobody was smiling. The bailiff called the room to attention and the judge entered. He gaveled the crowd to silence and looked at the jury, "Have you reached a verdict?"

The foreman, the Confederate veteran who had lost his right arm, stood and said, "Yessir, your honor, we have." He handed a folded paper to the bailiff who walked it slowly to the bar.

Neat suddenly found his left hand being tightly held by Goldsmith. He took a deep breath and very slowly exhaled. The sun had set and twilight dimly lit the sky outside. The only sound in the entire room was the hiss of the dozen coal oil lamps hung on the walls and distant voices in the yard below wafting through the open windows.

The judge unfolded the paper and read it, "Would the defendant please rise?" Neat and Goldsmith both stood. They were still holding hands and neither was self-conscious of the fact.

"Please state your verdict, Mr. Foreman."

"On the charge of murder..." He suddenly had a brief coughing spell, cleared his throat and repeated, "On the murder charge, we the jury find the defendant, not guilty by reason of self-defense." The pent-up tension in the room erupted in a roar of approval. Judge Ricard waited a reasonable time to let the noise begin to subside before rapping his gavel repeatedly.

"We're not through here," he shouted, "Quiet, by God, I said quiet!" He only waited for a reasonable ebbing of noise before telling the foreman to continue. He repeated the same decision on the charge of attempted murder and sat down. Before he had finished the sentence Neat's family and friends came through the swinging gate at the railing and were wrapped in a group embrace with Neat and Goldsmith crushed in the middle. Judge Ricard thanked the jury, the attorneys and the audience, rapped his gavel once more and announced, "The defendant is to be released immediately. These proceedings are adjourned." He got up and disappeared through the door into his chambers.

District Attorney Bergeron waited quietly at the edge of the Galvez celebration until Norman Goldsmith could dislodge himself. The elder Bergeron and

Mr. Hermann were on either side of him as Goldsmith approached to shake hands, "You were a worthy adversary, Mr. Bergeron. I thank you for your courtesy and consideration." Goldsmith said.

Bergeron took his hand with both of his, "And you, sir, are a gentleman and a fine example of our profession." He held onto the attorney's hand and pulled him closer. "I presume you have heard what occurred earlier in the judge's chambers. I was praying you would get your verdict before it leaked out. But now the word is spreading all over town. I would strongly suggest that you get your client out of the courthouse and out of town as quickly as possible. This is still a God-fearing community and they may not take too kindly to his dalliance with that young lady's virtue."

"I understand, sir." Goldsmith withdrew his hand, shook hands quickly with his uncle and Leland's father and turned back to the crowd around the defense table. He called Sherman out of the pile-up. "You have your daddy's big carriage here, don't you?" Sherman, still smiling broadly, nodded. Goldsmith grabbed him by the shoulders to get his full attention. "Get it right now. Bring it around to the back of the courthouse. I'll get Neat back there by the time you're there. I want you to take him around through the back of town and get him out of here as soon as possible without raising too much attention. Don't stop for anybody or anything. Get him home and keep him off the street 'til this stuff settles down, understand?"

Sherman, suddenly quite serious, nodded again, grabbed Pokey and Pierre by the arms and pulled them toward the rear of the courtroom.

XX
March 25th, 1877

Sunday dawned bright and clear, a perfect spring day. Neat awoke refreshed from a sound sleep on a relatively good mattress. His Friday night sleep had been restless after the harrowing day in the courtroom and the long ride from Napoleonville. Sherman and the family were busy all day Saturday with a May-ers' family reunion in nearby Samstown, so Neat slept most of the day. While awake he thought about the problems still besetting him.

The ride back from the courthouse had became doubly disturbing when Sherman told him of Amanda's revelation in the judge's chambers. "They told me Lawtell Pitre's head looked like it would explode. His eyes were bulging. His face was blood red. He wants to kill whoever is responsible and you look like the best, if not only, prospect right now. He hadn't figured out yet how you two got together but I reckon Amanda will tell him. That's when I got problems. I'm the one who brought her to you."

"Wasn't your fault, Sherman. Amanda and me did what we did because we love each other. I want to marry her. I know that between us, we can raise a baby. I'd love to start my life over like that."

Sherman tapped on Neat's door about six o'clock Sunday morning. Neat was out of bed but not yet dressed. He called Sherman in. "Neat, Maw and Paw want to talk with you. Get dressed and come on out for breakfast. Maw's making some cornbread pancakes and we got some good bacon from the boucherie we had in February." Neat quickly finished dressing. He ran his fingers through his hair, finished buttoning his denim shirt and joined Sherman in the hall.

Benjamin Mayers was already at the breakfast table with a steaming mug of coffee. Sarah was busy at the wood-burning stove. They both gave Neat a cheery "Good morning," and he relaxed a bit. *Maybe this ain't bad news. Maybe they just want to set some rules for living here.* Both boys got coffee from the drip pot on the stove and sat.

Sarah looked back from the stove and said, "Go on daddy, I'll just be a few more minutes, but I can hear you all from here."

Benjamin cleared his throat and leaned forward with his elbows on the table. "Neat, we're very glad you were acquitted. We can't say that we approve of what you done at that Mardi Gras ball, but maybe you had to. Anyway, the jury reached a decision and that's that. I'm also glad we were able to give you the money for the lawyer. I'm sure you intend to pay it back as we agreed." Neat nodded enthusiastically and started to speak but Mr. Mayers held a hand up. "We do have problems with what has happened as it relates to Miss Amanda. That is very wrong what you did. You took advantage of that young woman. I know, I know, you think you know all about love and life. I did too at your age but just hold on now. Mr. Pitre has every right to be in a raging anger over it. We got word last night that he and Mrs. Pitre are taking Amanda to Donaldsonville this morning."

Neat let out an agonized moan. "Donaldsonville? Why? What're they gonna do to her?"

Mayers raised his hand again to stop him from saying any more. "They're gonna take her down river to New Orleans. Father Hebert has connections down there with the Ursuline Sisters. You may not know about them but they been in New Orleans, oh, a hundred and fifty years. They gonna take in Amanda. She'll get more schooling there and when the baby is born, the Ursulines will put it up for adoption and see that it gets a good home."

Tears welled up in Neat's eyes. In a small, husky voice he said, "But that's our baby. That's Amanda's and mine. We can take care of it. This ain't right."

Benjamin became a little more stern, "It's right for the baby, Neat. It's what Amanda's mother and father feel is right for her, too. And they know what's right for their daughter. Now son, like I said, what you and Amanda did was not right but we're going to help you get a new start. You can stay here for the next few weeks but not permanently. Mr. Pitre would hold it against me for taking you in. He and Cora have been good friends of ours for a long time. I got some friends at the docks in Donaldsonville that can probably get you a pretty good job there. We'll see. Until then, I don't want you hanging around the Pitre home or going anywhere near Mr. Pitre. If you see him anywhere, turn around and go the other way. Avoid him at all costs. I'll try to see that he don't come around here looking for you but I don't want you giving him any excuse to do something crazy. Now I want you to go to church with us this morning, confess your sins, take communion and get yourself straight. Sherman, call your brother and little sisters to come eat."

Neat and the Mayers family, Sarah, Benjamin, Sherman and his younger brother Michael and the two little sisters, Elizabeth and Rachel filled out a pew in the small Catholic church in the center of White Castle. The Pitres were not in attendance since they were, presumably, en route to the Ursuline Convent on Dauphine Street in New Orleans.

Father Hebert chose a sermon of peace and forgiveness as a reward for honest confession and repentance for one's sins. Neat heard little of it. His mind was a whirl of thoughts about Amanda and their seemingly permanent separation. He was also trying to come to grips with starting a new existence in Donaldsonville. His discomfort was heightened by the looks given him by the congregation. They ranged from a furtive glance to hard, hateful stares. He noted that some of the young women gave him a slight smile when they caught his eye. Evidently the word had spread of Amanda's condition and the shameful flight of she and her family.

Like a zombie, Neat took his place in line for communion. Just as he was about to step to the altar rail he was bumped hard by a man he knew to be a close associate of Lawtell Pitre. "Watch yourself, boy. You ain't fit to be here with the rest of us." The man hissed under his breath.

XXI
AUGUST, 1877

Sister Camellia drenched the towel in the icy water, wrung it nearly dry and started again patting it onto the fevered brow of the young mother-to-be. She knew from the midwife that they were facing a very difficult night. First, according to all the calculations, this baby was not due for another six weeks. Second, the mother had been confined to her bed for almost a month because of intermittent cramps and occasional bleeding.

The only logical course of action was inaction. They would have to wait and pray that, with rest and nourishment, the fetus would be given time to mature more before birth.

Sister Camellia dearly loved her young charge. She had nurtured her since her arrival at the convent. Had she been a mother, this is the daughter she would have wished for.

The trip down river in late March was a disaster. Amanda's father was in a rage after the scene in the judge's chambers. He continued to rant on the long carriage ride home and through the packing and recriminations at the house. Father Hebert and Cora tried to console him. Amanda was closed up in her room weeping for hours. The priest proposed a solution. He could contact friends at the home of the Archbishop in New Orleans who would get her to the Ursiline Convent. The good sisters would not only take care of Amanda's immediate problems but would handle the embarrassing aftermath. He would immediately telegraph to New Orleans to have his associates aware of the impending arrival.

Lawtell was not to be appeased. In his mind, this worthless piece of trash, who called himself Neat, had destroyed the peace, tranquility and future of his family. His beautiful daughter's life was ruined. He, himself would forever live in shame while *Mr. Galvez* was free to pursue his own self-serving, irresponsible life. He continued his harangues all the way back to Donaldsonville the next day and onto the packet steaming for New Orleans.

Cora was beside herself. She knew she needed to comfort her daughter but she also knew that she must console her raging husband and get him to control his all-consuming anger.

The family booked two staterooms for the New Orleans trip. Cora shared one with Amanda. Knowing that Lawtell had brought on board a bottle of whiskey, Cora stood guard in the corridor throughout the journey to assure that neither of her beloved left their quarters. God forbid that they should meet at this stage. The situation was explosive. Amanda cried herself to sleep and awoke crying several times during the trip. She had no appetite and Cora was severely troubled that this would create health problems for herself and the child.

Two Ursulines, efficient as ever, were waiting for the family at the dock in New Orleans. A puffy-eyed Amanda, sleepless Cora and grumbly and terribly hungover Lawtell were transported to the convent. Amanda was engulfed into their midst, the parents were quartered overnight and, after a tearful parting with Amanda, were waved off on a departing steamer the next morning.

A physician and midwife examined Amanda. She was then assigned to Sister Camellia as her consultant and confidante. The young Ursuline, only four or five years older than Amanda, explained the simple rules and routine of the convent. She was given a tour including a reverential visit to the statue of "Our Lady of Prompt Succor" that had been commissioned and installed on the grounds several decades before in thanks to the answered prayers for help from France during one of the crises facing the nuns in New Orleans. She was then introduced, by first name only, to several other young women. Some were obviously in various stages of pregnancy. Others bore signs of physical and/or emotional abuse. Amanda was assigned laundry duties and cheerfully pitched into her routine.

Since arriving at the Ursuline Convent in late March, Amanda had become the darling of the nuns. Her Madonna-like beauty, her self-assured demeanor, her cooperativeness and loving nature endeared her to everyone in the convent.

She happily joined in to complete her assigned chores and gladly helped others in their assignments. She devoutly attended all the religious gatherings and services and enthusiastically participated with the other young women and nuns.

Few knew the sadness and heartbreak that weighed heavily on her. She knew that she deeply loved Neat and felt she could have a beautiful life with him. She truly felt that they could still have a wonderful family experience together; maybe not prosperous and opulent, but loving, happy and fulfilling. Not only did she look forward to the birth of this baby, she believed that she could convince the Ursuline sisters, or whoever could make the decision, that she should keep and raise this child with its rightful father.

A month after arriving at the convent, Amanda got the sisters to allow her to mail a letter to her friend, Elizabeth. The nuns always read letters from their charges before allowing them to be mailed. After Sister Camellia had read and approved the note to her friend, Amanda asked if she could close the letter with a wax seal her father had given her.

As she did so, unseen by the nun, she slipped another page into the envelope. This one was addressed to Neat. She knew Elizabeth would see to it that it was discreetly delivered. Knowing his reading shortcomings, she had carefully scripted it:

My darling Neat,

I am so happy that the court has acquitted you

And set you free. My prayers were answered.

I only wish that I could be there With you.

Please don't worry about me. The Ursuline sisters are wonderful to me. I am happy and healthy. And, I'm getting big as a sow. But, that's alright. It's our baby and it will be a beautiful baby.

I am praying and truly believe that I can talk the sisters into letting me (us) keep the baby. Please pray that I am successful. I know that's what I want and I fervently hope you do too.

Don't ever give up hope. We will be together again.

Be strong for us, Neat, and remember, I love you. I always have and I always will,

Amanda

In the humid, sweltering heat, the cramps started again around midnight. After an hour, Sister Camellia summoned another nun to send for the midwife. The delivery was still at least six weeks premature.

Everything that could go wrong did. When the midwife determined that the birth was going to occur with or without her help, she proceeded with a more careful examination and suddenly realized that the fetus was in a breech position. She frantically sent for a physician but could not delay the premature birth. The baby also had the umbilical cord wrapped tightly around its neck. It had been so for some time during the breech birth.

Suddenly, with the discharge of the fetus, Amanda started hemorrhaging. The physician arrived only in time to witness the disaster. Fighting to save the child from suffocation and the mother from blood loss, the attendants could do neither. Mother and child died.

XXII
November 7th, 1958

Bob Hudson did nearly a full page article on Neat's birthday, November 5th. The headline read: **B. R. Man, 100 Today, Credits Health to Diet.** Tess almost choked on her biscuit when she read it. She looked over at Louis, "Diet? What diet? You put it in front of him, he eats it."

There was a picture of the old man dressed in the dark suit and regimental tie Tess had outfitted him in the day of the interview. He appeared to be staring straight ahead through his steel-rimmed glasses. He was told many years ago that he should stand perfectly still, not even blinking, when having a picture taken. He saw a flash but didn't hear the muffled explosion followed by a cloud of smoke he had seen the last time he saw a real-life photographer.

Louis brought the paper out to the porch and read it to Neat, slowly and laboriously. Like his father, he was also undereducated having finished only three years of formal schooling. He had been needed on the sugar cane farm, education was not a priority. Neat listened unemotionally. Louis read:

> The old timer said there was one time when he didn't think that he would make it. Speaking of the only sickness in his life, he recalled he had smallpox and yellow fever when he was 16 years old. Since that time he has not been to a doctor except once two years ago, when he had a cold.
>
> Galvez believes he has lived to be this old because he eats right. He never overeats. And he has no particular diet and can eat anything that is served.

Neat thought, *it ain't that I got any damn choice anymore. I'm just like an old worn out mule. What they feed, I eat.*

Louis continued reading from the article:

He started working on the bayou when he was 12 or 13 years old. He wasn't old enough to work on a boat, so he would drive the mules that pulled the flatboats and barges through the shallow parts of the bayou.

He worked as a dockhand helping load sugar and molasses on the boats when he was about 14.

When his father died he returned to Brusly McCall to help his mother and four sisters on their small farm.

It is hard to believe that this man has already lived a century. His eye is keen, his manner active, his posture erect. He was prouder of the fact that he had been a scrapper and a handsome young man in his youth than of the letter he had received from President Eisenhower congratulating him on his birthday.

"I never drank much or ate too much. But I had a bad temper. If they'd tackle me, I'd fight," he said. His eyes flashed and he ran his fingers through his graying hair. (That's right. I said, "graying." At one hundred years of age he still sports quite a few black hairs.) "I'd tackle anybody that started anything. And I'd finish it." He shook his head, "Bad. Quick temper. But good. Never beat a coward though. You showed him my picture when I was young?" He asked his daughter-in-law sitting in for this interview. When she later brought out a picture of him at age twenty or so I saw a strikingly handsome man.

Galvez, known as "grandpa Neat" to his family and friends, has 9 living children, 31 grandchildren and 36 great-grand children.

He smokes a great deal, cigars and his pipe. He likes to play poker and watch TV, especially the Friday Night Fights. He attributes his health to "always working outside. No sit down jobs for me."

"And then it goes on to list all of your children's names and where we live." Louis said, "Ain't that nice, papa? Almost a whole page just about you."

"Yep, that's nice, but it's none of his damn business how much I smoke," he croaked. "What's for dinner?"

Louis's twenty-four year old son, Randy showed up about lunchtime. (This was "dinner" to Neat, the evening meal was "supper.") Randy worked for a radio station and had been talking about "getting the old man on tape" for several years. He knew his grandfather could tell detailed stories of life during the 1800's and thought it should be a part of the family's history. Like many well-intentioned projects, this one had never gotten off the ground. But when Randy saw the newspaper article, he was inspired to give it a try. He brought in a big Wollensack tape recorder, plugged it in on the side porch and set up a seven-inch reel of tape.

Over lunch of smothered liver and onions (not one of Randy's favorites but one his mother insisted on serving, "for your blood," at least once a week) they talked about the hottest topic in Baton Rouge and probably in all Louisiana. The Louisiana State University football team was undefeated and everybody was talking about a potential national championship.

"That Paul Dietzel is one smart coach," Randy said. "When he decided to recruit close to home he got the whole state behind him. Look what he's got. Billy Cannon, Warren Rabb and Johnny Robinson, all from right here in Baton Rouge all running first string on the White team."

Head Coach Dietzel had devised a unique system to overcome the limited and confusing substitution rules of the day. He formed three almost equal teams. All three played both offense and defense but with somewhat different levels of proficiency, the White (the "A" team with the best overall athletes) started the games, the Gold (emphasis on offensive talent) would relieve them on about the third offensive possession and the "Chinese Bandits" (named by Dietzel for a vicious gang of Asian pirates conceived in a comic strip) were defensive specialists substituted in selective situations to mop up the opposition's offense with fresh and inspired troops. Not only did the system and the unique labeling catch the imagination of the fans and the national media, it worked on the field.

"It's a good thing your birthday party's scheduled for the afternoon Saturday, Paw Paw, that night everybody not at the game's going to be glued to the radio."

Randy started explaining to Paw Paw Neat what he wanted to do with the tape recording. The old man nodded in agreement a few times and kept on carefully chewing his lunch. He really had no concept of what his grandson was talking about and, frankly, really didn't care. Just so long as this tape he was talking about wasn't going to be stuck on him and pull his hair when it was removed. While Tess was clearing the table, Neat wandered off to the bathroom then back out to his favorite chair on the porch. Tess immediately went into the bathroom and did a quick cleanup. Neat was not very big on hygiene.

As he lowered himself gingerly into the rocker, he looked suspiciously at the strange contraption Randy had plugged into the wall. Louis helped him light up a fresh pipe.

Tess called Randy to her side at the sink where she was washing dishes, "Now son, I guess this is a nice thing to do, your recording his voice and all, but just don't get him talking about some of that stuff he don't need to be talking about. You know what I'm saying?"

Randy knew what she was saying. He had grown up hearing whispered conversations of his grandfather's wild escapades. He had heard snippets of the story of the shooting of a carpetbagger at a Mardi Gras ball but no details, heard of his love for playing poker and the night he had smashed a coal oil lamp into the face of a young man who, Neat said, had threatened his life. He knew his mother considered all of those incidents embarrassing to the family and thus off limits. Don't ask, don't tell.

But, he had also heard of Neat's time traveling with a Minstrel Show and of his witnessing the near destruction by a tornado of a prison in Baton Rouge sometime before 1900. Randy had gone to the weather station at Ryan Field in Baton Rouge to look through records of storms and tornados during that time period. A tornado had hit Baton Rouge in July of 1891 but there was no description of its impact. He found those stories fascinating and wanted to get them on record. He knew it just seemed as if grandpa Neat was going to last forever. He had seen the rapid deterioration of the body, if not so much the mind, in the past year.

"You just stick to those funny old memories, Randy, and don't mess with that other stuff, you hear? Your daddy's gonna take me grocery shopping now. You take care of Paw Paw while we're gone."

Tess had not driven a car since she had an accident in the mid 1920's. She used the city bus service extensively and the grocery store still offered home delivery by boys on bicycles, but she would still rather choose her meat and poultry personally. Randy moved out to the porch and tested the microphone volume. As the car backed down the gravel driveway next to the porch, he pulled a chair up next to his grandfather's rocker, turned the machine to "record" and said, "Paw Paw, who's this Boyer fellow I've heard you talk about every now and then. Was he a friend of yours?"

Neat glared at him so Randy took off on another subject. They talked about growing up in post Civil War Louisiana and the family's circumstances after the death of Neat's father. Neat started getting a bit testy after the first twenty minutes of taping. He had never directly answered his grandson's first question about the "Boyer fellow" and whether he was a friend.

All he said was, "Never had a friend named Boyer. No. No Boyer was ever my friend." He said it very emphatically then looked off into the distance as his demeanor softened. "Had a good friend named Sherman. That was my best friend ever. Had a bunch of other friends, Pokey, Pierre. But Sherman's the boy that took Amanda out to the hideout to visit with me. That's how we really got in trouble, me and Amanda." He took a drag on his pipe and let out a thin stream of smoke. "Sherman got hisself killed in one of those new damn motorcars in about 1920. He was about sixty something years old. Shoulda knowed better than to try to drive one of those things at that age."

"You ever have a car?" Randy asked.

"Hell no. Never needed one. Never could've afforded one neither. By the time my son Edgar got one I was damned near seventy years old. He said he wanted to teach me to drive but that was just some of his foolishness."

Randy asked, "Paw Paw, your wife's name, my grandmother, was Marie. What happened to Amanda, the girl you told me once was your first and best love?"

Neat was silent for a long time. He puffed on the nearly extinguished pipe, glanced at Randy as if to determine if he was worthy of hearing the story. "Amanda died giving birth to a baby down in New Orleans. They shoulda never taken her there. Damn, boy, she was pretty, golden hair, skin white as milk and she loved me. She really did. She just was so open and giving and loving, but they took her away." Neat slowly related the story of Amanda going to live with the Ursuline nuns in New Orleans. "I got a letter from her. She was a sweet girl. I, I really, I mean, I really…I cared about her." Randy thought he was going to see his grandfather cry for the first time in their relationship. Neat squinted his eyes, sniffed loudly but no tears fell. "I never saw her again, not once after the trial. Sherman brought me the news. He said his mother heard about it when she visited with the Pitres. She helped them with the funerals. The little baby was a girl. Amanda woulda liked that. Hell, so would I. Sherman said it was something called a breech birth. The cord got wrapped around the baby's neck. They worked on it a long time but in the meantime Amanda was hemorrhaging blood and never did recover."

There was silence for a while. Randy asked in a small voice, "It was your baby?"

Neat gave him a look that could have melted steel, then looked away disgustedly. Randy said, "I'm sorry, I'm very sorry. I shouldn't have asked that."

Neat probably had not shed a tear in eighty years and he was not about to now. He pursed his lips and clenched his jaw as he shook off the sadness and the anger. "Life goes on. I had lots of other pretty women but none like Amanda. Didn't get married for another eighteen years. I was thirty-six when I met Marie. She was twenty-eight and all her friends called her an 'old maid' behind her back. But she was all right."

"What do you mean, all right?"

Neat closed his eyes. Randy thought he was falling asleep. He finally opened them and growled, "I mean what I said. She was all right. Nothing special. She was French, blue eyes, kinda blond hair, but not like Amanda's. She was not too bad looking. Kinda had a big nose, you know like some of the French do. Her grandfolks had come over here from Lyons, France. Hell, I wasn't no blue ribbon winner myself. Just a skinny little guy and dark like a mulatto. Marie didn't talk much, which was good. She was a damn good cook. Made the best fried chicken you ever want to eat. We served in a wedding together and kinda got together because of that. The new married couple kept putting us together, going on picnics, playing cards, things like that. Her folks had put together a pretty good dowry. They was ready for her to leave." He chuckled, "and she was ready to leave, too. She wanted children and she knew something about farming sugar cane and taking care of chickens and hogs. She seemed to like me and, well I guess it was 'bout time for me to more or less settle down and she was…all right like I said, so we did it. We got married. Then them babies started coming. That woman was more fertile than my cane fields."

"So you had forgotten all about Amanda by then, huh?"

"Boy, you just don't know nothing yet, do you? You never forget about a girl like that. You never forget any of 'em really. Many's a time when I'm going to sleep at night I can still see her and feel her just like when we was out in the swamp." He closed his eyes a few moments more. "'Course I do that with a dozen or so others sometimes, too, but," he winked at Randy, "Amanda's my favorite. Always was."

"So how long did you stay working the docks at Donaldsonville?"

"Well, I don't know, 'bout a year I guess. Long enough to pay Mr. Mayers back for that lawyer money. Worked on the docks and worked on his farm too. Paid him every cent. Then I had a little extra money for myself and to give to my mother and sisters. Two of 'em stayed old maids. Used to go visit them in Brusly McCall every other Sunday.

"'Cause of Mr. Pitre, I wasn't welcome up around White Castle for a long time so I kinda lost track of my friends. Sherman and me would see each other every so often when he could get away to come down to Donaldsonville. Pokey and Pierre and the others just drifted off to their own things. Some went up river to Baton Rouge to get jobs. Some down river to New Orleans.

"Sherman told me that Henry Gilmore, you know, the niggra sheriff? He moved down to New Orleans and got a good job down there on the docks. Then I ran into him a couple of years later." Neat stared off in the distance and shivered slightly.

Randy said, "What's wrong, something about Henry?"

It took Neat a few moments to respond, "Well, yeh, I guess but I don't want to talk about it now."

Randy decided to move on to another subject. "Okay, so how'd you get mixed up in singing and dancing in a minstrel show?"

Neat grinned a bit showing several of his few teeth. This was a subject that obviously energized him. "You see, I met a man in a saloon one night who started talking 'bout the minstrel shows. I'd heard about'em; white men blackening their faces with burnt cork or what they called 'grease paint' and putting on a show pretending to be niggras. I heard they was all the rage up north before the War Between the States but I ain't never seen one. This man said they was one coming to town, to Donaldsonville, and he'd get me in to see it.

"We went." Neat looked at Randy with wide eyes and slapped his withered old hand across his knee. "I swear boy I'd never seen nothing like it. All these men with black faces, black suits, white gloves and some wearing spats, you know them black and white funny looking shoes. They was all sitting in a semi-circle on the stage singing these funny songs, twanging on banjos and beating on tambourines and what they called castanets; they was made of bones. They was funny. Damn, they was funny. Never laughed so much in my life. I loved it. I said to my friend, 'They get paid to do this?' and he said, 'Why sure, we paid to get in didn't we? They make good money. But they travel all the time, do a show every night, it's hard work. They'll be in Thibodaux tomorrow night, Houma, Morgan City, you know that town they called Brashear City until a couple of years ago. They travel all over the place.' To me that sounded like more fun than chasing chickens at Mardi Gras. I couldn't wait to see how I could get to be a part of it."

XXIII
September 1878

Neat hurried around to the back of the saloon where he had just seen his first minstrel. He was flushed with excitement. Never had anything thrilled him as much as this show. He had to find out how he could be a part of it.

No one challenged him as he walked into the rear of the building. The men he had just seen on stage were in various stages of sitting around, smoking, drinking or changing clothes. Some had only undershirts on, some were using a cream to clean the burnt cork or grease paint off their faces, some were just sitting back relaxing with big tumblers of whiskey and cigars.

He walked up to one that he recognized from the performance, the only one that had not been in black face onstage. "Hello, I just wanted to tell you that I thought you were great up there, sir."

The man looked him over. He registered Neat as being very young with very old eyes, dark, very slim and dressed in cheap, though well pressed, clothes. "What's your name, kid?"

"They call me Neat, sir."

"I don't care if they call you sloppy or slovenly or whatever, what's your name?"

Neat was taken aback. "Well, sir, my name is Antoine, but everybody that knows me calls me Neat. That's it, sir, Neat, I'm sorry but that's what they calls me."

"Neat. Well, that's…Neat, I guess. What you doing back here, er, Neat?"

"I just wanted to meet some of you. You were Mr. Inter…Mr. Interlock-in-tator or something?

James Brady, thirty-two, a native of New Jersey and a twelve-year veteran of traveling minstrel shows, laughed, "It's Mr. Interlocutor, Mr. Neat. I'm the star of the show. Name's Brady, James Brady. In fact, it's my show. I get to ask the questions and I get to do the songs I want." Brady pulled a bottle of brownish liquid from a table next to his chair. He pulled the cork from the bottle with his teeth and took a slug. Through squinted eyes and puckered cheeks, he said, "You liked the show, huh?"

"Oh yes, I want to learn how to do this. I want to be a part of this minstrel show stuff, I really do."

"Oh really," Brady scoffed, "Can you dance?"

"Well, I, I guess so."

"You guess so? Great. Can you sing?"

"Sure, everybody can sing, can't they?"

"Ha, you'd be surprised. Can you play a banjo or a tambourine or bones?"

"No, can't play no banjo but I can pick a little on a guitar; and a tambourine ain't no more than clapping your hands together; and the bones looks like what my friend Sherman and me do when we play spoons."

Brady rolled his head back and laughed heartily, "Oh yeah, Mr. Neat. It's all so easy. You know I been doing this for twelve years and my daddy and uncle were doing it for twenty years before me, in New York City and Baltimore and Cleveland and all the big stages. You ain't even heard 'bout them places. You don't just get up on stage and perform. You got to be trained, got to be a part of what we call show business. You people down in the south damn near killed the business with this damn war you started but it's coming back real good."

Neat had a grin from ear to ear, "Mr. Interlocutator, sir. I'm a real quick learner and I really want to learn how to be a part of this show. Please sir? Will you teach me?"

"I told you my name's Brady, son, James Brady, how old are you?"

"I'm going on twenty, sir, but I been on my own since I was thirteen and I don't mind hard work."

Brady sized him up again: small, lithe, dark and not bad looking. Could probably be trained to tap dance pretty easily. Undoubtedly would work cheap. "Let me hear you sing something, Neat."

Taken by surprise, Neat started thinking feverishly, "Uh, uh, I can't rightly think of nothing…uh, wait a minute, how about," and he sang one of the songs he had just heard in the show loud and strong, "De camptown racers sing dis song, doo dah, doo dah, camptown races…" He thought Brady would fall off his chair laughing. He stopped singing, embarrassed. "Well, it's the only damn thing I could think of. Was it that bad?" He stood up to leave.

Brady recovered from his spasm, "No, no, not bad at all, Neat. I'm just amazed at your openness, your lack of self-consciousness. That's good. That's what we in show business are all about." He suddenly got serious, "You married? Children? Running from the law?"

Neat shook his head wonderingly, "Naw, not any more."

"Now what the hell does that mean? Not any more. Not any more wives, children or lawmen?"

Neat laughed, "Oh no sir, no wives, no children just that I figured I had to be honest and tell you that I stood trial for murder about a year ago for shooting a man. But I was judged innocent. It was self-defense."

Brady looked at him for a long time. "Shooting a man? How'd that happen?"

"It's a long, long story, Mr. Brady, but it was self-defense. The jury agreed too, it was self-defense."

"You were carrying a pistol at the time of the shooting, I guess?"

"Sure, still am, aren't you?" Neat pulled the Double Derringer from the small of his back to show him. Brady leaped from his chair and cringed behind the open door.

"Put that thing away, for God's sake! We don't allow firearms to be carried by our troupe."

Neat resettled his weapon and said, "I'm real sorry, sir, I didn't mean to spook you. It's just that, down here, we all gotta carry weapons if we want to live."

Brady reseated himself, "Look, Neat, I like you and I think you've got the presence, the look to make it on stage. But let's see a little movement." He got up and moved his chair over against the wall. "Get up. I wanna see you do this." Brady moved into a slow cross-step soft shoe shuffle then looked up at Neat. "Wanna see it again?" Neat nodded, wide-eyed. Brady repeated the move. Neat slowly mirrored his steps and looked up hopefully.

"Not bad, boy, not bad at all. Maybe you are a quick learner. I'm gonna give you a shot. One of my boys, the one you saw playing 'Bruder Tambo' tonight, is leaving tomorrow to join one of Lew Dockstader's troupes down in New Orleans. It's a real break for him, Dockstader's got the biggest minstrelsy network in the country. He's got troupes all over the states, but they only play the big towns. We little guys get to cover the backwaters." Brady finished rolling a fat cigarette and took another long swig at the bottle. "I'm gonna move one of my chorus boys up to the Bruder Tambo spot and let you fill in. You'll just be one of the chorus now, no solos until you learn the show. You'll have to leave with us first thing tomorrow morning. We'll rehearse on the boat going down Bayou Lafourche tomorrow and if you learn as fast as you say, you'll be on stage in Thibodaux tomorrow night. I'll guarantee you two weeks. If you work out we'll agree on longer terms. For the two weeks you'll get meals and lodging and a share of whatever tips the audience kicks in when we pass the hat after the shows. We'll talk about a salary after that. If you wanta do it, be here at seven tomorrow morning." He got up and walked out of the room.

Neat ran all the way through the dark streets of Donaldsonville to the tiny boarding house room he lived in near the docks. He packed his meager belongings into a small duffle bag then got out some note paper and a pencil. He meticulously and laboriously printed out several notes. One was to his employer, one to Sherman and one for Sherman to deliver to his mother and sisters. He explained his excitement at this opportunity of traveling with the show and making some money and a name for himself. He promised to let them know when the show came back near enough for them to come see him.

He felt as though he was being given a new life. Since he had been told of Amanda and the baby dying he had lived in a lost depression. He had no future, nothing really to live for. Suddenly, he was excited to be alive again. He sat up in his cot, fully clothed, until dawn. At one point he dropped into a fitful sleep and found himself rereading the letter Amanda had sent him shortly after she was whisked away to the Ursuline Convent. He fought his way through the reading of it though he was still having trouble interpreting script. She had closed with: *Be strong for us, Neat, and remember, I love you. I always will, Amanda.* Neat awoke with tears flowing down his cheeks. His eyes felt swollen. He poured cold water into a bowl and splashed his face with it, looked into the tarnished mirror over the chest of drawers and swore he would never, ever cry again.

XXIV
Fall–winter 1878–'79

A week after Neat joined the Brady Minstrel Show, the troupe of four chorus boys, two end men, Mr. Interlocutor, a piano player and two stage hands and gofers pulled into Morgan City at the mouth of the Atchafalaya River. They were scheduled for two shows there before moving up Bayou Teche. They had played the small towns of Thibodaux, Raceland and Houma since Neat joined them.

On the trip down Bayou Lafourche, Brady had drilled Neat relentlessly. He coached him over and over on rudimentary tap dance steps. Neat was, in fact, a quick learner and had a natural talent for dancing. He also was blessed with a true sense of rhythm and played the tambourines and bones like a seasoned veteran after just two days of training. The singing came harder. There were so many lyrics to learn. The first song Brady drummed into him was one of the basic classics of minstrelsy, *Jump Jim Crow*.

> *First on de heel tap,*
> *Den on the toe*
> *Every time I wheel about*
> *I jump Jim Crow.*
> *Wheel about and turn about*
> *And do jes so.*
> *And every time I wheel about,*
> *I jump Jim Crow.*

Of course the performer had to dance and sing at the same time; that created problems. From there they moved through *Camptown Races, O'Susanna* and *Old Folks at Home,* also known as *Swanee.* There was even a grand rendition of minstrel star Dan Emmett's *Dixie.* It had been one of the most popular minstrel songs in the North before the war and was later picked up by Confederate troops as a marching song.

Brady was pleased with Neat's progress but didn't want to praise him too much. He knew many performers who were great in rehearsal and bombed before a live audience.

The first night was rough. Neat was in awe of the response of the crowd to the first act. He caught himself smiling foolishly and looking around at the faces in the crowd. He missed a couple of cues and failed to respond to some of the jokes flying back and forth between *Bruder Tambo, Bruder Bones* and *Mr. Interlocutor.*

Neat had learned that the typical show consisted of three acts. In the first, *The Minstrel Line,* the troupe assembled in a semi-circle and sang a couple of songs. *Mr. Interlocutor,* the only member of the cast not in black face, thus obviously the leader, then yelled, "Gentlemen be seated." That's when the Endmen, the *Bruders Tambo* and *Bones* would lead the ensemble in a series of jokes, songs and dances. The Endmen spoke in a comic caricature of black colloquial speech. Brady explained to Neat that, in contrast, his speech on stage as *Mr. Interlocutor* would always be in a florid eloquence that was a spoof of white upper class condescension.

During the ten-minute intermission following act one, Brady pulled Neat aside and whispered heatedly to him, "Get your head out of your ass, Mr. Galvez. Stop looking at the audience. Pay attention to what's happening on stage. Focus. I don't want to have to warn you again."

Act two was called *The Olio.* The stage was draped at the back with a painted backdrop usually depicting a formal garden. This was the segment when each individual of the troupe got a chance to show his stuff. They sang and danced and told quick stories. *The Olio* ended with a sort of stump speech by one of the Endmen, *Bones* one night and *Tambo* the next. They took satiric pokes at political figures and current happenings in the nation and, when they had a chance to research it, local issues. They fed on information they gleaned from any of the locals they came in contact with: innkeepers, liverymen, theater owners. They found the more irreverent they were with local, well-known people, the bigger the laughs.

After a second intermission came the *One-Act Musical*. Brady taught Neat that this segment usually burlesqued a popular topic, novel or play. Two stock blackface characters were almost always depicted: *Jim Crow*, an ignorant country Negro harshly humiliated by a character named *Zip Coon*, a city slicker whose exaggerated self-assurance always led to his comic comeuppance. The chorus boys participated by reacting with exaggerated facial mugging, guffaws and foot stomping. Neat loved every minute of it.

After the finale featuring the entire troupe, they took two bows to a standing, applauding, appreciative audience. Singing, dancing and laughing in public places was not a normal occurrence in post-war Louisiana.

Neat came through his two-weeks probation exhausted but satisfied. Brady clapped him on the back after the performance in the tiny village of Lafayette. "You know what, kid?" he said, "You're pretty damn good. I'm gonna start paying you a regular wage from now on in addition to the split on the tips. If you think you're ready, I'll give you a solo during the *Olio* up in Opelousas in a couple of days."

Not only did Neat charm the audiences; he threw in a twist that had not been seen before in minstrel shows. Baker and the piano man coached him for the singing and dancing routine to Stephen Foster's *Old Folks at Home* or *Swanee.*

> *Swanee, how I love you, how I love you*
> *My dear old Swanee*
> *I'd give the world to be among the folks in D-I-X*
> *I even know my mammy's waiting for me,*
> *praying for me*
> *Down by the Swanee*
> *The folks up north will see me no more*
> *When I get to my Swanee shore*

His solo was well received and Baker was pleased with it. Then, in a performance a couple of weeks later, with a lot of Cajuns, Creoles and Hispanics in attendance, Neat surprised everyone, including Mr. Interlocutor. He sang the second verse in French and the third in Spanish. He brought the house down. After the performance, the troupe went through the audience passing the hat for tips. That night Neat filled his hat with currency and coins twice. It was probably the only multi-lingual *Swanee* in minstrel history and it stayed in the show.

Two months later, while performing in Baton Rouge, the veteran performer playing the part of *Bruder Tambo* tripped on a step leading down from the stage and broke his hip. The troupe gathered at the back of the theater to watch their friend being carried by stretcher into the back of an ambulance carriage. Brady called Neat aside. "You ready to take his place, *Bruder Tambo?*"

Neat could hardly breathe. "Me, take his place? You bet I'm ready. I'll need your help. I'll need to rehearse a couple of times before the next show." *Mon Dieu, am I ready?* It was the first week of December, 1878.

Through the winter of '78 and '79 the Brady troupe traveled the Southern Gulf Coast from Galveston, Texas to Mobile, Alabama. It was grueling, numbing work but Neat was good at what he was doing, getting better at it and loved every minute. At one of the stops in Alexandria in late November a well-dressed, older gentleman came back stage asking for Neat. He introduced himself as an associate of Lew Dockstader, the famous minstrel producer. He said the Dockstader people had heard about this young, limber, multi-lingual end man and he had been sent to scout him out. The gentleman gave him a card and asked that Neat visit with him in New Orleans sometime around the first of March when Mr. Dockstader himself would be in town. He would stage an audition and he was sure Neat would soon be on the biggest stages in the nation.

One night in early January, Neat and the troupe finished a show in Ponchatoula, Louisiana. They were scheduled to stay in the little town overnight before moving up the Illinois Central Railroad to other dates as far north as Jackson, Mississippi. The crowd had been very responsive and appreciative especially when Neat as *Bruda Tambo* and Robert Barclay, who was in his third year as *Bruda Bones* improvised a skit on the naming of the town.

Ponchatoula is a Choctaw Indian word for "flowing hair." The Indians used the word to describe the beautiful Spanish moss that was so prominent on the lovely oak trees in the area. Neat fashioned a wig of moss and Barclay used a clump of it as a beard. When they hit the stage as long lost lovers with their new "flowing hair" or "Ponchatoula" jokes and songs, the audience went wild.

Neat was removing the black makeup by lamp light back stage after the show. He was still smiling to himself at the reception their improvisation had received. It was unusually balmy for a January night so he had opened the outer door of the dressing area for fresh air. He suddenly became aware of a tall, dark figure standing in the doorway just beyond the lamplight. Neat slowly continued swabbing his face as he calculated the distance to the pistol he had stashed in his duffel bag at the end of the table. A deep voice chuckled, "Ain't no use going for your pistol, Neat. This darkie ain't gonna harm another darkie like you, no how."

Neat recognized the voice, whirled off his stool and reached out for the man, "Henry, Henry Gilmore, you old son-of-a-gun. Come on in here, boy. Let me look at you."

Henry came in grinning. Neat reached out to shake hands with him but Henry moved in and wrapped his long arms around him and nearly lifted him off the floor. "You see, it ain't all bad to be born with black skin. You wouldn't have to make up like a girl every night."

They laughed and talked for several minutes while Neat finished cleaning his face. Neat said, "What the hell you doing up here in redneck country? I thought you were heading north, going up to one of them big towns where you darkies get rich and live with the white folks."

"Well, that's what I was goin' to do. When I got to New Orleans I moved in with an uncle until I could save enough money to get me a steamer to Chicago. My uncle runs a couple of the wharves down on the riverfront. He put me to work down there for 'bout a month." Henry drew up a chair and sat down. "Turns out I be 'bout the only man in my crew that can read and write. I had to read most of the paper work for my boss." Henry's gleaming white teeth flashed in a grin. "Fore long my uncle done put me in charge of a couple of the crews. We busy like bees since the feds left town and making pretty good money. I figure I can't do better than this up north. So here I am."

"Damn, that's great, Henry. And you look good, too. That work must be good for you. But, what the hell brought you across the lake up here?" Henry was dressed in jeans and a western cut shirt and jacket. He had on a beret-like cap with a short brim and was wearing well worn but well-shined boots.

"It's kinda a long story, Neat." He looked around at the back stage dressing area. "You through here? Can we take a little walk?"

"Sure thing. And I even got a bit of bourbon stashed back here. It'll be like old times." Neat grabbed his bottle and a jacket and they headed out. Neat told him the troupe was staying overnight in Ponchatoula before catching a mid-morning train north for the next week of shows.

"Thas good, cause I got something I want to show you." They started walking slowly toward the front of the theater. "You remember Lucille Chatagnier?" Henry asked.

Neat thought a moment and said, "Yeh, little Lucy. Her daddy was one of the field bosses up at Nottoway. Pretty little brunette. I didn't see her much the last few years though." He looked at Henry with a gleam in his eye. "You know I was kinda 'away' for a while there."

They both laughed and Henry said, "Yea, Neat the swamp rat. Well, Lucille and her mother moved to New Orleans when her daddy died in the winter of '75, just before you got into your mess. She went to a Catholic school in the city and ended up working in the Customs House for an export company." Henry's voiced softened, "I met her one day down on the dock. We were loading a ship owned by her boss and she came down to deliver some papers to the captain. We shared a lunch together and talked a long time 'bout old times in Iberville Parish and, well, after that things just kinda happened."

Neat stopped walking. "Things just kinda happened? What things? Henry, you didn't." He tried to see into Henry's eyes but it was too dark. "You did." Neat spun around in astonishment. "Damn, Henry, people like you get killed for that sort of thing around here."

"I know, I know but it's a little different down in New Orleans. They's been a lot of mixing over the years down there. Lot of us darkies ain't so dark and are passing for white and everybody sort of looks the other way, you know, if you don't brag about it or rub their noses in it."

Neat shook his head in wonderment, "So how long has this been going on? You're not married, are you? They ain't that reconstructed in ole Orleans are they?" He pronounced it a la Francais: Or-lay-on.

"We been together now 'most a year. No, we ain't married but if we do, I'm calling you down to be best man."

"Unh, unh man, I ain't hangin' with you. You marry that pretty little white gal, you doin' it without my permission or, how'd that lawyer of mine put it? 'Without my prior knowledge.' So, again. Why you up here?"

"I was getting to that. Lucille's mamma's older sister, her aunt (Henry said 'unt') lived up here just outside of town. She was an old maid, never married. Well, she died last month and left everything she had, a little house, some furniture and some livestock to her sister. Mrs. Chatagnier has been sickly all year and she asked Lucille if she would come up here and settle the affairs. She suggested that Lucille take that nice darkie she's seen helping her out. Said he looked good and strong." He winked at Neat. "She don't know the whole story of course. She wants Lucille to put the house up for sale, sell the livestock, let her niggra friend clean the place up. She said I could sleep in the shed out back. Oh yeah! She said we should pick the best of the furniture and things in the house and ship them back to New Orleans. You see, Mrs. Chatagnier thinks Lucille is living with a girl friend out on the edge of the Quarter in Marigny. That's a pretty mixed district. Uh, well, you see, that's where we living. Lots of couples like me and Lucy. My uncle was good enough to give me some time off to come up here to help."

Neat blew out a long breath. "Hey, Henry, whatever makes you happy. Just, for God's sake, be careful. You know some folks just can't accept that kinda thing, especially outside of Orleans. And especially up here in the 'Florida Parishes.'"

"You wanna come see her? You wanna see Lucille? I gotta a little horse and buggy 'round the corner. It'll take us about half an hour to get out to the unt's house. Then I can take you back later, or you can sleep out there." He laughed and nudged Neat with an elbow, "They's a shed out back that I ain't using. I can run you back in time for the train in the morning."

Neat considered for a moment, then said, "Sure, what the hell. Lemme just go tell Mr. Brady. I'll be right back." When he ran back into the theatre Neat went back to the dressing area to pick up his things but they were gone. He saw Robert just leaving the stage door and called after him. "Hey, Robert, where's everybody? Where's my clothes and stuff?"

"Oh there you are, Neat. We've been looking all over for you. Brady figured you'd picked up on that pretty, young redhead in the third row that was throwing you kisses. He told the boys to bring your things back to the boarding house. You know we leave at ten in the morning."

"Damn, I never even saw the redhead. Wish I had. Throwing kisses, huh? Well, I'm going out in the country to visit a friend of mine. I'll either get back later tonight or catch up first thing in the morning. Tell Brady not to worry, I'll make the train. Besides, he hasn't paid me for this week yet and I'm too broke to go anywhere."

Robert slapped him on the back, "You take care now. We'll see you tomorrow."

Neat trotted up the street to catch up with Henry. He had intended to take off his spats and his bow tie and at least retrieve his pistol before leaving the theater but he trusted the group with his belongings and figured everything would be all right on his little tour with Henry.

Henry was waiting in a tiny, two-wheel buggy hitched to an old, brown, swayback mare. Neat hopped in and Henry popped the reins on the horse's loins. She took off at a slow trot. Henry said, "See, that's why it'll take a half-hour to get out to the house. With a real horse we could make it in fifteen, twenty minutes." They laughed and Neat popped the cork out of his bottle, took a swig of whiskey and passed it on to Henry.

Twenty minutes later Henry pulled the nag off the main road and onto a narrow, rutted lane crowded on both sides by woods and underbrush. "I don't know how the old woman got along all by herself out here. It's really isolated and lonely. I tried to talk Lucille into coming into town with me but she didn't think that would be wise and said she still had a lot of packing to do. We're going back day after tomorrow. Been here nearly a week. Of course we had to ride in separate cars on the train coming up and then she got a ride with the unt's lawyer out to the house. Practically had to beat him with a broomstick to get him to leave her alone at the house. I got a ride out after dark." He looked at Neat, "See, we being careful. You learn after a while. The only brush we had was when one of the old woman's friends sent her son over to see if Lucille needed anything. We were just getting up and he almost caught me coming out of the bedroom with her. But, I'm sure he didn't see anything. I just shuffled my feet, grabbed a broom and started sweeping the kitchen and said yassuh and nosuh to him."

They bumped along for a few minutes with the horse now slowed to a walk. There was a half moon that barely lit the lane but Neat noticed a glow coming through the trees ahead of them. "What's that, Henry. Lucille burning some trash or something?"

Henry peered ahead, "I don't know. She shouldn't be doing that at night like this. Somebody might come out to investigate. I just don't know." He popped the reins on the old mare and she moved to a slow trot again.

As they came closer, it was obvious that what they were seeing was the glow of a large fire. Finally they broke out of the woods and into a clearing some two hundred yards from the house. It was totally engulfed in flames. The horse stopped abruptly and tried to turn away. Henry wrapped the reins around a peg on the buggy's dashboard, leaped out and started running toward the house. He was screaming, "Lucille, Lucille! Oh my God, Lucy!"

Neat was frozen in the buggy. He could not comprehend what was happening. He thought he heard a woman's scream from the direction of the house. As Henry got within a hundred yards of the house, he was holding his hands out in front of him to shield the withering heat. Four horsemen came galloping out from behind the house. One of them shouted, "There's that nigger, get him." They seemed to be wearing flowing white robes and, it looked to Neat, as they were silhouetted against the roaring flames, that they wore peaked hats. *Klansmen!* The word burst in Neat's head. They quickly surrounded Henry.

One of the men swung a thick object at Henry's head and he went down immediately.

Neat knew he had to get out of there. There was no way he could help Henry against the Klansmen but maybe he could find help somewhere in time. He slipped out of the buggy, used it as a shield between himself and the house and sneaked into the underbrush at the edge of the clearing. As he looked back, two of the men had lifted Henry's unmoving body onto one of the horses and they rode slowly around to the rear of the house. He could hear them laughing.

Neat stayed on the edge of the trail back out to the main road. He turned north toward the town of Ponchatoula some four miles away. It was already near midnight. He continued trotting toward town as long as he could. Every five minutes or so he had to stop and catch his breathe. Even a minstrel man was in no shape for this. He finally saw the buildings of the center of the town and ran toward the theater where they had appeared that night. The boarding house where the troupe was staying was a couple of blocks further up near the train station.

There did not appear to be anyone at the theater but some lamps were still burning inside. Neat ran through the front double doors and startled an old Negro man who was sweeping the center aisle. "What you want, mister?" the old man yelped. "Can't you see we's closed? Ain't nobody here but me."

Neat yelled back at him, "I'm not here to hurt you. I need to find the sheriff or a deputy or somebody. Some Klansmen are about to kill my friend."

At the word "Klansmen" the old man dropped the broom and headed toward the exit, stage left of the auditorium. "Wait, wait. Where can I find a sheriff?" Neat yelled.

Over his shoulder and without breaking stride the old man called out, "'Cross from the train station at the jail. They's a deputy lives upstairs." His voice trailed off as he sped through the door.

Neat ran to the small frame building with the sign "Jail" painted on a hanging shingle. He bolted up the outside stairs to the quarters above the jail. He beat on the door for almost a full minute before he saw the swinging light from a lamp sweeping under the door.

Deputy Horace Kirby yelled through the door, "Who the hell is beating on this door and do you know what the damn time is?"

Neat called out that he needed help and that a friend was about to be killed.

Kirby opened the door. He stood there holding the lamp in his left hand, a .44 in his right and a holster belted around the waist of his long nightgown.

Neat related the problem as quickly as he could while gasping for breath. When he said he thought "Klansmen had waylaid his friend" Horace raised the lamp closer to Neat's face and took a better look.

"Your 'friend', he's a niggra?"

"Well yea, but he's a good one. And he's an old friend."

That brought a deep laugh from the deputy. "Well, hold on and lemme get some clothes on and we'll go see about that old niggra friend of yours those bad ole Klansmen are scaring."

Neat lowered his voice to keep his rage under control. "Scaring my ass. They probably set that house on fire with his girl friend in it and they probably looking to kill him unless we get out there right now. Fact, it might be too late. They took him before midnight."

The deputy seemed to take an inordinate amount of time to get dressed. Fifteen minutes later he came down the stairs to where Neat was waiting. He was wearing jeans and a military style shirt with a star on it and his gun belt tightened under his overhanging belly. "My horse is out back and we can use one of the others for you." He paused and looked at Neat's citified outfit. He still had his spats on. "You *can* ride a horse, can't you?" Neat didn't even deign to answer.

Twenty minutes later they entered the clearing where Lucille's aunt's house lay in smoldering ruin. Embers were still white hot. Flames licked the foundation and chimney and a few standing walls. Thick smoke curled upward. Neat thought, *Lucille is probably smoldering in there also, and maybe Henry.*

"Aw, shit," Horace breathed out, "they sure did it up good, didn't they?" He had questioned Neat on the way down. Neat told him of his connection with the minstrel and how he had come to know Henry. "Come on, you're kidding me, this niggra you came out here with was once a sheriff?" When he asked whether or not Neat could describe any of the four men or even their horses or what they were wearing, he seemed relieved when Neat said he only saw them from a distance and then only in silhouette against the fire.

As they circled around the house they came downwind of the soft breeze that was carrying the smoke toward the rear of the property. A sharp, acrid odor hit the two men and Horace said, "Smell that? I believe either your friend or that woman you said was in the house done joined the ashes."

Neat saw it first and the back of his throat filled with bile. The tall, slim figure was hanging from a sturdy limb some nine or ten feet off the ground. The body was swinging ever so slowly from a perfectly executed hangman's knot.

Neat guided his horse up close and stood in the stirrups trying to release the noose. "Could you please help me with this, deputy?"

"Sure, buddy." He rode over, took an extremely sharp-looking Bowie knife from a scabbard on his saddle and sawed through the rope. Henry's body collapsed in a heap. "Look at that there noose. Looks like them boys sure knew what they was doing." Horace could hardly hide a slight hint of pride in his voice.

Neat was numb with shock. The deputy helped him lift Henry's lifeless body on to Neat's horse, draped him over the haunches behind the saddle and unceremoniously tied him to the saddle with the same rope that had been used to lynch him. He picked up Henry's cap, held it up to see better and chuckled, "Now ain't this cute."

If Neat had remembered to bring his gun he would have shot him on the spot. He whispered hoarsely, "This happen a lot around here?"

Horace didn't even look at him as he remounted his horse, "Naw, not a lot. But then, you just don't see many niggras stupid enough to be running around with white women."

Neat stopped halfway up on his saddle, "How the hell did you know there was a white woman involved in this?" he breathed.

The deputy snapped a quick look at Neat and said, "Well, I just figured, I mean, well, you know, I knew who lived out here and just figured whoever burned up in there probably was a white woman." He gave Neat a sickly smile. He quickly turned his horse away and called over his shoulder, "That's why I'm a deputy sheriff, cause I know shit like that. Now let's get on back to town. I'm gonna have to wake up the sheriff and he ain't gonna like all this going on in his parish."

Neat got back to the boarding house just before sunrise. His eyes were bloodshot and his clothes dusty, disheveled and smelling of smoke. He knocked on Brady's door and obviously woke him up. "What the hell is it, Neat? You wanta brag about getting into that little redhead's pants? Damn boy, where'd y'all screw in the middle of the road?" He sniffed the air. "What'd you do, light a damn campfire? Look at you. You're a disgrace to the troupe."

"Hold on Mr. B., you won't believe what has happened." He clenched his teeth to stop the tears welling in his eyes. Brady opened the door wider and pulled him inside.

After he had related the whole story, he said, "and now the sheriff is saying that the best thing to do is just to forget the whole thing since I can't identify nobody. He says if I don't do that he will have to hold me as a 'material witness' or something and I might be in Ponchatoula for a long time. He said his advice is for me to just get on that train with you and the boys and put it behind me. What am I gonna do, Mr. Brady. I can't just forget Henry and Lucille. How can I just walk away and let that bunch get away with murder?"

Brady suddenly felt very sorry for Neat. He realized that this young man who seemed so mature for his age was still just beyond childhood and in serious anguish.

For the next hour the man comforted, soothed and counseled the youth. He guided Neat to his room and pulled out some clean clothes from his bag while Neat cleaned up at the washbasin. By the time the two joined the rest of the troupe for breakfast, Neat seemed almost serene. Brady didn't know if it was from his fatherly efforts or merely the severe fatigue and shock setting in.

Before they boarded the train, Brady paid for telegraphs to send the terribly disturbing news to Henry's uncle and employer and to Lucille's aunt in New Orleans. Neat's performances over the next few weeks reflected the horrible experience. He was not as funny, not as nimble. He just could not forget the smell of the burned house and the sight of Henry dangling from that tree.

Other disturbing news was also traveling the Gulf Coast. Another major outbreak of Yellow Fever was spreading out of New Orleans. By February, 1879, officials estimated that over 4,000 people had died in Louisiana, Mississippi, Texas and even as far north as Shreveport, Louisiana and Memphis, Tennessee in the past two months. The plague stretched tensions so high that Mississippi and Texas officials were threatening to tear up railroad tracks on their borders with Louisiana and open fire upon boats trying to enter their ports.

In the Crescent City, carbolic acid and sulfur were burned to keep away the fever. Charity Hospital patients were given saltshakers filled with calomel, a compound of mercury used as a strong laxative. The patients were urged to take a pinch whenever they felt like it. The attempted cure may have been as damaging as the disease. Nearly fifty people died every day in New Orleans as family carriages or "dead wagons" piled high with wooden coffins made their way to the cemeteries.

Mardi Gras celebrations in New Orleans, all the parades and balls, were cancelled because of the epidemic. The Brady Minstrel Show was doomed. Performances were cancelled as authorities quarantined town after town, banning public gatherings. They were forced to travel farther and farther inland from New Orleans and the Gulf Coast to get bookings. Attendance was small and unprofitable. As the inevitable dawned on the cast of the show, alcohol abuse among the troupe, always a problem, increased. Brady himself was starting most of the shows somewhat inebriated and many of the cast were joining him. Their condition translated to sloppiness on stage instead of the usually sharp repartee and timing that was vital to the success of the performance. One or two of the cast members missed several shows because of their afternoon drinking sprees.

Finally, during a particularly disastrous performance in a small town in central Mississippi, the frustrations and drinking problems exploded into a fist-fight on stage between a member of the chorus and *Bruder Bones*. It came at the end of the last act just before the finale. Bones adlibbed a joke about a "fast" woman he had met. Unfortunately, he used one of the chorus member's wife's name when describing the street woman. Both men having too much to drink, they went at it on stage. At first the sparse audience thought it was part of the show and were standing and cheering as the two men slugged away. But when *Bones* hit the floor headfirst and blood started seeping, everything went deathly quiet. Brady signaled frantically for the curtains to be closed.

Word of the unprofessional incident spread quickly and the next several stops were cancelled. A couple of mornings later, a member of the troupe found a note tacked to Brady's door announcing that he was broke and couldn't pay the cast for the last week. He wished them luck. His room had been cleared of all his belongings. Brady was long gone.

Neat and several of the crew who had previously survived yellow fever and thus were immune, hopped a train into New Orleans and tried desperately, without success, to hook up with one of the Dockstader troupes. The agent that had contacted Neat in Alexandria a couple of months ago had left town with no forwarding address. The Dockstader groups had all disbanded and left the state.

Neat decided he had experienced about all the fame and glamour of show business he could stand. He had managed to save a little money in the past several months. He used part of that to book passage upriver to Donaldsonville. It was time to go home.

XXV
November 7th, 1958

"So you went back to Donaldsonville and started selling supplies to sugar cane refineries again for the next few years. Is that when you ran into this Boyer fellow?"

Neat gave his grandson a withering look over the steel rims of his glasses. "You just keep chewing on that name like an old cow with a cud, don't you? I'll tell you about young Boyer when I'm damn well ready," he flashed.

He was quiet for some time and Randy wasn't about to prod him again. Finally, Neat stirred and asked for some tap water and for Randy to restock his pipe with tobacco. When they had settled down again and the tape recorder was rolling, Neat said, "I got lucky. I couldn't complain. Those were pretty good days for me, boy. I had a nice little place to stay near old Fort Butler in Donaldsonville. I traveled up and down Bayou Lafourche, sometimes all the way over to New Iberia and St. Martinville, now that was a sweet little town, and beautiful women? C'etait si bon! They liked to wear what they called 'les chapeaux;' frou-frou little bonnets with flowers and lace and what all. But, man, could those St. Martinville women kiss and make love. A lot of them had come over direct from France. They did things to a man nobody else could do. Only got over there a couple of times a year but it was worth the wait."

He sucked on the pipe for a few seconds. "I was making pretty good money and I was winning a lot in poker games. We'd have a big game every Saturday night in Donaldsonville or if I was traveling on Saturday, I'd find me a game. I saved a lot of my money cause I knew that I'd have to slow down sooner or later and settle down with a piece of land." His expression changed and he seemed to lose some of his energy. "But, damn it all, I still missed her."

"Who, Paw Paw?"

"Amanda, boy. No matter how much fun I was having, with the women or the poker table, whenever I thought of my sweet Amanda it took my breath away. They shoulda never sent her to that damn convent." Again he went silent for several minutes. Randy switched off the tape recorder and waited.

"Then that little fool showed up." He sat up a little straighter. "You wanted to know. I'll tell you. Ain't told hardly no body 'bout this for over fifty years. It was the summer of 1886. I was twenty-seven. I had just put some money down on a few acres of sugar cane land owned by the family of a friend of mine. His father had died and the widow woman wanted to get off the land. My friend wanted to get his share of the money and move to Texas. It was back of White Castle. Pretty good gumbo soil, black and rich. We'd agreed I'd move out there and take over the farm in February of the next year and finish paying the woman off. I'd be just in time to get the fields set up for a new crop for harvesting in the fall. We had a big showdown game set up for that Saturday night at the saloon when he showed up to spoil everything."

XXVI
July 1886

The young man looked old beyond his years. At age twenty-two he had already severely abused his body and mind. In the sweltering humidity of the Philadelphia waterfront, he was scrounging the waste barrels for scraps of food. Earlier he made the rounds of the eating establishments frequented by the merchant mariners, offering to clean up the kitchens, sweep the dining rooms, wash the dishes or utensils, anything for food or funds.

He was recognized by most of the regulars. They called him "Sambo." Even while getting their kicks annoying or teasing him they still felt pity for him. It was said that he had lost his father during the War Between the States, that he was orphaned. Whenever Sambo heard such talk he protested violently, "I ain't no orphan. My mama's a hard-working lady up in Pottstown. I just ain't gonna be no burden on her. And my daddy didn't die in the war. He was murdered. Shot down in cold blood back in Louisiana by a runty piece of trash by the name of Galvez. But I'm gonna get him. I'm gonna get him yet."

Samuel Boyer spent most of his mid-teen years in a home for troubled boys in Philadelphia. By age fourteen, his mother and grandmother determined that they could not handle his tantrums and rebelliousness. They turned him over to the authorities after he trashed a merchant's store in downtown Pottstown when the owner refused to sell him tobacco. It was another in a long string of incidents. The local Episcopal minister intervened and had him committed to the St. Mark's School for Wayward Boys at the corner of Front and Arch Streets in the heart of Philadelphia.

It was a tough life. The headmaster and his staff believed in hard work and harsh physical discipline. Samuel was beaten, denied food and confined to a cell on a regular basis in attempts to restrain his temper and unruliness. His rage seemed to feed on the abusive punishment. He escaped the home four times in four years only to be brought back by police after committing another felony or misdemeanor. The punishment increased. When he reached age twenty-one he was declared emancipated. The St. Mark's authorities had no qualms about washing their hands of him. Good riddance. He was just another reminder of the failure of the system.

Samuel worked menial jobs up and down the busy waterfront frequently crossing over to Camden on the New Jersey side of the Delaware River and living there with other derelicts and castoffs for months at a stretch.

While sharing a hovel with several other men, he met a man named George Hampton. In spite of his circumstances the thirty-year old Hampton was handsome, suave and carried himself with a sophistication usually inbred. Like Samuel, he had left home at an early age. Unlike Samuel, he had sought his fortune by using his looks and his charm on a young woman from a prominent Philadelphia family. In spite of the protests of her family and only because her out-of-wedlock pregnancy would have caused the family more embarrassment than a mismatched marriage, Hampton found himself at the altar swearing the marriage vows that would take him into the high circles of Philadelphia society. His dangerous flirtation with nirvana only lasted six years. His brother-in-law, Clay Thornton, caught him in a highly compromising situation with one of the family's young male servants. An attorney was called, Hampton was given a small cash settlement, signed away all marital and parental rights and was banished from the family.

He blew through the cash quickly and found himself, like Samuel, on the streets, groveling for work and subsistence. Also like Samuel, he was bitter. Sitting on a pier at night sharing cheap alcohol, they would vow to wreak vengeance on those who had brought them to this level of existence.

On a hot Saturday night in June, George clapped an arm around Samuel's shoulder and slurred, "'Sambo', it's time to take care of our business. You help me and I'll help you. Like they say, 'you scratch my back and I'll scratch yours.' We're gonna kill that rotten son-of-a-bitch brother-in-law of mine; then we're going down to Louisiana and take care of that murdering Mexsin of yours."

"Right, how we g-g-gonna do that, Georgio?" Samuel stuttered back and lifted his bottle in salute. They were sitting in an open bay of a warehouse a block off the waterfront.

"Well, I'll tell you. Back when I was a respected member of society, brother-in-law Clay used to take me along with him ever so often when he'd go to his favorite whorehouse and poker establishment. It's just about a mile from the family mansion. If the weather's decent, he walks down there most every Thursday night. The bastard's a damn good player. He carries a lot of cash and he usually wins. We can take him when he comes out of the building and starts for home. You help me, we'll split the money and head for Louisiana to settle your score."

"And how we gonna get there, swim or walk?" Samuel giggled.

"Nope, got that figured out, too." He punched a finger in Samuel's chest. "Pal of mine is working for a steamer company looking for hands for a trip to New Orleans in a week or two. They got stops in Savannah, Tampa and Mobile. He can get us on. We'll take care of brother Clay, score his stash, make a little money on the way, hit New Orleans, have some fun then take care of your business and get out of there. Maybe go to Mexico or wherever. Shit, the whole world's out there waiting for us! Ain't that Gonzalez guy down there around New Orleans?"

"Galvez, name's Galvez, not Gonzalez. But they all look alike." Samuel almost lost a mouthful of liquor snickering at his own joke. "Yea, he's around New Orleans, I think. We lived about a day trip upriver from there. He's probably still around there. Probably too damn dumb to leave." Samuel took a long swig of the whiskey then laid back on the deck, "You're serious, ain't you?" He stared at the starry night for several minutes. Suddenly he sat up and shouted. "You know what? I like it. I like it a lot!"

George started laying out the plan step by step. Monday, he and Samuel visited his friend at the freight office handling the New Orleans trip. They were hired on to ship out the following Sunday. They would trap his brother-in-law Thursday night and lay low until they could board the steamer.

The days of steady drinking and plotting crept by. At eleven on Thursday evening, a light mist was falling on the streets of Philadelphia. Samuel and George, armed with seven-inch stilettos, waited in an alley a half block from "The Chanticleer Rouge," a bar and gambling house on Front Street.

Though the weather was marginal, Clay Thornton strolled down the street and into the establishment at 7 o'clock. The two rogues spotted him, clapped each other on the back with glee and proceeded to consume most of a bottle of cheap whiskey while waiting. The front of the establishment was well lit with gaslights but the rest of the street was quite dark and the mist added to the low visibility.

"Here he comes." George grabbed Samuel's sleeve and pointed to a figure emerging from the front door. He peered anxiously through the gloom. "Damn, there's somebody with him," he hissed.

Clay was laughing and talking animatedly with another man as they casually strolled away from the inn.

"Good. He's laughing. He must have won. That's why he quit early. He's a smart one, he is. We'll track them for about a block. If the other man doesn't go off, well, that's just his tough luck," George said.

Samuel didn't like it, "Unh, unh George, we can't take the chance of doing 'em both. Besides, we don't have to kill him, do we? Let's just knock him out and take the money."

"No, that's not the deal," George said angrily. "He's got to go. You want your revenge down in Louisiana? Well, I want mine here. That boat's leaving Sunday with or without us and this is our last chance." He grabbed Samuel's arm. "Come on, stay close to the buildings."

The two men ahead of them were obviously in no hurry. They were strolling along, talking and laughing loudly with no idea they were being tailed.

George grabbed Samuel's arm, "Clay's got to turn left at the next corner to head home. This next alley cuts behind the corner and will put us at the center of the block where he'll be passing. Let's go." He pulled the younger man with him into the alley and started running as quietly as he could through the cluttered passage. Small, furry figures scurried through the debris ahead of them. A couple of minutes later they arrived at the alley entrance on the cross street. Both were breathing hard and trying to do so silently. George peeped around the corner of the building and jerked his head back quickly. "He's coming." He chuckled fiendishly, "He's alone."

The two assailants had rehearsed the attack. Samuel, not known by Clay, would step out of the alley as if drunk, which wouldn't be hard considering the liquor he had already consumed. He would stagger in front of Clay and ask if he had a light for a cigar. George would take him from behind and cut his throat.

It didn't quite happen that way.

When Samuel emerged stumbling from the alley, Clay stopped and backed away toward the street. He told Samuel to get away from him and drew a small pistol from his jacket. Somehow, the schemers hadn't considered that possibility. Samuel started talking crazily, gesturing wildly and circled around Clay, keeping his distance but effectively getting him turned with his back to the alley way. Behind him, George couldn't see the pistol. With his impaired judgment, he still thought he had the advantage over their victim. He leaped out of the alley with the stiletto held high and rushed him. Clay spun around and fired just as George got to him. They both went sprawling into the street. The gun slid across the cobbles into the gutter. Samuel sprang into action. He whipped out his stiletto, grabbed Clay by the neck and stabbed him deeply in the side. Clay screamed and Samuel stabbed him again, this time higher up in the chest. The wounded man slumped over, started coughing and fell to his knees. Samuel kicked him viciously in the side of the head. He trembled violently for a few seconds before toppling over, unconscious.

Samuel saw George still lying in the street several feet away. He dropped to his knees and rolled him over. George's eyes were open and there was a tiny hole in his forehead oozing blood.

Samuel started shaking uncontrollably. He tried to run but his legs weren't functioning. He let out a loud moan and crawled back to Clay's body. Looking up and down the street for signs of witnesses, he quickly searched the man's jacket and found a large wad of bills. He stuffed them into his pants pocket then ripped a gold pocket watch off the man's chest and ran reeling through the streets.

Boyer lived under a bridge for two days venturing out only at night for food and drink. Watching furtively for the signs of police searches or other strangers, he counted his newfound wealth over and over. At times he giggled out loud. Adding the pay he expected from the coming voyage he calculated that he could live a good life for at least a year. His clever mind told him to hide the money and the watch. He stuffed the loot into an old sock and stuck it between two beams at the foot of a bridge near his encampment. Saturday morning two Philadelphia uniformed policemen were making the rounds of the camps along the river and called upon him.

They did a perfunctory search of his meager belongings finding them filthy and disgusting and were on their way in minutes.

Early Sunday morning, before dawn, Samuel retrieved his priceless sock and made his way to the dock of the "Beau Terre," the steamer he was boarding for the trip to New Orleans. He explained to the steward that his friend George had changed his mind about joining the crew. No further questions were asked.

By two in the afternoon the boat was under a head of steam heading downriver for Delaware Bay and the Atlantic Ocean.

Philadelphia police concluded that Clay Thornton and his estranged former brother-in-law were the victims of a fatal robbery. The family insisted that Clay would never have voluntarily met with George but Clay died on the way to a hospital without recovering consciousness. Police suspected that the brother-in-law may have been involved as a perpetrator in the incident but never could tie the loose ends up. They discovered that Clay had been a modest winner that night at "The Chanticleer Rouge" and that he owned a valuable pocket watch that was missing. However, they were never able to ascertain the presence of another person at the scene.

Meanwhile, Samuel Boyer, cash in hand, was on his way back to Louisiana and his fateful confrontation with Antoine Galvez.

XXVII
August 1886

It was near ten o'clock in the evening and the heat was finally beginning to subside. A piano player at the back of "The Green Door" saloon in Donaldsonville was noodling around on the keys and the kerosene lamps were turned up to full brightness. A large crowd of men and women were laughing and talking loudly around the thirty-foot-long bar.

Neat and four of his associates had been at it for over two hours. Everyone else at the poker table had taken off his jacket and loosened his tie. Neat was still fully clothed, cool and unruffled. He also had a hefty pile of chips in front of his place at the table. Stefan, a large, usually jovial German, shoved away from the table with a grunt, "Shit, you're too damn lucky tonight, Neat. And it's too damn hot in here. I gotta take a break and go on out back. Just hold on to the cards for a few minutes." The men at the table all agreed. Several stood and stretched.

One of the barkeeps, Jeremiah, took the opportunity to come over to tidy up the table. He leaned over and whispered to Neat, "Don't know if you might be acquainted with that young man over there sitting by himself at the corner of the bar, but he's been asking about you all afternoon." He nodded his head in the direction of a fair-haired, neatly dressed man in his early twenties. "Been sitting at the bar sipping rye and watching you since you came in."

Neat squinted through the gloom, "Looks vaguely familiar but I don't believe I know him. Anybody else know anything 'bout him?"

"Nope. Seems like he rode into town about noon and has just been riding around looking. Went out in the country for a while, too. Said he wanted to see a couple of the large plantation homes. I told him they wasn't much to see anymore. Done got pretty ratty looking over the years since the war. Ain't nobody 'round here with no money to keep'em up. Don't know why but he kinda got a kick outta that." Jeremiah went back toward the bar and watched as the stranger squared his hat and stood. He swayed ever so slightly, righted himself, then walked toward the poker table. Neat, seated in a chair with his back to the front wall of the saloon, was the only player still at the table. The man stood just off the side of the table a couple of feet away from Neat's chair.

"Something I can do for you, sir?" Neat asked.

"Matter of fact there is," the stranger said in a low voice.

Neat waited. He shifted slightly to get a better grip on the arms of the chair, "And what would that be?"

The man stared straight into Neat's dark eyes. Moments passed. "You could start by saying you're sorry, you son-of-a-bitch." It was almost a whisper.

Some of the players were returning and stood in shock around the poker table when they heard the strangers taunt of Neat. The tension rippled through the room. The piano player picked up the vibrations and stopped in mid-song. The whole saloon was eerily quiet. Neat suddenly realized that, for one of the few times in public, he was not armed. The atmosphere in the town had been so genial for several years that, on a night like this, gambling with friends, he felt safe. Now, he wasn't so secure. He could not detect the bulge of a sidearm on the young man. "And who are you, sir, and what should I be sorry for?"

The man leaned ever so slightly forward. "My name is Samuel, some call me Sammy. But you can call me *Mister* Boyer, you miserable, murdering piece of shit!" Neat heard the zing of metal on metal and realized that Boyer had unsheathed a stiletto from his belt. He caught the glitter of the blade in the man's hand. He lifted himself on the arms of the chair and kicked both feet into the man's midsection knocking him back several feet. Women in the crowd started screaming. Neat grabbed the chair and held it up as a shield.

Stefan made a grab for Boyer but the young man slashed the blade toward his face and drove him back. He turned back to Neat. His voice went up an octave, "You killed my father, you son-of-a-bitch. I swore I'd never forgive or forget. You've never paid for that but you will now." He grabbed a chair leg and tugged it forward. The move caught Neat off balance. He lost control of the chair and fell against the wall. Boyer lunged for him with the stiletto thrust forward like a small sword. Neat cringed sideways as the blade ripped through the cloth of his jacket. It passed under his left armpit and nicked his side. With his right hand, Neat pulled one of the kerosene lamps off the wall and smashed it into Boyer's head. The glass lantern shattered into the man's left temple. Oil splashed out of the lamp and suddenly exploded into flames. Boyer screamed and fell backward, his head and left shoulder ablaze. Several men threw coats on him and eventually managed to stifle the flames but the horrible damage had been done.

❦   ❦   ❦

"Damn, Neat. You just can't keep yoself outta trouble, can you?" Henry Gilmore's six-foot three-inch frame, topped by a ten-gallon hat, towered over the crowd in the saloon. Drinks had been set up 'on the house' in order to calm the nerves of the crowd after the carnage.

Gilmore was no longer high sheriff, the new administration was not quite that liberal-minded yet; but he had been named chief deputy for the Donaldsonville office. It was his reward in consideration of the warm relations he had maintained during the transition period as the reconstructionists pulled out. "What the hell you want me to do, Henry?" Neat held up his jacket with the armpit ripped out. He showed him the streak of blood down the side of his shirt. "The crazy bastard was gonna stick me like a pig."

"I don't guess you coulda just hit him with a chair or something. No. You gotta 'most kill him. Doc Branson said he never seen such a mess. The whole left side of his head and face is cooked. He's gonna lose that left eye. They ain't no ear on that side anymore and besides, he lost a lot of blood. Doc say he gonna ship him down to New Orleans in the morning. He done asked me if one of my guys can go down with him. Doc say he can't handle a case this bad. I'm sending Adam with him."

"Well, he shoulda knowd better than to come after me with that pig sticker. He talk to anybody 'bout how he got here or what his plans were?"

Waldo Johnson piped up from the back of the crowd. "I had a couple of drinks with him this afternoon. He was buyin'. Said he had been traveling a couple of weeks down from Pennsylvania. Got in this morning and picked up a horse over at Stanley's stable. Said he used to live around here and wanted to go see where he and his family used to live. Then he said he had some unfinished business he had promised his mama he'd take care of."

Gilmore glared at Neat, "You know who he is, don't you? That's the Boyer's little boy all grown up and still mad as Hades. He sure knows how to carry a grudge."

Neat snorted. "I hope he knows his business is finished around here now. I should have killed the son-of-a-bitch. I done been tried and acquitted. He's got no right to be coming after me like that. You got any more questions for me, Henry? I'm tired. Need to get to bed."

Gilmore removed his hat and scratched his already salt and peppered short hair, "Naw, guess I ain't got no more questions, Neat. Guess you done gone and committed self-defense again." He tipped his hat and turned away, "You be careful now."

XXVIII
April 1887

The terribly scarred figure went about his chores on the second floor of the hospital. His mop circled and sloshed the floor as he worked his way through the corridor and through the endless day. This one had started before dawn as he awoke, in pain as usual, in his tiny room in the shed behind the medical facility.

His daily ritual started as he carefully removed the petrolatum-infused bandages from his head and face, dipped a rag in the washbasin in the corner and did a perfunctory washing of the unscarred right side of his face and over his body. Dressing in his shapeless clothing, he donned a floppy black hat that effectively hid most of the burned flesh on the left side of his head that was now almost totally healed but still extremely sensitive to the touch and to changes in temperature. The scar tissue covered the entire left side of his head and face. It was taut and multi-colored. He put the patch over his left eye and looped the string over the back of his head. He was ready for another tedious day at Touro Infirmary in the now-deformed life of Samuel Boyer.

It would be hard for Boyer to acknowledge, and most people would be surprised to know it, but he had received some of the finest medical treatment available anywhere in the United States at the New Orleans hospital. The facility had matured swiftly after its founding as the Hebrew Hospital of New Orleans in 1852. Judah Touro, one of the leaders of the close-knit Jewish community was the funding and guiding force in establishing the facility. He crafted the mission statement that called it "a charitable institution for the relief of the indigent sick."

During the war, some of the most talented physicians, surgeons and support technicians in the south, and indeed, from the nation, practiced their skills in the small but rapidly expanding hospital. The horrors of war exacerbated the need for and development of new surgical and treatment techniques.

One such treatment for burns was the use of a relatively new substance derived from oil. Its discoverer, Robert Chesebrough, had heard of drilling rig operators using a nuisance residue that collected on their machinery as a healing substance for various disorders of the skin, including burns. By 1859, through experimentation at his lab in Brooklyn, Chesebrough distilled enough of the substance to prove its amazing healing powers. Variations of the substance were used with great success at clinics, hospitals and on the battlefields of the war. With the confusion and pressures of the times, Chesebrough didn't get around to applying for a patent on his discovery until 1872. It found great popularity in a variety of uses from friction reduction to treatment of severe abrasions and burns. Petrolatum later was renamed to the more consumer-appealing petroleum jelly. Even later it became more commonly called by one of its brand names, Vaseline.

The doctors and staff at Touro were a hardy and battle-tested breed. They had seen the ravaged bodies of war victims, the brutally injured targets of street violence, the inhuman results of negligence, starvation and abuse. Still, the arrival of Samuel Boyer in August of 1886 was a day many would not forget.

A wire had been received that a badly burned patient would be arriving from Donaldsonville accompanied by a deputy sheriff. A request was made for transportation to the infirmary since the victim would either be unconscious or delirious upon arrival.

Not only was Samuel delirious, he was suffering such incredible pain that two male nurses and the deputy fought for fifteen minutes to restrain him long enough to strap him down tightly to a gurney. The hoarse, agonized screams of the man had ripped through the packet on most of the trip downriver to New Orleans and continued through the streets of the French Quarter and into the hospital.

It took every iota of patience, expertise and experimentation to finally calm the patient enough for doctors to drug him into unconsciousness and begin treatment. He would, mercifully, remain in that semi-comatose state for over six weeks.

The practice of skin grafting in burn cases was still a relatively new procedure in the United States. Even with their combined expertise, the staff of Touro had not yet mastered the procedures. Instead they chose the more conventional methods of dead skin removal and constant saturation with petrolatum. The damaged eye was removed to prevent infection.

In the ensuing months, other than the massive disfigurement, Samuel recovered more and more of his normal functions. It was obvious, however, that his mental state was highly questionable. Some of the doctors were at odds for the reason for this. Most assumed it was a temporary condition brought about by the extreme trauma of his injuries. Some, however, feared that the use of massive pain-killing drugs and extreme treatment methods could have caused permanent brain impairment.

Whatever the reasons, Boyer seldom spoke. When he did it was only with the barest amount of words. He gave his name and little else. The hospital administrators had decided several months ago that they couldn't turn him loose on the street. He couldn't, or wouldn't give them the names of any family members or even his place of birth. So they assigned menial tasks that he could do while continuing his treatments. He went about his chores at the hospital, took his meals alone in his tiny room and, to the relief of most of the staff, kept to himself at all times. Soon, Samuel Boyer was just a shadow in the halls of Touro. He was another piece of furniture. No one paid much attention to him or hardly noticed his almost constant presence in the halls.

Boyer's mental condition was undoubtedly altered by the catastrophe but it wasn't necessarily diminished. If anything, his hatred and anger seethed even more. He soon was beginning to plan his return for his revenge on Antoine Galvez. Now, however, the vengeance would be two fold. Galvez would pay not only for murdering his father but also for the irreparable damage he had wreaked on Samuel.

After four years in his almost invisible existence at the hospital, Samuel was about ready to set out again on his quest. He no longer had any money of his own nor access to earning any. During the years he had found that he could very cautiously and carefully steal small amounts of cash from the wards, patients' rooms and the doctors' and nurses' dressing rooms without detection. The key was patience and restraint. The amounts had to be very small. He could not afford to be greedy. Time would reward him. He kept the cash hidden in his cell. No one ever visited that space. No one dared.

By the end of 1890, his stash totaled over two hundred dollars, a very healthy sum. In one of his few trips away from the hospital, he had visited a pawnshop on Conti Street and purchased a beautifully crafted knife known as a Bowie Knife. Such knives were named for the famous frontiersman Jim Bowie who had carved a wooden model of the knife he wanted made by a master blacksmith in Arkansas. The overall length of the knife was about fifteen inches with a blade almost ten inches long. The blade was two inches wide. The cutting edge was easily honed to razor sharpness and the top of the blade was sharpened for the front four inches. Boyer also purchased a honing stone so that he could keep the knife at scalpel sharpness.

Samuel left Touro Infirmary on January 1st, 1891. He just took his few belongings and walked away. He wasn't missed for several days. When inquiries were made about his whereabouts among the staff no one knew where he might have gone. Most could not remember the last time they had seen him. The unspoken emotion was, "Poor fellow, good riddance."

XXIX
November 7th, 1958

"Jeez, Paw Paw, that's incredible. Did he live, have you ever seen him again?" Randy asked.

"Oh, yea. The bastard lived. He wasn't very pretty, but he lived. I gotta give it to him, he was a determined little cuss. He came back at me again. Even with all the scars and problems he must have had, he really hated me."

"Damn," Randy was in awe. "When did he come back? Oh, wait a minute, let me get the tape turned over. I've run out on this side."

While he was resetting the tape he heard the crunch of gravel as his father's car rolled up the drive. "Uh oh, Gramps, we got problems. My mother can't know about what we've been talking about or I'll be barred from ever talking to you in private for the rest of both of our lives." Randy wasn't sure the old man fully understood the problem. "Let's start talking about something else. What about that zephyr you told me about? What was that?"

He got the tape rolling just as Tess and Louis came to the door of the porch. Randy held a finger to his lips to indicate that he needed quiet and Neat, right on cue, said, "Yep, that was a night. I was in Baton Rouge that time. Had me a room at the boarding house on North Boulevard down by Front Street right across from the State Capitol building. That was a nice little place. Little stable in the back for the horses. Four or five rooms on the top floor and two on the bottom with the owners' rooms, a kitchen and a eating room. I liked it. Stayed there ever time I was in that town. I had rode all the way up to St. Francisville and back that day. Left at the crack of dawn and didn't get back 'til after sundown. I was burned out, plum tuckered. They had a good meal of white beans and pork sausage with rice and I got to bed early after taking care of my horse. I was gonna head for home the next day."

Tess and Louis got interested in the story and quietly moved out on the porch and sat down to listen.

"Then, by damn, I'm sound asleep when the whole sky lights up. Lightning striking and thunder banging and a sound like the biggest train I ever done heard. Now, we was right across from the train station but they was never no trains at that time of night or morning or whenever it was. It was still dark, 'cept for the lightning. I'd heard about 'em but never seen or heard one. They calls 'em zephyrs. This thing just roared on for a long time then seemed to go on north and east of the boarding house.

"I get up and pull on some trousers and go downstairs. Everybody in the place is up. They was all down in the kitchen and everybody was talking at the same time. 'What the hell was all that?' I says.

"Old man Bunker who owns the place is still in his nightgown carrying a kerosene lantern. 'You know what I think?' He says, 'I think that was a tornado. I heard about 'em but never came close to one, thank God. They calls 'em twisters, too. Everybody all right?'

"I says, I calls 'em zephyrs. We was all in one piece so I go round back and check on Pretty Lady, that was my horse then. She was a little spooked and wide-eyed but fine so I went on back to bed. The next morning we was havin' breakfast when an old man came in and started telling us about some people being killed and hurt by that there zephyr and about it tearing up the prison out east, way out of town. I decided to go see for myself. Figured I'd take a look before headin' home."

Tess leaned over to Louis and whispered, "I'm going to start supper."

Louis got up with her. "I'm gonna go get a bath. I done heard 'bout this zephyr thing since I was ten years old." They both went back into the house.

Neat watched them, turned back to Randy and the microphone and whispered, "It was when I got back that crazy, scarred-up son-of-a-bitch was waiting for me."

XXX
July 16th, 1891

The boarding house gang discussed the night's events and the old man's news over a breakfast of grits and eggs. Neat's curiosity got the best of him. His business in the Baton Rouge area completed, he intended to leave that morning, Thursday. He'd ride down the river road south for twenty miles or so then hop on a ferry to cross the Mississippi to Donaldsonville. But he couldn't pull himself away from the reported catastrophe of the overnight storm. He saddled Pretty Lady and rode up the hill heading east on North Boulevard. The imposing state capitol, designed like a medieval castle, loomed over him on the right. On the left was the new water works building with its seventy-five foot brick chimney and even taller metal standpipe.

The forty-four year old gothic capitol building had been through difficult times. The official site of the state capital had been moved in and out of Baton Rouge repeatedly. The occupation by Federal troops in 1862 forced a retreat of the state government offices first to Opelousas, then to Shreveport. The Union eventually declared New Orleans the capital. During the war, Union soldiers vandalized the building while using it as a barracks. They ended up gutting it and setting it on fire. It lay abandoned for seventeen years.

In 1877, when President Hayes cut his deal with the new Democratic state government, the decision was made to move the capital back to Baton Rouge from New Orleans. Funding was authorized for a major rebuilding project in 1879. The towers and cupolas were restored and huge, new cast iron turrets were installed atop the crenellated parapets.

The skies were still dark and threatening and a stiff breeze whipped over the muddy streets as Neat and Lady slowly moved into the Baton Rouge business section. Neat had heard about the big penitentiary east of town, but had never ventured out to it. When he got to the newly installed Confederate Monument with a statue of Johnny Reb on top, he pulled Lady to the left and headed north on Third Street.

The business district was buzzing. Men and women of both races were standing on the wooden sidewalk in front of the Verandah Hotel and Saloon. Neat slowed to pick up on the conversation. It was all about the death and destruction out east of town. He turned east on Florida Street. He could see a stream of carriages and horsemen going out and coming back from the prison.

On the corner of Church Street, that in later years he would know as North Fourth, he heard loud voices coming from a crowd gathered in front of the big Heroman building. It was a huge three-story structure with wrought iron railings encircling the second floor. It had recently been renovated for the Louisiana Institute for the Deaf and Blind. Some in the crowd were using sign language to convey the general gist of the news. A young man yelled up to several people standing on the second floor gallery, "There are dozens of them prisoners dead, I tell you! One whole wall of the building is collapsed. Their uniforms is everywhere!" Across the street, nuns and orphans stood in groups on the grounds of the Saint Joseph's Convent and Academy.

When Neat rounded the corner three blocks up on Saint Anthony Street (later North Seventh) he pulled Lady to a sudden halt. "Sacré coeur," he said aloud. The destruction on the penitentiary grounds was breathtaking. The prison building was a huge three-story rectangle with an open courtyard in the middle and a huge smoke stack towering over it. One entire corner of the building was ripped open, exposing the courtyard. Bricks, mortar and all manner of debris were strewn for hundreds of feet around the gaping hole. Ancient oak trees on the grounds were uprooted, branches and leaves covered every foot of the property.

But, what really caught Neat's attention were the black and white striped uniforms. They were everywhere, stuck to the sides of the building, plastering the nearby trees, lining the streets. *Where are all the bodies? He thought. Have they already picked them up? Mon Dieu, how many could there be? It looks like hundreds.*

Work crews were laboriously sifting through the havoc. Baton Rouge's population of about thirteen thousand had a ratio of sixty percent Negro. That was reflected in the makeup of the volunteers on the scene. Neat hitched Lady near the road and approached one man working feverishly to clear the rubble in the prison wall. "Can I help?" He said. Without a word, the Negro man reached down and handed him a flat-bladed shovel.

Neat started digging in. After a few minutes, sweat already pouring from his brow, he asked the man, "Did all these people die? Where are all the bodies? Their clothes are all over the place."

In spite of the situation, the man threw his head back and started laughing uncontrollably. Neat looked around with embarrassment. *What the hell was so funny?*

When the man finally caught his breathe, he looked solemnly at Neat and said, "They's was only a few prisoners killed. This here corner of the pen? Where the funnel cloud hit? It's the laundry! Those were just empty uniforms." He started laughing all over again.

Neat worked with the volunteers cleaning up the sight and repairing the damage as best they could through the day. Nuns from the convent brought the workers food for lunch and buckets of water. He hadn't worked this hard in years. At dusk the laborers started wandering back to town and Neat guided Lady back to Bunker's boarding house. He looked in the front door briefly to let Mr. Bunker know that he needed supper and a room for another night.

Then he walked Lady back to the stable. Bone tired, Neat unsaddled the young mare in the fading light, filled her trough with food and was wiping her down with the saddle blanket when he noticed the silhouette of a man standing at the opening to the stable. The first thing Neat thought was that the man was awfully overdressed for a night this hot. A long topcoat was draped over his shoulders and a big black hat with a soft, wide brim flopped down around his head.

Neat nodded to the man, "Howdy, mister. Ain't you hot in all them clothes?" There was no answer. Neat grew a bit uneasy. "Anything I can do for you?"

The figure took a couple of steps into the stable. The man was now standing at Lady's haunches. "I don't know," he said, "you might tell me where White Castle, Louisiana is. You see, I'm from Pennsylvania, but I've heard a lot about that little town." He took another step closer to Neat.

The hair on the back of Neat's neck stood on end. *That voice. There's something familiar about this man. And not very friendly. What is it?.* Neat stepped away from Lady's head toward the side of the stable. He knew there was a small shovel in the corner used for cleaning the area. *I knew I shoulda carried my goddamn Derringer. Just didn't think I'd be out this late today.*

"Now that's interesting. You're looking for White Castle? I just happen to be from around there. I can tell you exactly how to get there." Neat edged toward the corner of the stall.

"And you *just happen* to be Antoine Galvez aren't you, sir? Mr. Bunker said you'd be back here." Neat didn't answer. "Ah, I don't blame you for not admitting it." The stranger took another step closer. He was now blocking Neat's way out of the stable. Neat considered rolling under Lady to the other side of the stable but figured he'd still be jammed in the stall. The man suddenly shrugged the topcoat off his shoulders, flipped off his hat and whipped out a huge knife. "We also *just happen* to have unfinished business, sir," he hissed.

Even in the poor light, Neat cringed at the sight of the man's mangled face. The left eye was covered with a patch. The hair was long, stringy, oily and swept over his head from the right to partially cover the horrible, shining baldness of the left side. A stub of an ear protruded between the strands of hair. The whole left side of the face was a multi-colored, purplish and white scar.

"What's wrong, Antoine? You don't like your artwork? You did this, you miserable slime. First you killed my father in cold blood, then you scarred me for life." He choked in a sob. "You don't think you should die?"

Neat watched the movement of the knife. Samuel Boyer swept it back and forth, back and forth. It was as large as some knives used in butchering. *He's moved up a notch*, Neat thought. Neat knew it was what people were calling a "Bowie Knife," named after a legendary frontiersman who had lived in Opelousas and died some fifty years ago in San Antonio, Texas at a battle historians were calling, "The Alamo."

Boyer moved slowly closer. "I'm going to slice you apart you miserable scum." Neat was now trapped in the back corner of the stable. Lady continued to serenely enjoy her evening meal. Neat knew the shovel he now gripped in his left hand was too short to reach Boyer and that, if he swung, he would be exposed to the huge blade. He made a snap decision. He swung the shovel from behind his hip and walloped the side of Lady's head. The shovel rang with the force of the blow. Lady reacted as any animal would. She jerked away from the pain and lashed out with her hind legs first then reared up and thrashed the air with her forelegs. In the melee, the fifteen hundred pound horse's rear end crashed into Samuel Boyer. He was sent reeling into the side of the stable. Neat immediately pounced. He smashed the shovel over the top of the man's head, not once but twice. Neat grabbed the knife from a seemingly lifeless hand.

Lady's whole body was trembling. Neat tried to calm her but she jerked her bloody head away from him. Trying to catch his breath, Neat felt Boyer's neck for a pulse. He wasn't sure. He thought there was one but, *what the hell, who cares*. He stumbled to the front of the stable and looked around. Nothing was moving. He went back in and wrapped the inert body in the great coat, picked up the hat, put the knife in his belt and dragged the body out of the stable. Boyer was not a big man but Neat was handling dead weight. Working very carefully and quietly, it took him the better part of an hour to drag the body out of the stable, behind Bunker's place and the house next door, across Front Street, over the railroad tracks and up and over to the bottom of the levee. He threw the coat and hat over the body and staggered back to the stable.

Lady's bruised head was not as bad as it first appeared. Neat washed the wound and soothed the still-frightened animal. It would take her a while to get over the trauma of the attack. When he had taken care of Lady and straightened out the stable, he went up to his room and collapsed on the bed.

He slept fitfully and got up at dawn. He had paid his rent the night before so he just threw his clothes into a duffle bag, grabbed a biscuit and some coffee in the kitchen, saddled up Lady and headed out. He stopped when he reached the top of the levee and looked for the body. He stood in the stirrups to get a better view. A light fog was swirling at the water's edge. There was nothing in sight. He scanned up and down the levee as far as he could see but, other than clusters of debris, there was nothing. *Did somebody find him? Get him to a hospital? Police? An animal maybe? Time to go home, Neat. Henry was right, I gotta stop getting into this crap.*

XXXI
January 1898

New Orleans City Alderman Sidney Story had a brilliant idea. It wasn't totally original. The German and Dutch had established legal "Red Light" districts in their major ports years before for the purposes of controlling and limiting prostitution.

It was the age-old reasoning of "people are going to do it anyway, so let's legalize it so we can control it." That logic had been and would continue to be used for years in various efforts including the control and limiting of gambling.

A rotund, balding forty-five year old, Sidney was serving his second term. He had many friends who were "entertainers." That term stretched from musicians to jugglers, to saloonkeepers to prostitutes. Though Bertha, his wife of fifteen years, and her lady friends did not have the right to vote, they were very vocal in their protests of the prostitution industry flourishing in the French Quarter and spreading throughout the port waterfront.

Bertha confronted Sidney one October night in 1897, "Sidney, I don't question you when you're gone most of the night. I know you have duties to the people as alderman. But, I also know what is happening in the quarter. Now, don't you look at me like that. I know that you, all of you men, are weak when it comes to sins of the flesh." Sidney feigned shock and outrage. "Oh don't try to fool me. Bernadette and Virginia and I have been talking with a lot of other wives and we all feel that, since you're an alderman, you can make a name for yourself by introducing an ordinance making prostitution illegal."

Sidney gagged on the mouthful of hot, chicory-laced coffee he was sipping. "What are you talking about woman? Nobody can stop that kinda thing! That's like saying that going to the outhouse is illegal."

Sidney and Bertha argued over the concept for the better part of the morning. In the afternoon, on his regular rounds of the neighborhoods and bars, Sidney tentatively mentioned to his friend Bernard, "Do you know what Bertha and your wife Virginia have been talking about? They want me to propose an ordinance making prostitution illegal." Bernard starting laughing uproariously. Several men nearby, who had overheard the conversation, joined him.

"Great idea Sidney," Bernard managed to wheeze, "you didn't want to continue to be an alderman did you?" The men at the bar roared with laughter. And so the idea subsided. Sidney continued his surreptitious visits to his favorite prostitute at Mahogany Hall, a high-class brothel on Basin Street owned by Lulu White.

However Bertha Story was not to be denied. She and her friends started talking to others and the concept spread like a ripple in a pond. Soon the priests and preachers were agitating from the Sunday pulpits.

By December of 1897, many of the saloon keepers, who also were brothel and crib owners gathered in a secret meeting with Story and several other alderman. After many beers and other alcoholic beverages, Franklin Bercegeay stood and asked for quiet. "Listen well to what I say. The time is coming when such a thing as attempting to outlaw this natural act of man will happen. It's happened in other places. We can't afford to let it happen here. We must beat them to the punch. I propose that Alderman Story draft an ordinance doing exactly what the women and the preachers want. He will ban prostitution throughout the city and parish." The crowd of bar owners gasped. Bercegeay raised his hands for quiet. "Hold it now! Hear me out! Sidney will then acknowledge how difficult such a law will be to enforce. So brother Sidney will then wisely suggest, and the wives and preachers will have to agree, that this nasty business be limited to a small area here in the quarter where it can be controlled and regulated and not allowed to expand throughout the city." Bercegeay's suggestion was met with mixed emotions. "Listen to me," he shouted. "We will still have the businesses that we all now run and, and…listen to me, *and* we will have shut down any competition from spreading to any other areas." There was a loud "Aaaah." The attendees started gabbing among themselves as Story, Bercegeay and other leaders put their heads together. By the end of the evening a consensus was achieved.

Two weeks later a carefully worded ordinance, No. 13,032, was introduced. It absolutely forbade any and all prostitution in New Orleans outside of a tightly defined district just northwest of the French Quarter. It included twenty blocks bounded by Basin Street and Claiborne Avenue. St. Louis Cemetery

Number One anchored the northwest corner of the district. It became the only part of the entire United States to, in effect, legalize prostitution.

Sidney Story was hailed as a defender of morality and virtue. His wife, Bertha, was proud of his valiant efforts in spite of the fact that she truly wanted the entire practice of prostitution outlawed. At least her Sidney had isolated it to a relatively small section of the quarter where it could be controlled.

At first the area was simply known as "The District" but it wasn't long before someone had named it Storyville. In spite of Sidney's protests the name stuck.

New Orleans gift to the world, jazz music, migrated into Storyville, making the district even more famous. Establishments in Storyville ranged from cheap "cribs," rooms furnished with little more than a mattress where low-priced prostitutes turned tricks for as little as twenty-five cents, to more expensive houses. At the top of the scale was a row of elegant mansions along Basin Street for extremely well heeled and well-connected customers.

Many young women were virtually enslaved in Storyville. But they were not the only ones. Many young Negro men and indigent white men were used by the brothel owners to clean and maintain their facilities. They were cooks, waiters, maintenance men and bouncers, whatever the madams and pimps needed. Some of the younger boys were also used in bizarre sex rituals. Most of the males were beholden because of debts or because of various problems with the law. In many cases their choices were to work for the panderers or go to jail.

One of the more pitiful cases was Samuel Boyer. No one seemed to know where he had come from, nor did they care. Benjamin Moresi, a New Orleans policeman assigned to the district, quietly ran a white-slavery ring. He would find derelicts, have them booked, bail them out and sell them to the bordello owners. Some he would find already in jail under relatively minor charges but with no means of making bail. Moresi bailed them out for a pittance and then he owned them. Some he sold, others he rented out.

Boyer had been picked up on a Mississippi River wharf and held for vagrancy. He couldn't or wouldn't tell the police his name or where he had come from. Dockworkers surmised that he had stowed away on a steamer that had recently arrived from Baton Rouge. His face was grotesquely scarred and he was terribly emaciated. He said he had not eaten for at least a week. He spent several nights in jail ranting about being left for dead on the levee several years prior. At first Moresi decided the man was too bizarre and too weak to serve his purposes but, one of his clients was desperate to add another man to her clean-up crew. Samuel Boyer was sold to Lulu White of the infamous

Mahogany Hall. At least he was working for one of the most elaborate mansions in Storyville.

Samuel turned out to be a quick learner. He took to his new life surprisingly well. He was assigned to work with a large black man called Nebbie, short for Nebuchadnezzar. He and Nebbie were two of the brothel's clean-up crew that worked the prostitute's rooms. When a trick was finished and the couple left the room, the two would rush in, carry out the washbasin and empty, clean and refill it. They would remake the bed, change the linens if necessary and generally straighten things up in preparation for the next customer. For their work they got their meals, a cot to sleep in and a few coins a day left for them by the working girls.

The girls of Mahogany Hall were considered to be the best of the district, best looking, most experienced and most innovative. Many were natives of France. They specialized in novel sex practices considered off-limits by many of the other professionals and were anxious to fulfill any of their customer's unusual desires. Samuel found that there were several rooms in the big house that had peepholes in the walls. Several times a night he would sneak off from Nebbie and watch the action in amazement.

The Mahogany Hall women loved Samuel. Because of his gross appearance, they felt sorry for him and treated him with utmost kindness. Many of them went out of their way to spend time with him between customers, smiling and joking with him and sometimes holding his hand and caressing him.

The Madam, Lulu White, was not as impressed with him. She warned him several times not to fraternize with the women. One night she caught him peeping into one of the rooms and beat him severely with a walking cane.

Nine months after starting to work at the hall, Samuel's life collapsed again. He had become secretly enamored of a nineteen year-old prostitute who Lulu had personally trained. Myrtle was blonde, blue eyed and petite. Although she had been working at the trade for two years, she still had an aura of innocence and youth. She was especially nice to Samuel, giving him small gifts of chocolates or trinkets. He cherished her attention.

One of Sidney Story's fellow alderman, Henry Degeyter, was a frequent visitor to Mahogany Hall. Myrtle was his favorite. One Saturday night around midnight, Henry and his companions showed up in the downstairs parlor. The three men had been drinking heavily and were loud and unruly. Lulu rushed to the parlor to quiet them and suggested that she escort Henry to the second floor where he could meet with Myrtle.

When they arrived at the sitting room on the second floor, Lulu found that Myrtle was already occupied with another customer. Henry was enraged. It was if he had never thought that his sweet, innocent Myrtle was really a prostitute. Lulu could not calm him down. He was almost in tears, shouting down the hallway for Myrtle to come out and be with him. Lulu yelled for one of her bouncers to come upstairs. Meanwhile Samuel and Nebbie, hearing the commotion, ran into the room intending to help Lulu. She waved them off and continued trying to reason with Henry. After several minutes Myrtle came out of one of the rooms. She had a negligee over her shoulders and ran, barefoot down the hall to the raging Henry. At first he embraced her tightly and started weeping. Then he suddenly stepped back and hit Myrtle in the face with his fist. "You good for nothing bitch," he shouted "you've made a fool of me." Myrtle fell to the floor, her nose bleeding profusely.

Samuel exploded. He grabbed a poker from the front of the fireplace and slammed it over Henry's head. Blood and tissue splattered all over the room. Henry went down in a heap. Samuel hit him again before Nebbie grabbed him in a bear hug. For a moment there was absolute silence except for the sounds of jazz wafting from the ground floor parlor. Then Myrtle and several other women started screaming. The bouncer ran in just as Samuel attacked. He helped Nebbie subdue Samuel.

Lulu raced downstairs and sent one of her most trusted girls to find Officer Moresi.

It cost Lulu White a lot of money but it was worth it. Alderman Henry Degeyter's body was found the next morning three rows deep in the St. Louis Cemetery. Moresi's police report attributed his death to an assault and robbery. It was just another of the many that occurred in and around Storyville.

Samuel was whisked away by two of Moresi's men. He was held for several days in the New Orleans jail then sent, by order of a judge in Moresi's network, to the East Louisiana Mental Hospital in Jackson. He was adjudged to be criminally insane and locked away from society for more than half a century.

XXX
April 1950

Louisiana Governor Earl Long was not being magnanimous. He was not personally concerned with the well being of the inmates whose lives he was changing drastically. He was just trying to balance a budget. His economic advisors were unanimous in the prediction that the state's expenses would far exceed its income in this fiscal year. Under state law, that could not happen though it seemed to occur with maddening regularity. The governor was charged with the responsibility to balance the budget. Like those before him and those to come, he broke out the smoke and mirrors and began the process.

Considering the constituency that had elected him, he could not and would not reduce the state's welfare payments. For the same reason, he would not reduce the number of state employees in the highway department or the bloated charity hospital system. He would not turn his back on his base constituents, the poor and black voters, the state employees, the unions, the public school teachers and the rural electorate. It was these voters who still believed that any governor with the Long name, the martyred Huey or his brother Earl, were the best friends they ever had.

As a part of the cost-cutting part of the formula, the governor issued an executive order that did not get wide publicity. The mental hospitals in the state, in Pineville, Jackson and Mandeville would immediately commence a deep and all-encompassing review of every inmate or pending case. They were ordered to purge the rolls of patients who were: borderline, considered benign or judged to be improving enough to be considered for release in the next six months. Also targeted were those considered too old to continue to treat. When the review was completed, the patients found to fit the criteria would be released.

The numbers were expected to be in the hundreds. Many in the medical and psychological services communities were outraged. "It proves to me that this governor is himself mentally incompetent if he would prescribe such a scenario," said Doctor Owen Svenson, former dean of the Tulane University Medical Center.

In spite of the protests, inmates of the mental hospitals were being released daily. In some cases their families were elated, in most they were chagrined. Ruth Oberlin, interviewed by the Baton Rouge *State Times* newspaper, was described as, "weeping almost uncontrollably when advised that her brother, Bradley, was being released from the East Louisiana Mental Hospital in Jackson. 'He's not capable of living with us. We're not capable of handling him. He's violent. He crippled my father. What are we supposed to do with him?'"

The hospital administrators were doing everything they could to properly place the patients. Some families found private facilities; some took the drastic action of moving to other nearby states that still had adequate mental hospitals to handle the problem. In the case of the elderly inmates, there weren't many options. In most case there were no families to which they could return. Private individuals and charities were enlisted but it was a daunting task.

No one seemed to know the age of the scarred old veteran. He had been an inmate for most of his life and longer than most of the staff's service time. The records on his case were very scanty and incomplete. He had outlasted two hospitals and almost everyone connected with them. It was believed his name was Samuel Boyer. He had first been incarcerated around the turn of the century in Baton Rouge. The scrawled, faded writing in his folder said he had been committed by a New Orleans judge who labeled him criminally insane. The report said the burn scars and loss of his left eye preexisted his incarceration. He would offer no information on his previous life if, in fact, he had any memory of it.

It was learned that between 1891 and 1898 he had been arrested repeatedly for various misdemeanors and felonies in and around Baton Rouge and New Orleans. Boyer spent several years off and on in jails and the penitentiary in Baton Rouge before the New Orleans judge finally committed him. He was an embodiment of the forgotten inmate. Now in his eighties, Samuel had lived in the mental institutes over fifty years. As at Touro Infirmary in New Orleans, he had come to be a piece of the furniture, a nonentity who was only recognized during a headcount. He had been assigned chores through the years and, in most cases, had quite efficiently fulfilled his simple duties. Occasionally, his record related, he showed irrational temper tantrums and injured other inmates and guards in wild displays of anger. Such behavior had subsided over the years.

Now that the decree had come down that he and others like him would be released, the staff of the mental institute was determined to find adequate housing and care. In Samuel's case, his safe haven came in the form of an angel in the Baton Rouge community, a wealthy attorney, who volunteered to place and pay for the subsistence of two aging inmates. They would be housed in the YMCA on Fourth Street in downtown Baton Rouge. Several other patients, in the same category as Samuel, were also placed in the "Y" due to the philanthropy of other wealthy Baton Rouge citizens.

Totally disoriented, Samuel, his new roommate, seventy-two-year-old Horace Bateman, and the others were transported to the "Y". They were settled into fairly comfortable rooms on the second floor of the four-story structure. Fortunately, the building had recently been equipped with elevators.

The inmates were allowed reasonable access to most of the building's facilities with the exception of the indoor swimming pool in the basement. They were not allowed to leave the building except on supervised trips for shopping and sightseeing in the downtown area. Their days were spent playing cards and board games, reading newspapers or scanning magazines, listening to the radio and arguing about subjects that few of them knew anything about. None of the former inmates housed at the YMCA had family so they were totally dependent on staff, volunteers and themselves.

Samuel soon took new interest in his surroundings. He appeared to have a restored awareness of his situation. In truth, a dim memory had seeped up through the half century of confinement. He somehow knew that he had to find a man named Galvez. He realized that this man had caused all of the misery in his life. All of the horrific memories came flooding back: the shooting of his father, the long, sad trip back to Pennsylvania, the turmoil of his teen years, the murder of his friend George's brother-in-law in Philadelphia, the search for the worthless man named Galvez, the pain of the coal oil lamp bursting over his head, the years at Touro Infirmary, his escape to Baton Rouge, the awakening, half dead, on the levee. He lay awake at night remembering the period of time he had spent in Storyville and the satisfaction he had felt in killing the fat pig that had hit the pretty, young girl named Myrtle. For some reason, most of the years of confinement after that were a blur. He figured he had enough memories to sustain him. It was not worth the effort to try to add more.

He asked for writing materials and stamps. Intuitively, he wrote to newspaper reporters in Baton Rouge and New Orleans. He wrote that he was an old, lonely man with no family who was desperately seeking news or the where-abouts of a dear old friend. He didn't even know if his old friend was still alive. No one found it unusual that he was especially interested in any news of his older "friend" by the name of Galvez. He even wrote a letter and addressed it simply to: Antoine Galvez, White Castle, Louisiana. Even with that incomplete address, Neat received it but never showed it to anyone. It read:

> I am going to find you, you murdering
> bastard. You cannot live forever and I
> will find you before you die.
> You will pay for what you did to my father
> and you will pay for what you did to me.
> Look over your shoulder, I'm coming.
> If you have any guts, I'm waiting for you.
> I'm at the YMCA in Baton Rouge. I dare
> you to come and get me.

As before, Boyer embarked on a systematic scheme of stealing money from the other occupants of the YMCA. Stealing very insignificant amounts at a time, he practiced the patience and discipline he had learned in New Orleans. The inhabitants at the "Y" were, with the exception of Samuel and several other former mental inmates, a transient group. Most stayed only several days to a week. Once they were on their way they rarely returned. Therefore, Boyer shrewdly surmised, if they were on the road again leaving Baton Rouge before they realized that a small portion of their funds was missing they seldom took the trouble to come back. By carefully watching the comings and goings of the "Y"'s clients, he knew when to make his moves. Going about his assigned chores of emptying trash containers and cleaning the rooms, after several months, he had a significant amount of cash hidden in his room. He was care-ful not to use it openly or otherwise call attention to his modest stash.

As time wore on, Boyer's health actually improved. He loved to walk and eventually convinced the supervisors at the "Y" that he could be trusted to take long walks in the downtown Baton Rouge area without an escort. He especially enjoyed walking north on Fourth Street from the "Y" toward the magnificent Louisiana State Capitol building soaring twenty-seven stories up in an art deco design overlooking the downtown Baton Rouge district. He would always stop in the ancient St. Joseph's Church to light a votive candle and say a brief prayer.

He didn't recognize the irony that he was praying to a kind and forgiving God to help him find and kill Antoine Galvez.

He strolled through the gardens in front of the Capitol that Huey Long had commissioned to resemble the Gardens of Versailles. Always dressed in his long black coat and floppy hat, he soon became a familiar and thus, non-threatening figure on the streets. His mysterious-looking outfit still frightened young children but their parents always assured them that he was just a harm-less, if eccentric, old man.

The owner of the Capital City Pawn Shop on Third Street, Stan Taylor, had seen Samuel walking the downtown streets for months. Stan was a little sur-prised the day the old man stopped for the first time in front of the window display then came into the store. "How are you, my good man?" Boyer said as he entered. His voice was low and smoky, "Could an old man look around a bit at your wares?"

"Why certainly, sir. Take your time. Just let me know what I may help you with."

Boyer roamed around looking into the display cases that surrounded the room. He looked up into the wall cases. "Oh my," he said, looking down into one of the displays. "May I see that camera, there? I believe I owned one of those back in the thirties."

Stan was happy to open the case that held the bellows camera. "You don't see many like this anymore. I can let you have that at a really good price."

Samuel looked through the eyepiece of the camera, slid the bellows back and forth and opened the rear. "Gosh, I had a lot of fun with this old camera. Got some wonderful pictures of my wife, God rest her soul." He bit his lower lip for a moment then brightened as he looked back into the case, "Hold on, what is that? Is that an old Colt thirty-two revolver? Oh, my God, I haven't seen one of those in years. Could I see it, please?"

"Yessir, that's the one they called the Single Action Army, it's actually a Model 1570. Got a seven-and-a-half-inch barrel. You don't see that much any-more except on target pistols." Taylor pulled the gun out of the case and handed it to the old man. He pulled his hand back reflexively when the man's hand brushed against his. Boyer still had his floppy hat on but in the course of their conversation, the shopkeeper had gotten a glimpse of his customer's glass eye and the hideous scarring. He was getting a little uncomfortable.

"Do you think this thing still works? I remember seeing one like this when I was just a kid, and that wasn't yesterday, you know? Not that I'd want to fire it or anything but it would be interesting to know if it still worked."

"Oh yea, it still fires. The original models go way back into the eighteen hundreds, but this piece is really not all that old, probably thirty years or so but it's been well taken care of. I took it out to the firing range with some of these other guns one day just to be able to assure anybody that buys one that they work. Can't hardly let you try it out in here, you know." He cut short a nervous laugh. "And, I have most of a box of bullets for it."

"Really, why that's quite amazing," Boyer said. "Damn, this would make a fine addition to my collection. I've collected old pistols all my life, you know. I'll have to look it up but I believe Colt started making this thing when I was just a tyke. That would be way back in about 1870 or so." He looked conspiratorially at Taylor, "Do you suppose an old man like me could afford this little piece of history?"

Stan opened up a ledger he had taken from the display case. "Well, let's see what I've got invested in that little beauty. Uh huh, took it in a little over a year ago." He flipped a few pages, "Owner never claimed it of course, gave him a fair price for it. Hmmm, I guess I can let you have it for thirty dollars. That's a real steal."

Boyer looked crestfallen, "Oh my, let me see, I don't believe I have quite enough money on me. No, I really couldn't pay quite that much. Oh dear, I did so want that little piece to add to my collection, but," he shrugged, "I guess I'll just have to pass it by. So sad." He started to hand the pistol back to Taylor.

"Well, hell, look, I want you to have it. You got twenty-five dollars? I'll throw in the box of bullets. Ain't no good to me without the pistol."

"Would you really? I do so appreciate that. I might be able to scrape together just enough. Thank you so much." Samuel reached into his pocket and started counting out bills. He only had singles. When he got to nineteen he reached in his other pockets and brought out a handful of change. He finally counted out twenty-four dollars and seventy-eight cents. He looked sadly at the owner and shrugged.

"Ah, what the hell, take it, it's yours," Stan said, pulling the bills and coins across the counter. He was anxious to be rid of the old codger as well as the old pistol. He had made him happy and he had made a sale, his only one of the day. He offered a limp hand to Boyer and wished him well.

❦   ❦   ❦

Several weeks later, Boyer's correspondence with the media paid off when a Baton Rouge reporter to whom he had been writing for several years noticed an article in an area paper about a one-hundred-year old gentleman named Galvez. He clipped the article and dropped it off at the YMCA that was just a half-block away from the offices of the Baton Rouge Morning Advocate and State-Times.

Samuel held the clipping in shaking hands. Antoine Galvez was celebrating his one-hundredth birthday. There was a party planned at the American Legion home in White Castle that Saturday. He clenched his fist and looked heavenward, "There is a God."

Boyer started recruiting everyone he knew at the Y that had a car. He finally cornered seventy-eight-year-old Roland Hebert. Roland was still in fairly good health and had a relatively late model, drivable automobile his daughter had given him when he was released from the mental hospital.

Boyer invested two hours methodically losing checker games to Roland. He wanted him in a really good mood. Finally, with his adversary yawning and obviously ready for bed, he said, "Roland, my good friend, you can do me the greatest favor of my life." Hebert was wary. "My dearest friend in all the world is having his one-hundredth birthday party this weekend in White Castle. Can you believe that? One-hundred-years old! I've got to be there. Would you be so kind to drive me to the party? It's only a few miles down river from here. I'll pay all the gas, the ferry fees and buy you a nice meal on the way home. Would you please? Please?"

It took more cajoling, more stroking and the promise to play a lot more checker games with him before Roland finally agreed.

XXXIII
November 8ᵗʰ, 1958

"Is that old coot still hanging around down here?" Neat rasped.

Randy's wife, Paula, seated in the back of their second-hand, white Plymouth sedan, shushed him, "Paw Paw, he'll hear you. Randy, roll his window up before 'The Prophet' hears him and gets mad. You know how he can rant and rave when he gets started." Their three-year-old daughter, Nancy, had her nose pressed against the window staring wide-eyed at the tall, gaunt, middle-aged Negro standing on the side of the road.

Randy was driving his small family and Neat to White Castle for the birthday celebration. His parents had gone down earlier to help prepare the hall, lay out food and ice down cold drinks and beer. Neat was sitting on the passenger side of the front seat.

They parked on the ramp and waited for the ferryboat that would take them from Baton Rouge across to Port Allen on the west side of the river. "The Prophet," who's given name was George West, had become a fixture at the riverbank for several years. Wearing a once-white robe, a soiled white skull cap and carrying a hoe-handle he called a "staff," the man had labeled himself, "The Messiah of Jesus." He also carried a bucket of water and a well-worn Bible.

He preached to the occupants of the cars waiting for the ferries. He preached to the pedestrian traffic waiting on the floating dock. He preached to the sky, he preached to the water. He offered redemption through immersion baptism. Randy, nor anyone he knew, had ever seen him or even heard of him baptizing anyone, but he was always there with his bucket, just in case.

Once they got on board and started the twenty minute crossing, Paula and Nancy went upstairs to the passenger deck of "The City of Baton Rouge" for a better view of the voyage. They both loved riding the ferry. The chugging and hissing of the huge steam engine driving the rear paddle wheel was hypnotic.

Randy used the time to continue his interrogation of Neat. The old man was in a talkative mood and obviously a bit energized about the upcoming gathering.

"When my mama died, that was about a month after that zephyr thing in Baton Rouge, my two old maid sisters figured they'd move to Beaumont to live with my other sister. She'd lost her husband in a boating accident, poor thing. My other sister died in childbirth early on. So, I sold their little farm. I divvied up the money with my sisters and used my share to close the deal on the farm I had paid down on a couple of years before. That's the one I told you about that was back of White Castle. It was thirty-three arpents then. Already had some cane on it and I added to it every time one of my neighbors died or wanted to sell out 'til I ended up with nearly ninety arpents."

"I forget, Paw Paw, how big's an arpent? What would ninety arpents be in acres?"

"They tell me that was right at seventy-five acres, least that's what I ended up turning over to my son, Edgar. That boy made out like an outlaw. Got out of going to that big war 'cause he claimed he was farming my land. He was considered 'vital' or something or other. Then, a couple of years ago, damned if they didn't drill a well and up comes oil or gas or somethin' down on the southwest corner. Hear tell he's got more money than Rockefeller. Wouldn't know it by me. He ain't saying nothin'. Wouldn't give me or his brothers and sisters a dime of it. Says he 'earned it.' Bull shit. One of my smart mouthed daughters said I should had some rights to minerals or something. Hell, I don't know. What's a mineral? Ain't that water?"

"Naw, don't worry about it, Paw Paw. So you got married in about, what, 1894?"

"Yea, it was 'bout time to settle down. I was thirty-six. Like I said, Marie was a decent gal. Her family was antsy for her to get married being over twenty-five and all. Not bad looking, blonde, blue eyes but," Neat looked around furtively and whispered, "nothing like Amanda. That there was a beauty." He smiled and with both hands traced the silhouette of a small-waisted woman. Then he fell silent for several minutes. The ferry was completing its arc across the river and slowing for the docking in Port Allen.

Paula and Nancy came tripping down the stairs and back into the car.

The long, straight road from Port Allen to Plaquemine was lined with twenty-five-year-old live oak trees planted about a hundred-fifty feet apart.

Many called them "The Huey Long Oaks." The legendary populist governor had made a point of claiming that he had paved or graveled every road in the state and had planted rows of oaks on many of them. On hearing of Long's assassination in 1935, Neat, then seventy-seven years old, remembered the governor as a "goddamned outlaw…but a good outlaw."

During the ride, Neat continued to answer Randy's endless questions. They talked about the difficulty of farming in the unmechanized years when mules and humans were the only sources of power. They talked about the birthing of the children. All were born in the front bedroom of the wood framed farmhouse. Neat related in a sorrowful voice that the house had never really been finished. "By the time we put up the cistern, built the two-hole outhouse and the barn, I just couldn't afford to put up a lot of the walls on the inside. 'Course we could always use the exposed studs as little shelves."

"Randy had always wondered why his grandparents home had few interior walls. He and his family had spent the night there a couple of times. He had considered it an adventure. Other than the big bedroom where the parents slept, only the kitchen and parlor had interior walls. The rest of the rooms had exposed framing. Naturally, there was no inside plumbing. A washbasin in each bedroom was filled during the evening hours for cursory washing before bedtime and in the morning. A pot, commonly and not very tastefully called a "slop jar," was emptied during the day and placed under the bed for nocturnal excrements. Other calls of nature were made at the two-hole outhouse, across the chicken yard. It was amply supplied with Sear's catalogs and other available paper.

The water to the kitchen came from the story-and-a half high cistern that trapped rainwater from the roof. The kitchen included a large wood-burning stove and oven, a tin basin and a couple of waist-high tables. A pot-bellied, wood-burning stove was placed in a corner of the parlor and vented through the wall.

Randy would like to have spent more time at the old farm. Living in Baton Rouge seemed a century removed from the old place. He enjoyed feeding the chickens and "slopping" the hogs. Other than the odor, he even got a kick out of using the outhouse. The old, lethargic mules let him run his hand down their sides and across their broad brows. He walked through the rows of sugar cane that started just behind the farm house yard. There was a spur rail track used to pick up the cane during the cutting season that led through a wooded area and across a trestle over a small slough. For a boy who had grown up in

Baton Rouge, it was almost like stepping through a looking glass. He was always on the lookout for a white rabbit.

Randy had researched the period of Neat's life around the turn of the century and was fascinated by how quickly the freed Negroes were disenfranchised by the newly empowered, all-powerful Democratic elected officials. As they sped along the road to White Castle, he asked Neat if he was aware that there were 145,000 black voters in the state in 1896 and by 1904 new literacy tests and other qualifications had reduced that to only 1500. The old man looked at him strangely. He didn't answer but he thought, *Why the hell would I know anything about that? I couldn't vote either. Never tried. I knew they had them tests to see if you'd gone to school or could read or whatever. Besides, why would I give a rat's ass if a niggra couldn't vote? I was the same as them. Pretty damn dark and with no learning. Only difference was, they shoulda all been back working the fields like I was, far as I was concerned.*

Randy persisted with his historic quiz. "Ever play the Louisiana Lottery, Paw Paw? You know, the one being operated back around 1890 or so?"

"Yea, I tried buying a few tickets now and then but I never had enough money where I could figure I could afford to lose it. I knew I had a better chance playing poker. Now, I won me some money doing that."

"From what I read not many people won anything in the lottery, that's for sure," Randy said. "Matter of fact in twenty-six years of operation the lottery never paid the top prize one time. Not once! And they were pulling in twenty to thirty million dollars a year. Man, that was really big money back then."

Neat nodded agreement. He couldn't even fathom what a million dollars was in those days, or now for that matter. He started talking about how tough it had been to make any money with the farm and with having nine children to raise. "Raised most of our own food, meat and vegetables," he remembered. "Marie made all the clothes by hand." He reminisced that they had never had modern plumbing in his house. Through the World War Two years, and several years beyond, they still used the old two-hole outhouse and still drank rainwater collected from the cistern at the side of the house. "Now my son Edgar, he built a big ole brick house right next to mine. He had everything modern over there. Something that heated water before it came out of the tap. Didn't have to pump nothin', just turn it on. I mean that was some house. It had everything."

Neat proudly related that, in spite of living near poverty at times, he always took good care of his family, providing them with adequate food and clothing. Marie kept a good house, was a good cook and seamstress and all they asked of their children as they grew up was a good day's work in the fields or around the house and respect for their elders. He worked hard and Marie never questioned him when he left the farm every Saturday afternoon for an evening of poker with the men in town. It was almost a tradition with the Galvez men. Randy's father, Louis, still spent every Saturday afternoon at the American Legion Home in Baton Rouge in a game of low-stakes poker.

It was one o'clock in the afternoon when they arrived at the little American Legion Hall in White Castle. A dozen or so cars were already parked in the small parking lot. Tess and Larry and several other of Neat's children and their families were putting the finishing touches on the food table. Everybody broke into spontaneous applause as Neat shuffled through the front door.

They placed him in a comfortable stuffed chair in the center of the back of the room. Louis declared it "The seat of honor." Tess helped him with a chicken salad sandwich and lemonade sipped through a straw as guests started arriving.

The event was scheduled from one-thirty to four. Two and a half hours would be about all Neat and some of his older friends and relatives could take. People brought greeting cards, small token gifts, old photos, newspaper clippings and memorabilia of all kinds. Neat sat gazing through his glasses, more or less acknowledging each of them as they filed past.

"Doesn't he look wonderful?"

No, I look like a wrinkled-up old piece of shit.

"He hasn't changed a bit."

Goddamn, you mean I always looked this old?

"Hi, grandpa, remember when I used to sit on your lap?"

Who the hell are you? Got nice legs. Wanta sit on my lap again?

"You're looking good, young man!"

There's something wrong with your eyes, you old fart.

"You're going to live another hundred years, you old coot!"

And you're gonna die before you're sixty, you little shit.

Hell, I don't know any of these people 'cept my kids. They just all here out of curiosity. What's a hunnerd-year old man look like? Can he walk? Can he talk? Can he hear? Can he see? Can he screw? Come see the freak.

Around three, one of Edgar's teen-aged sons tapped repeatedly on a glass to get the attention of the crowd. As things quieted he welcomed everyone. He held a piece of notepaper in his shaking hand and started introducing the immediate family. The crowd politely applauded as each was introduced. Then the young emcee introduced his fourteen year-old sister who, he read from his notes, had recently won a speech contest at White Castle High School and had written a speech in honor of grandpa Neat for this occasion.

The petite, dark young lady was dressed in what probably had been her confirmation dress. Her coal-black hair framed a round face accented by full eyebrows that met in the middle. There was a dark fuzz beginning to develop on her upper lip. She stepped to the front, straightened the hem of her dress, cleared her throat and loudly read from her script, "This is your life, Antoine 'Neat' Galvez." After ten minutes of pedantic reading, the crowd began shuffling their feet and whispering. Some near the entrance quietly slipped out. She went on, "Then came a mighty event across the broad Atlantic Ocean. It was called 'The war to end all wars.' No one knew then that it was World War One for World War Two was still many years down Neat Galvez's halls of history."

Neat shifted uneasily in his chair. He squinted over his steel rimmed glasses at the girl. *Who the hell wound her up? Damn, I gotta pee.*

"Thirty-six men served as governor of the great state of Louisiana during his lifetime." *Yep, and only about three of'em was worth shooting. Matter of fact two of those got away. We only shot Huey.*

"Twenty great men have held the office of President of the United States since grandpa Neat was born." *The onliest one ever did anything for me was that Rutherford Hayes, far as I'm concerned.*

"He saw the first automobiles, the first airplanes, the first..."

Hell, I remember when I saw my first indoor toilet and, come to think of it, I really got to pee, now! Neat saw Randy standing a few feet to the left of his chair. "Hey, Randy." It was louder than he thought. The girl stopped reading and all eyes went to Neat. He looked around with agitation. "Well, damn it, a man's gotta piss sometime," he croaked. The crowd roared. Randy helped him out of the chair and toward the back of the room to the hall leading to the restrooms. As Neat passed the young orator, he whispered, "You just keep on reading while I do my business. I won't miss anything, I already know the story." She kept on reading.

The crowd was beginning to thin by three forty-five. The speeches and accolades were over. Cake and punch and cold drinks and beer had been served. Mercifully, the organizers did not try to put one hundred candles on the cake. One big one was symbolic enough. In spite of himself, Neat was beginning to doze off amid the buzz of the crowd. His head nodded, waking him from a brief snooze. As his eyes blinked open he saw a hauntingly familiar silhouette moving slowly toward him. It was a man with long, stringy hair dangling from below a large floppy hat. He was wearing a knee-length, old-fashioned frock coat and had one hand stuck in a front pocket. Judging from his posture and his short steps and gait, he had to be the second oldest person in the room.

Is this a dream? Neat looked around at the people nearest his chair. No one was paying any attention to him. They were talking, eating and drinking. *Oh, mon Dieu, this must be a dream. That couldn't be him. That old son-of-a-bitch can't still be alive. He can't still hate me.*

Neat was frozen with terror. He tried to cry out but no sound came. He tried to lift himself out of the chair but couldn't. The man was now directly in front of him. His age-bent posture brought him almost face to face with the seated Neat. He lifted the brim of his hat with his left hand as he slowly drew a long-barreled revolver from his coat with his right. "Left me for dead, didn't you, you miserable piece of shit?" The man grunted through clenched false teeth. His breath smelled like putrid fish. "Killed my daddy, tried to kill me twice. You don't know what I've been through waiting to find you again. You made my life a misery. Told you I'd find you. I swore I'd get you, you rotten old bastard and now I will." Boyer was gasping for breath. "You think you're gonna live forever? Well, I'm not going anywhere 'til you're gone." He pointed the pistol at Neat's chest. "They said I was crazy. Well, I'm just crazy enough to kill your sorry ass." The withered old hand holding the weapon was shaking wildly. He tried to stabilize the gun with his left hand and was squeezing with all his might to pull the trigger.

Two of Neat's six-year-old great-grandchildren came tearing through the crowd. The boy in the lead was waving a toy pistol over his head and looking back over his shoulder. The chaser was yelling, "Give me that. That's mine." They both ran full speed into Samuel Boyer just as he succeeded in firing the gun. Boyer, the Colt revolver and the boys went sprawling on the floor. There was a split second of silence, then pandemonium. Most of the crowd ducked to the floor with the sound of the gunshot. Many went screaming for the exits. Several of the young men grabbed the two scared boys and a couple others bent over the strange man now lying across Neat's feet. At first, no one looked at Neat.

Plaquemine Times reporter Bob Hudson was across the room sipping a beer and trying to impress a pretty young woman with his tales of journalistic prowess when he heard the firecracker-like pop. He looked across the room and saw the commotion. People were dropping to the floor or cringing behind chairs and tables in fear. He immediately realized that Neat was slumped back in the big chair provided for the honoree and a pile resembling black rubbish was draped over his feet.

Hudson grabbed his twin reflex, Rolleiflex camera off the table at his side and raced across the room bumping into and bouncing off people running in the opposite direction. He got to the scene just as a couple of men rolled the mound of ragged black clothing over to reveal the form of an emaciated old man. The floppy black hat covered the face and head, but Bob and the others noticed the withered hand holding an ancient, long-barreled revolver. A wisp of smoke escaped from the end of the barrel. Bob started shooting film as fast as he could aim, focusing and cranking forward to the next frame.

Edgar carefully picked up the pistol, "Would you look at this? That old fool just fired this thing." Suddenly looking at Neat, Edgar realized the old man was unconscious, slumped in the chair with a small trickle of blood beginning to stain the right side of his white shirt. Edgar shouted, "Get a doctor, call an ambulance! My Paw's been shot."

One of the crowd of family members was a doctor practicing in Norco, Louisiana. He pushed his way through the crowd and quickly confirmed that Neat had been shot. "Let's get him out of that chair. Put him on that table. Ladies! Clear that table off for us right quick, please." Several men gingerly lifted Neat's frail body out of the chair.

Meanwhile old Ruth Fontenot, a White Castle native and a friend of the family for years was morbidly drawn to the figure on the floor. She carefully pulled the hat away from the man's head. An audible gasp escaped the crowd gathered around. It was almost like looking at a fleshless skull. A woman fainted and children ran to hide behind their nearest parent. Another of Neat's relatives, a registered nurse from Lutcher, held her fingers under the jaw line for several seconds and said, "I'm sure he's dead" The badly mutilated left side of the assailant's face lay exposed, the glass eye glaring into the ceiling. The long greasy hair had fallen away from the skull revealing the glossy, mottled burn area with the stub of an ear protruding.

Bob Hudson kept pointing, shooting and cranking until he ran out of film. He jammed his hand into his jacket pocket and cursed when he realized he had not brought an extra roll. Who would have thought something like this would occur. He started asking anyone who would listen if they knew whom the assailant was. No one seemed to recognize the grotesque figure. Finally, Neat's youngest son, fifty-three-year-old Edgar, whispered, "That's gotta be that

Boyer fella. His name's Samuel. Paw thought he was dead or in prison or an asylum somewhere. He's been trying to kill the old man for over eighty years."

While the doctor tended to Neat, men and women were crying and comforting each other. They gathered their families together and prayed. Edgar's preliminary identification of the black-clothed body whispered its way around the great hall.

Hearing the name Boyer lit up a memory in Hudson's news-oriented brain. He could hear Neat's voice at the end of his interview, *"I wonder if that Boyer kid is gonna make it to the party. He's been following me around off and on for damn near eighty years. Probably not even still alive. He'd be getting pretty old by now, somewhere in his '90's. Not many of us live to be that old. Wonder if he ever got his face fixed. Damn shame what happened to his daddy. But, hell, I couldn't help it."*

Bob knew he was on to something other than just a shooting. This was the shooting of a one-hundred-year old man, on his birthday, for God's sake, by a man almost as old. Why? He couldn't make the connection between the two. He knew there was a story here but didn't know exactly what it was. Edgar was pulled away by his weeping wife and kids and was off with them in a corner of the room. Bob looked around to find an ally. Tess was standing between him and Neat's outstretched body now lying on a table. The look in her eyes said, "No more pictures. No more interviews."

As the ambulance wailed to a stop outside the hall, Hudson saw Randy Galvez standing at the foot of the steps. Randy had once worked at a small "one-lung" radio station in White Castle. They had met briefly when Hudson was reporting on a murder-suicide in Brusly that Randy was also covering. Bob had not realized the family connection until now. He knew Randy was now with a big Baton Rouge station and, thinking competitively, Bob was somewhat reluctant to approach him for information. But he had no choice.

"Hi. You're Randy Galvez, right?"

"Right." Randy saw the camera and notepad. "You're the guy that wrote that newspaper article about my grandfather. Hudson?" Bob nodded. "You did a nice job. Man, this is terrible. I can't believe what happened."

"Yea. I'm sorry about your grandpa. He was a good old man, a good interview, too. Is he badly hurt?"

"Don't know yet. My cousin, the doctor, thinks the bullet might have lodged in his lung but he can't tell how much damage it did. It was an old, old gun."

"Any idea who the guy is that shot him?"

"Well," Randy looked around cautiously, "come over here." He walked around the corner of the building. "The family never liked to talk about it but I think that's a man by the name of Samuel Boyer. He's the son of, well, he could be the son of…Look, I shouldn't be telling you all this."

"Aw, come on, Randy. After something like this there ain't gonna be no more secrets. Besides, I got pictures and all and I'll eventually get the rest. And, look, you've got an exclusive for your radio station. Being a weekly, my paper won't print it 'til next Wednesday. 'Course I'm gonna feed AP with it but they probably won't use it 'til late tonight or early tomorrow. If they use it tonight, nobody'll know it 'cause there's that LSU football game on and they're going for the national championship, and tomorrow is Sunday and none of the radio stations use any real news on Sunday."

Randy kicked a rock out of the grass back onto the gravel parking lot. "Yea, you're right. But look, don't quote me. My mother would die. You got this on your own." He proceeded to tell Hudson the sketchy details that he knew: about a dozen years after the Civil War, when grandpa Neat was about seventeen, there was a gunfight, Neat killed a man who was the head of the area's reconstruction organization called the Freedmen's Bureau and seriously wounded another carpetbagger who was his top aide. The dead man had a wife and two kids. Neat hid out for a year or more back in the swamps. He finally came in and was tried and acquitted in the case.

"I just don't know much else. My mother wouldn't hear of any of us talking about the incident or asking grandpa questions. I got to talk with him about it for just a few minutes one time. I know he mentioned a couple of other things. He said the carpetbagger's family had moved back to Pennsylvania before the trial and that the son was about five years younger than him. And, now this was pretty slim, but he hinted that the son had stalked him off and on all his life, that he had come after him with a knife twice. The first time, Neat hit him with a kerosene lamp and scarred him up pretty bad. The second time he left him for dead on a levee in Baton Rouge. He heard later that he had lived but was pretty screwed up, took to drinking, been incarcerated for some misdemeanors and minor felonies around Baton Rouge. He said the last he had heard of him the 'old coot,' as he called him, was mentally deranged and committed to an asylum. Last time he talked about him he just said, 'good riddance'"

The sound of the ambulance siren split the air, startling both Randy and Bob. Randy said, "I've gotta get going. I think they're taking him to Our Lady of the Lake Hospital in Baton Rouge. I know the family will all be gathering there." He shook hands with Bob. "Remember, I never said a word." Randy took a couple of steps then turned back with a slight smile, "You know, the old man will really get a kick out of this. He's never been in a hospital in his life and now he's going to the one where his favorite outlaw, Huey Long, died."

Samuel Boyer was declared dead at the scene. The doctor gave the cause as simply "heart failure" until a more thorough examination could be made. He was believed to be well over ninety years old. The only identification he had was a tag with his name on it attached to the key to his room at the YMCA in Baton Rouge. In his pockets were a few one-dollar bills and some change and an ancient laminated daguerreotype photo of a round-faced, fair-haired man of about thirty. No one could determine how Boyer had made his way to White Castle and the American Legion Hall. Roland Hebert, the man who had driven him was too scared to acknowledge that he knew him. He left the hall as soon as he could, drove back to Baton Rouge and never again mentioned Boyer's name or acknowledged the fateful trip he had taken with him. Authorities were not able to find a living relative. He was buried in an indigent's grave in Iberville Parish.

Bob stuck around the Legion home for another fifteen minutes talking with stragglers. Nobody could add to the story. Nobody was old enough to know much about either the victim or the shooter. He finally drove back to Plaquemine where he wrote and filed his story.

At the Baton Rouge hospital, a bullet was removed from Neat's right lung but no other vital organs were damaged. The surgical team agreed that the gun and bullet were so old that they lacked the power to do much damage. Neat went home to Tess and Louis's home four days later.

The Associated Press used Hudson's story as its lead for the entire weekend. It hit the national wire on Monday and photos were published throughout the United States the following week. The story of a ninety-five year old man's attempted revenge on a one-hundred year old captured journalists' imagination all across the nation.

Bob Hudson was nominated for a Pulitzer Prize. He took home three awards at the next annual Louisiana Associate Press meeting in New Orleans. Within six months he was on the staff of the Baton Rouge State-Times.

XXXIV
1959

Randy kept searching for the true story of his grandpa Neat; kept trying to separate fact from folklore. He knew his grandfather could not last forever. Since the shooting he was visibly weakened and disoriented. Randy wanted to find out more about that period that had been so preciously guarded by his mother and others. If the man named Samuel Boyer was so determined to kill him, was Neat truly not guilty of murder? Was it really self-defense?

It was useless trying to talk to the old man. He was off in a world to himself. Randy tried one afternoon, again sitting in their familiar setting on the screened side porch. "Paw Paw, can you hear me? I wish you'd help me out on this. I'm trying to understand what really happened back there when Boyer's papa was killed. Can you remember? Tell me about the Mardi Gras ball. How did you get in? Did you have a mask? Did you say something wrong to Mr. Boyer? Did he or his men shoot at you first?"

Neat sat silent, the rocking chair creaked slightly. *Sure as hell I remember. Ain't telling nobody nothing, never, ever again. Next thing you know some other crazy good-for-nothing yankee'll come along and try to kill me. You'd think after all these years a man could get some Goddamn peace. It's over and gone. Way, way gone. I can't bring nobody back. The man was throwing me off his property. I know I shouldn't been there but he didn't have to come after me like that with those other men with their pistols. What woulda happened if I'd a just stood there? "Oh, 'scuse me, sir. You're right. I wasn't invited. I forged my invitation. I'm so sorry. My name is Neat Galvez and I have some friends and a very pretty girlfriend here. I just wanted to show off this mask. I'm sure you understand." They woulda shot me, that's what. I know Goddamn well they woulda shot me.*

Amanda, God bless her beautiful soul, she saved my butt. Didn't have to. I know she didn't see nothing. Wasn't out on the gallery yet when it happened. But, by Jesus, she loved me and she was ready to swear what ever she needed to.

Why's all this coming back now? I wasn't hurtin' nobody. Ain't done nothing but raise sugar cane and kids the last sixty-five years. Hell, I'm gonna be dead soon. Would be already if it was up to that burned up Boyer kid. Tried to be a good father, good husband, good farmer…hee, hee, good poker player. Can't help it if I just liked my poker as much as I did. Didn't really hurt my family. Got myself through all that trouble, saw my boys off to two wars and they all made it back. Only one came back with some scars and some metal still in him. Made it through that Goddamn flood in the twenties, through what they was calling the "depression." Hell, we made out all right. Three of the boys was working for the government post office and never had a problem with jobs during what they was calling a depression when everybody else was laid off and near broke.

Go through all that, live to be a hunnerd and then what? "What happened eighty years ago, Paw Paw? Did you really kill that man in self-defense?" Shit, ain't nobody's business no more. I ain't saying nothing, nothing, no more.

Try as he might, Randy couldn't get Neat to talk.

He tried another tact. He called his reporter friend Bob Hudson, met with him for coffee and asked for his help in tracking down any newspaper stories that might have mentioned the 1876 shooting of a reconstructionist administrator and a subsequent trial. Nothing. Both he and Bob ran into dead ends at the local papers in the Plaquemine, White Castle, Donaldsonville and Napoleonville areas.

Randy went to the courthouse in Napoleonville. After an hour he asked an elderly clerk why he could find nothing before 1895. "Well, sonny, I suppose that's because the old courthouse burned down in 1894. I should say the new one burned down. The old one burned in 1884. They built it back and durned if it didn't burn down ten years later. Lost everything. Not a folder, not a record was saved. That created havoc around here for years; lost birth certificates, deeds, property transfers, court records even marriage licenses. Hee, hee, there was some guys kinda happy about those being lost."

It was obviously an impossible task. Randy decided, when it came to the defining incident in his grandfather's incredible life story, he would never be able to sort out fact from fiction.

XXXV
February 29th, 1960

"I don't think it'll be very long now. His heart is mighty weak. He's been through a lot in the last year or so, and we all know he's lived a long, long eventful life. After all, he *is* a hundred and one years old. He's more or less in a coma now. There's nothing else I can do for him." Doctor Harrison folded up his stethoscope and slipped it into his black valise. The family members gathered around the bed in Louis and Tess's house were grim-faced. Neat's frail body was outlined under the white sheet, unmoving except for the barest hint of shallow breathing. He had been like this for two days, since Saturday.

"It's been downhill ever since he was shot at his birthday party," Louis said. "First the collapsed lung, then, by the time he finally healed, he was almost too weak to walk or do anything. Then this pneumonia hit him around Christmas. He just never had a chance to bounce back."

Neat could hear every word. *You're right, absolutely right, boy. Once that crazy son-of-a-bitch plugged me I've been on my way out. It's a damn good thing his heart quit on him that day 'cause this time I woulda really had to go after him and made sure I'd killed him. I shoulda done that years ago.* Neat's body was dormant but his mind was still churning.

I just love the way these doctors like to say, "He's lived a good life." How the hell does he know what kind a life I've lived. He just started prodding around on me a couple of years ago. Hell, I was seventy when he was born. Truth be known, life hasn't been so damn good now for at least twenty years. It's just been so damn lonely. No women, no friends. Can't play no cards anymore, can't drink. Oh, I been healthy. I could open my eyes right now, just don't want to. Ain't nothing left that's worth seeing.

That's the real problem. That's why I never "bounced back" as Louis said. What's there to bounce back for? Bounce back to what? Sitting in a rocker all day? Sucking a pipe that tastes like charcoal? Got no wife. She's been gone nearly twenty years. No friends still living. Haven't had any friends around since old Jordan passed on in about 1940, that was a long time ago, and he was just another old codger I knew, not a real close friend.

Some of them ole boys been gone a lot longer than that. Poor Sherman killed himself trying to drive a damned automobile. And then there was Henry. Best ole niggra that ever lived and look what happened to him. Just 'cause he fell in love with the wrong color woman. I hope those good-for-nothin', murderin', kluxing Klansmen burned in hell just like they burned sweet little Lucy. Henry shoulda gone on to that Shee-ca-go place where he said people treated niggras like real people. Hell, I thought we all treated him like real people, except for that crazy bunch wearing robes and peaked hats. But we all treated him right. Just 'cause he couldn't come with us to some places, couldn't buy a drink in a bar, couldn't eat with us, couldn't look back at a pretty white gal and had to use different out-houses, ride in different railroad cars and things like that. That was just the natural way, wasn't it? Some men are more equal than others, I guess. You're born one way, you're stuck with it.

What else they want me to open my eyes and get up for? Sure ain't no women gonna give me a serious thought. Some of my kids're still around but I think even a couple of them might be dead. I don't know. Never see 'em. Must be dead. One's still here got their own families. I'm just an extra problem, an extra mouth to feed, extra trouble for 'em.

If I could just saddle up a good horse by myself and mosey in to town. Betcha I could find a hot poker game and some good bourbon. Might even find a good, soft, willing woman. Ain't nothin' better. The boys would say, "Come on, Neat. Hope you brought lots of money. Pour my friend, Neat, a drink and let's deal the cards." Now that'd be something worth living for.

Can't do nothing I used to do. Use to sing and dance. Put on that burnt cork. Had to use some white grease paint around my eyes and mouth since I was so dark already. I was even taken for a niggra a coupla times. Now that didn't bother me none, long as they didn't keep me from going into the bars and all that other stuff niggras couldn't do. "Mammy, how I love you, how I love you, my dear ole mammy." Damn, that was fun. But it's gone. All gone. Never comin' back. "Wish I was in the land of cotton, old times there are not forgotten, look away, look away, look away Dixieland."

That's another problem. Old times ain't forgotten, dammit. If I could forget the old times then I might not care that I've lost 'em. I just keep reliving 'em over and over all night long, memories, memories. Mosquitoes in the swamp, the sting of that cottonmouth when he bit me, the taste of that fresh-caught fish cooked over the wood fire, Amanda, oh Lord, Amanda, sweet, soft, warm. That first time with Amanda, I could have died right there and been happy. Hell, every time we laid together was like the first time.

Sherman's been gone almost forty years. That was a friend. Couldn't have lived that year in the swamp without his help. And if Henry Gilmore hadn't covered for me, I'da sure 'nuff swung from a rope just like he did before I was twenty. Ole Pokey. He went off to New Orleans around '90 and never came back. Somebody said he died in that last big yellow fever outbreak in '97. And Pierre got himself a big spread when he married that rich Larimore gal up around Natchez. Had a big house, couple of hundred acres and then the damn flood came in 1927.

Mon Dieu, that was almost as bad as the War Between the States. Never seen so much water in all my life. I mean ALL my long life. They say the damn Mississippi was a hundred miles wide in some places and just stayed up there forever. They told me a man could take a boat all the way from Baton Rouge to Opelousas and never see no dry land. I know it took out my little farm. Ain't made no crops that year. It was all I could do to keep my family and me together, just surviving. Had to move everybody to Baton Rouge and live in that School for the Deaf for weeks and weeks.

First, it took the South a good fifty years to start recovering from the Goddamn war, then that flood wiped it all out again. But man, that soil was good when the water went away. We could grow some sugar cane then.

'Course, after the war they wasn't no slaves to do the work. Oh, some folks got 'em thinking one day they could own something by being a "sharecropper." Never happened. By the time they had worked their butts off and the crops was sold, they owed most all of their little shares to the owners for food and stuff they had to have all year long. They fooled 'em all, dumb darkies and dumb poor white folks, too.

After them gasoline engine machines came in, the big farmers didn't need as many hands to make a farm work. That flood though, that was the end. No machines could fix that and by the time the water was down and the land good enough to grow something, all the darkies had packed up and headed north. They all went off to Deetroit and Sheecago and places like that. Well, I hope Henry's folks got treated like real people up there. But, I doubt it. Damn, I miss old Henry, that was a good darkie. He was a good sheriff. I loved that ole niggra boy.

Tess said, "I'll come back and check on him in a bit. Let's go have supper." Neat heard the family leaving the room and the click of a light switch.

Ya'll go on. Ain't hungry. Ain't thirsty. I'll just lay here a while longer. I been by myself so many years it just don't matter no more. All I got left is the loneliness and the memories. I guess I could put up with the boredom a while longer. Nothing to do. Can't hardly hold a conversation no more. Who's interested in what a dried up old noodle has to say, even if they could understand me. Keep saying "What's he saying? What's he talking about? What's a gallery? What's a zephyr? What's a slop jar? What's a cistern? Did he say the word nigger? He can't say that word no more!" They just don't know nothing! Talking about me like I'm not even here. I'm here. Well, some of me's here.

Don't give a damn what's going on anymore. Ain't even interested in reading the newspapers or watching those people talking on what they call the TV. Louis was telling me something about some Russians throwing something 'bout the size of a basketball up in space. What the hell is that all about? I don't suppose you'd throw something down to the ground. Where else you gonna throw something but up in space. And, a basketball? What's happening to this world?

They told me Huey's little brother Earl's been governor three times. That's hard to believe. Said he's acting like he's going a little crazy now. That ain't no news. All them politicians go crazy after a while. They'll shoot him too if he don't watch out. Then they's talking about fighting a war in Korea? Don't even know where that is. Don't care. Must be up there around Deetroit or Sheecago.

Tess listens to the radio all day. Can't understand what they're singing. Men singing like girls. Too much noise. You don't need all them horns and stuff. Banjos and guitars and tambourines is fine. Then you could hear the singing. 'Every time I wheel about, I jump Jim Crow.' Never did figure what that damn song was about. But it was fun singing and dancing to it with the minstrels.

So what am I doing just lying here hanging on? There's nothing left. No friends. No fun. No life.

Ah, but there's always Amanda. Just Amanda and me. Just gotta relax my mind now, kinda drift and let her come to me again. The sun is going down. Pretty pink and orange clouds. Amanda. So warm. So soft. The scent of lavender. That silky hair covering my face. Feathers tickling inside my stomach when she touches me. That sweet breathe on my cheek. Those damp lips on mine. Amanda, you've always been here for me. You've always been my only love.

"Yes, I always have, I love you, Neat. I always have. I always will. Now, let the lights go dim. I've been waiting for you so long, my darling. Hold me close. Slowly,

slowly, it's nice and cool and getting dark, very dark. Let's go to sleep, my darling. Let's go to sleep."

Just drifting off, just me and Amanda, deal the cards, sip the whiskey, laugh and sing. So many years, so many good times. So many memories.

"Sleep my darling, sleep, sleep…peaceful sleep."

Author's Note

My grandfather, Antoine "Neat" Gomez was seventy-six years old when I was born. Naturally, neither one of us paid much attention to the other for several years. But when I was about fourteen and he was ninety, I became more aware of the grueling, but darkly interesting life he had led.

My mother was the epitome of a perfect Catholic, God-fearing woman. Motherless from age twelve, she was one of nine children in a French speaking home that coveted religion, peace and tranquility. She never fully accepted my father's boisterous, braggadocios siblings and was especially careful not to let her children listen to too many tales of grandpa Neat's early escapades. She considered her father-in-law's early life embarrassing at best; reprehensible and scandalous at worst.

Thus, I was fascinated with the old man's vivid memories of those early days. He described in great detail the "zephyr" of 1891. I found evidence of it in old weather records. Driving with him through downtown Baton Rouge in the mid 1950's, he pointed out the boarding house he was staying in when the tornado hit. The small, two story brick building near the corner of North Boulevard and Front Street was finally razed around 1970. Its foundation is still visible.

The "shooting incident" was shrouded in great secrecy. I could never get him to talk about it in detail but other older family members had gleaned bits and pieces over the years. The fact that the victim was a carpetbagger and that it occurred during a Mardi Gras function is pretty well established. Other than that, I had to depend on period research and literary license for the book. And, there was no Amanda. Or was there?

Two things I found during research particularly fascinated me: The bizarre presidential election of 1876 with its profound affect on the future of Louisiana as well as its uncanny correlation to recent presidential elections. The other was the history of and the making of a minstrel show.

I only wish I could have further explored that wealth of knowledge hidden away in Neat's century-old memory bank before it was too late. I was thankful for the two newspaper articles written on his 100th birthday that are combined and quoted verbatim in the text.

His lack of education and speech skills and my lack of language skills in anything but English greatly hampered our communication. What he did reveal led me to believe this was a man whose one hundred years of unique history should be written…even if in fiction. Thank you for sharing it.

978-0-595-37051-1
0-595-37051-9

Printed in the United States
50803LVS00005B/142